Amanda James has wri
asked her parents for a typewri
imagined her words would ever be published. In 2010
drea

Please return/renew this item by the last date shown.
Items may also be renewed by the internet*

https://library.eastriding.gov.uk

* Please note a PIN will be required to access this service
this can be obtained from your library

... a child and even

... She never

... 2010 the ...

... her

beautiful

Cornwall

THE FORGOTTEN BEACH

AMANDA JAMES

One More Chapter
a division of HarperCollins*Publishers* Ltd
1 London Bridge Street
London SE1 9GF
www.harpercollins.co.uk
HarperCollins*Publishers*
1st Floor, Watermarque Building, Ringsend Road
Dublin 4, Ireland

This paperback edition 2022

1

First published in Great Britain in ebook format
by HarperCollins*Publishers* 2022

A catalogue record of this book is available from the British Library

ISBN: 978-0-00-855061-5

This novel is entirely a work of fiction. The names, characters and
incidents portrayed in it are the work of the author's imagination. Any
resemblance to actual persons, living or dead, events or localities is
entirely coincidental.

Printed and bound in the UK using 100% Renewable Electricity
by CPI Group (UK) Ltd

To my wonderful grandson, Ronan, with all the love and hugs in the world. Thanks for your enthusiastic brainstorming session last summer which helped shape this story!

On the forgotten beach at the edge of the land,
lies a forgotten treasure beneath the sand.
A cup of kindness for Auld Lang Syne,
Sweeter than the finest wine.
In a parting glass from years gone by,
Dwells a magic strange to you and I.
Sup it down before you part,
to find the truth within your heart.

Chapter One

The September morning greets me with woodsmoke, birdsong and the gentle kiss of a salt breeze. I lock the door to my flat and take a moment to gaze down across the town of Polzeath. The Atlantic Ocean is sketching a hazy line across the horizon, dividing itself from the lighter blue of the sky, and a few gulls are having an argument as they turn lazy circles over the rooftops. Not to be outdone, nearby, a grumpy crow yells at me across a field. Work calls, but there's a familiar yearning in my chest, because I want to be out by the sea. I give a little sigh and set off down the hill into town.

It's exactly the kind of day for a walk on the beach, and along the path to Port Isaac. But then walks along the beach don't pay the bills, do they? The nip in the air is the perfect partner to the mellow sunshine drenching the Cornish coastline. It cools my face as I stride along, taking in the colours, smells and sounds of my beloved locality. It's only a ten-minute walk between my flat and the shop, but the brisk walk is invigorating, allowing feel-good endorphins to flood my system and lighten my step. My heart lightens too as I think how lucky I am to live and work in this beautiful little village in north Cornwall. How many people can say they are their own boss and do a job they love too?

Outside *Sea Spray Gifts*, I cast a critical eye over my display in the shop window. Maybe I should change the latest selection of plates and bowls I made in June. The bold blue and bright yellow designs are a bit too summery for September. A tickle of excitement replaces my beach yearnings as inspiration throws a tumble of ideas around my mind's eye. Burnt umber, russet and mustard will be more in keeping with the season for the plates and bowls, and a moody ocean scene or two for the hanging plaques will be ideal. My reflection in the window gives me an encouraging smile and, ready to get started, I flick my long plait over my shoulder and unlock the door.

At eleven-thirty, I flick the kettle on, to grab a quick coffee before the next customer. I've not even had time to do a sketch of my new ideas, as it's been incredibly busy, which is unusual outside the main tourist weeks. I make a mental note to order in more scented candles and handmade soaps as stocks are low, and maybe some more lovely sea glass pendants. I set my favourite seascape mug on the counter and trace a finger across the lighthouse standing sentinel in a rough ocean. It's one of the first I ever made, and I'm so proud of it. I pour a good slosh of the coffee I got from the deli the other day, and inhaling the smoky aroma, take a grateful sip. But as I do, the tinkle of the shop bell puts paid to another. Oh well. Mustn't grumble. I'd be wishing for busy days like this when winter comes knocking. Painting on a polite smile, I step out of the little kitchen and back behind the counter. My smile stretches when I see who's come in.

'Hi, Mum!' I say.

'Hello, sweetheart. You look nice!'

I glance down at my unremarkable denim dungarees over a white T-shirt. 'I do?'

Mum nods and waves a hand at my face. 'Yes, you look all pink-cheeked and glowing. Sets off your seaside blues and lovely smile.'

I chuckle. Mum has always called my grey-blue eyes 'seaside blues'. Says they remind her of the sea on a misty day, or mizzly, as we say here in Cornwall. She describes my hair as the colour of wet sand too, which adds to the imagery. I prefer to call it honey-blonde.

'Thanks,' I say. 'I'm probably glowing because I've been running around like a mad fool all morning. It's been so busy. Just let me grab my coffee while it's quiet a minute.'

I come back out with my mug and take a mouthful.

Mum tilts her head to the side and narrows her green eyes, catlike. 'Hmm. Glowing because she's been busy, she says … not preggers, then?'

I nearly spit out my coffee at this. 'Pregnant! No. Thank goodness.'

'Would it be so bad?' Mum holds me in her steady gaze as she runs her hand through her short caramel curls and folds her arms. 'I was only saying to your dad the other night that I reckon you'd be settling down soon with Josh. You've been with him two years now, haven't you?'

I dismiss this with a wave of a hand. 'Yes, but there's no rush. We're only twenty-five.' Well, he's twenty-six next week, but that's neither here nor there. I don't like the look in her eye, or the topic of conversation. She's hit a tender spot. More than once, I've raised this exact subject with him too. But Josh always answered me with what I've just said to Mum.

She gives a smug smile. 'Me and your dad were married at twenty-three and twenty-four. Had you the year after.'

'And?'

'And I'm just saying it would be nice for you to settle down soon.' She fiddles with the zip of her lime-green waterproof. 'That's why I popped over on my way to my shift at the Post Office. How about coming over for Sunday lunch with Josh? We've only met him about four times, and it would be nice to get to know him better. Your dad's got a day off from the restaurant, and he'll cook us a nice salmon steak.'

I picture Sunday lunch at my parents' with poor Josh being grilled like the steak by Mum's probing questions. He'd hate it. So would I. Josh's a free spirit, hates been pinned down to times, places, people. That's why he's a surfing instructor, he's much more at home in the waves than in an office. Social occasions for him normally involve having a barbeque on the beach with friends and a few beers. Formal Sunday lunches are a no-no. I remember he once told me that life's too short to be doing things you don't want to. That's why he's only seen my parents a few times. He doesn't see his own much either.

Mum wouldn't get this. She'd see it as rudeness, so thinking quickly, I say, 'He's off for a surfing competition up the coast on Sunday, unfortunately. I'll come over though. I haven't seen you properly for a while.' The lie warms my cheeks and I pretend my coffee has gone down the wrong way to distract her from my guilt.

By the look of Mum's crestfallen expression and hard stare, I think I failed. 'Ri-ight. Funny that he always seems to have something on when we ask him over.'

I avert my eyes and look for something under the counter. 'Yeah, well, he's busy.' I pop back up with a roll of Sellotape and a gift box. The tender spot she's hit is becoming an open wound. Only last night I was toying with the idea of broaching the subject of moving things on with Josh the next time he was in a good mood. Possibly on his birthday. Mum's like a dog with a bone when she latches on to something, and I can't deal with this right now. I give her a smile and say, 'Anyway, I must get on and wrap these earrings before the next customer comes in.'

Mum picks up her bag and sighs. 'Okay, Sennen. See you on Sunday. About one?'

'Yes, thanks. That will be lovely.' I lean across and kiss her cheek.

At the door, she turns round and says, 'Oh, yeah. I almost forgot. When you come over for lunch, you might like to look at some old photos and bits and bobs in your grandma's treasure box. I was clearing out your bedroom, as we're going to decorate it, and found the box at the bottom of the wardrobe. I know you love all that old stuff.'

Warm memories of my grandma swell my heart. She's been gone three years and I really miss her. I give Mum a big smile. 'That would be lovely.'

There's a mischievous twinkle in her eye as she adds, 'I might even share a special secret of hers with you too … if you're lucky.'

'Ooh, that's sounds intriguing…' The rest of my sentence is left on my tongue, however, as I watch her step through the doorway and hurry away down the street.

The house I called home for ten years stands at the end of a tiny bramble-lined lane, overlooking open countryside and the ocean beyond. As I drive towards it along the twisty little lane, I think about how it was left to them by my paternal grandparents when they passed away. Dad's dad was a fisherman, and when he first bought the house and the bit of land surrounding it, the place was a little ramshackle, just an old fisherman's cottage really. But over the years, he and Grandma saved up and extended it. Nowadays, because of its location and land, it is a very desirable property. I smile as I pull up outside. Lucky for my parents it was a gift. No way would they be able to afford it even with Dad's head chef job.

Outside the car, a grumpy offshore breeze smacks my plait across my face and I wonder whether it's time to opt for a shorter style. I haven't cut my hair for eight years –

well, apart from a trim – and it can get on my nerves – like now, as the wind tries to use it as a blindfold. Josh loves it long, though, and I must admit it's nice being able to style it in lots of different ways. I hook my bag over my shoulder, grab the bunch of roses and bottle of wine sitting on the passenger seat and slam the car door.

Turning to face the front door, I find myself smiling again. The house feels like it's offering a welcome because there's a red curtain waving at me from a half-open upstairs window. I take a deep lungful or two of salt air and wonder if it's missed me since I moved out. But how can it? It's just a house. An inanimate object. Cornish grey stone, slate roof, big picture windows, like eyes in a glass conservatory looking out over the ocean, its foundations standing stout and solid in the ancient pastureland. But sometimes old buildings have a character, a personality, don't they? A 'feel' about them. Perhaps the energy of past dwellers has seeped into their walls, formed a spiritual layer under the bricks. Whatever the truth, I reckon it does miss me a little. And if it doesn't, never mind. I miss it, and tell it so as I walk up the path and open the door.

'Hello! Mum, Dad, it's me!'

'Hello, sweetheart!' Dad appears grinning in the hallway, rubbing his unruly salt and pepper hair with a towel. 'Just got out the shower.' He hoiks a thumb over his shoulder. 'Your mum's in the kitchen; come through. We'll have a glass of wine.'

I follow him through to the conservatory, the familiar view beyond lifting my soul. While Dad gets the wine, I step through the French doors out onto the lawn so I can get a sweeping view of the beach and Polzeath village to my right, while directly ahead, a cool azure ocean sends white horse waves galloping in to shore. A few nervous clouds breeze onto the stage, but only have a walk-on part, thanks to the strengthening September sunshine. God, it's beautiful. I take a big breath of sea air and walk back to the conservatory, briefly allowing a snippet of an idea for the future to settle in my mind. A place with a view like this, me and Josh on the lawn playing with a couple of kids, happy, laughing … could it come true?

Dad comes back in then, and the idea scarpers. He's got two very full glasses in his hands and his black bushy brows are furrowed in concentration as he tries not to spill a drop. 'I've poured a nice Merlot. I know you're partial, and we're having roast beef, so it will go nicely.' He sets both glasses down on the glass table just inside the door.

'Blimey, Dad! I'll be comatose if I drink that before lunch. Besides I can't, I'm driving.'

'Your mum says she'll pop you back and you can get the car tomorrow. She's not a big afternoon drinker as you know.'

'Neither am I, to be honest. And roast beef? Mum said you were cooking salmon?'

He waves a hand and plops his big frame down on the plump red leather sofa we've had since forever. 'We were. But I cook every day of my working life and get a bit sick of fish to be honest. Your mum decided to give me a break.'

'Sick of fish. Granddad wouldn't be happy to hear that,' I say, pulling a mock-serious face and wagging a finger at him.

'True.' Dad laughs. 'He taught me all I know about catching and cooking the damned things. But now and then it's nice to eat something else.' He takes a sip of wine, his eyes – the twins of mine – growing round in appreciation. 'That's a proper nice drop, Sennen. Get it down you, maid.'

I follow his orders and discover he's correct. But unless I have some nibbles with it, I'll be asleep all afternoon. I put my glass down and go off to the kitchen to find Mum. She's racing around like a dervish, stirring, prodding, checking the meat in the oven, her curls damp in the nape of her neck. I have a hunch she needs help.

'Hi, Mum.' I place my hands on her shoulders and kiss her hot cheek. 'What can I do?'

'Hello, lovely. No need, thanks. It's all coming together now,' she says in her high-pitched 'I'm not coping, but pretending everything's fine' voice.

I peer through the glass door of the oven. 'Well, I could at least turn the roasties, and maybe put the Yorkshire pud in?'

She turns her pink, shiny face to me and puffs a curl out of her eye. 'Oh, would you? That would be great. But don't let your dad see you. I wanted to do this meal all by myself, but always get in a flap. He makes everything looks so easy when he's cooking.'

Incredulous, I say, 'But that's his job! I expect if he did a shift in the Post Office, he'd be in a flap too.'

Mum smiles and pats my arm. 'I expect he would. Thanks, Sennen.'

I pour her a drop of Pinot Grigio and then tackle the

potatoes and Yorkshire pud with the speed of a ninja before Dad comes noseying.

We eat in the conservatory and talk about everything and nothing. And we laugh. A lot. Okay, the wine might be part of the reason, but I'm having a much better time than I imagined. Mum hasn't given me the third degree about Josh – in fact she's hardly mentioned him – and Dad's been talking about doing a bit of travelling when he retires. He's been to a few Spanish language evening classes at the library and loves them. I can't see him retiring any time soon though. He's only just fifty, and though he moans about cooking, he once told me he couldn't wish for a better job.

My younger brother Ruan comes up in conversation a few times too. He's in the dog house as usual with my parents because he hardly ever visits. But then to be fair, poor Ruan is working all hours building up his hairdressing business in Plymouth. We speak on the phone often as we've always been thick as thieves, but he said to me the other day that he's always felt there was too much pressure on him from our parents. Especially Dad. Once again, this afternoon, I have to acknowledge that Dad hasn't really got over his disappointment about Ruan opting for hairdressing instead of cheffing with him. The dream of Ruan joining the family business had been in Dad's mind since my brother was born, I think.

After we clear the table, Dad's left to the dishwasher and

sink, while Mum and I take our coffee into the garden and settle down on the old weather-beaten bench overlooking the ocean. The sun is still out, yet the breeze reinforces the message that summer is now behind us. 'That was a great meal, Mum.' I lean across and tuck the old yellow blankie we're sharing over her knees.

'It was.' Mum gives me a cheeky wink. 'Even if I do say so myself!'

Slipping my arm through hers, I sigh and watch the sun and clouds paint light and shade across the surface of the ocean. 'You learned from the best though, eh?'

She chuckles. 'I certainly did. Your gran was the master of the Yorkshire pudding. Or I should say mistress.'

'And the sticky toffee pud, and apple pie!'

'She could cook anything. Even once beat your dad hands down at *moules marinière*.' Mum touches my arm and lowers her voice, even though Dad's washing up. 'It was never said out loud of course,' she says with a giggle. 'But your dad's expression when he put a forkful in his mouth spoke volumes.'

'I was there! It was on his birthday, and you and Gran decided to cook for him. I must have been about sixteen, I think.'

'So you were. Funny, it was that long ago … I could have sworn it was when you were away at uni. Time flies by so fast, doesn't it?'

The catch in her voice puts a lump in my throat. I squeeze her hand as we sit staring out at the scene, because I know we're sharing similar memories. We're both wishing Gran was sitting here with us too. Then a thought suddenly occurs. 'Oh, I just remembered. You mentioned you'd found some of her things in my old room. And what's this secret you mentioned before scuttling away from the shop the other day?'

'I mentioned her things? Don't remember…' She pauses, nipping her finger and thumb together and draws them across her lips in a zipping action, laughter dancing in her eyes.

'Come on, tell me.'

'Okay!' She giggles. 'Yes, I found her old treasure box. I remember finding it once before, under an old blanket in the wardrobe when I was little. Before I could open it, Mum shoved it quickly away, saying she'd show me what was in it when I was older. I was always curious, but never snooped. Then when I was about sixteen, she let me look through it. There were just mostly old photographs of her family and her as a kid and teenager, odds and ends really. I couldn't understand why she'd never let me look at her things before, as it all appeared very normal. But then' – Mum wiggles her brows and leans in close – 'she lifted the false bottom of the treasure box and handed me an envelope.' She stops, looks at me, her eyes shining with mischief.

'Well, don't keep me hanging!' I exclaim. 'What was in it? Is that the secret you were on about?'

She raises an eyebrow and folds her arms. 'Might be … but I'm not sure I should tell you. It *was* her closest secret after all.'

'Mum!' I pretend to strangle her.

She laughs. 'Okay. It was a keepsake, a very precious

one. And she told me the whole story behind it. Made me promise not to tell Dad I knew, though.'

'Ooh, sounds intriguing. Tell me more.'

'I'll do better than that. I'll show you.' She ruffles my hair. 'Come on.' Mum gets up and heads for the door with me close on her heels.

Chapter Two

On the bed in my old room sits a battered old wooden box. It must have been blue at some point judging by the sides, but the paint on the surface is so faded it looks more like a washed-out winter sky. Mum and I perch on the edge of the bed and she hands me the box; it's light and as dry as sandpaper. Opening the lid, I pick up a sepia photo of Gran aged about six. She's on her dad's shoulders on the beach, he's in rolled trousers and braces, laughing out loud as she holds onto his head, her hair flying in the wind, an expression of utter joy on her face.

Emotion rushes up from my depths and I take a moment. The laughing child and the man both gone now. 'Oh, bless her. Where was this?'

Mum smiles. 'Must be about 1944 or '45, in St Ives, I think. My granddad was from there. He was exempt from the war because he was a farmer.'

Next there's a series of similar photos and when Gran is older, in the 1950s. There's a cork, presumably from a champagne bottle, and a silver key with a pink 'Happy 21ˢᵗ' ribbon tied around it. Two dun-coloured tickets for *The King and I* in London, and a programme too. Then a photo of Gran and Granddad on their wedding day and a few of Mum as a toddler. As I reach the end, Mum points to a little finger-hole to the right of the bottom of the box and gives a nod. I push my forefinger into the hole and pull. The false bottom comes away easily and I see two items. One is a thin, delicate and yellowing piece of card, its edges threaded with blue and white ribbon, upon which is a poem of some sort in light-blue spidery longhand. The other is an oval photo in a red Bakelite frame of a man in uniform.

I pick up the photo and take a closer look at the dark-haired moustachioed young man with the half-smile and twinkly eyes. 'Who's this, then?' I ask Mum.

Mum nods to the piece of beribboned card. 'Read that first, and I'll explain the whole story.'

Though the ink is as faded as the paint on the box, I trace each word with my finger and read aloud:

> *On the forgotten beach at the edge of the land,*
> *lies a forgotten treasure beneath the sand.*
> *A cup of kindness for Auld Lang Syne,*
> *Sweeter than the finest wine.*
> *In a parting glass from years gone by,*
> *Dwells a magic strange to you and I.*
> *Sup it down before you part,*
> *to find the truth within your heart.*

'What does that mean?'

'Look on the back.'

I do as Mum asks, and see a pencil-drawn love-heart with the names 'Morwenna' and 'Jory' written inside it. 'Morwenna was Gran, so is Jory the soldier?'

'Not a soldier, a Naval pilot based at RNAS Culdrose down the coast. Jory Nancarrow was your gran's first love. They'd met in the summer of 1955 when she was seventeen. She had a job in the local bakery and used to walk across the south-west coast path every few days to deliver fresh bread to Nancarrow House at Daymer Bay. Jory was the youngest son of the Nancarrows, a wealthy landed family who had lived there for generations. Your gran said they'd bumped into each other, literally.' Mum laughs. 'She'd been coming round the corner of the house, and he'd been running the other way and knocked her and the bread basket flying! Love at first sight by all accounts. From that day they were inseparable.'

'Wow! How romantic. So how come they separated, and what has the poem got to do with their story?' The wistful, sad expression on Mum's face tells me this story doesn't end well. But then logically I know it doesn't, because Gran married Granddad. I don't want to hear what happened, but I can't not hear it either.

Mum takes the photo from me, traces the love-heart with her finger and sighs. 'They knew the fact that they were in love wouldn't go down well with his grandparents. They looked after him and his brother Edward after their parents died. Even though it was the 1950s, their attitude was of a century earlier. People didn't marry out of their class, according to them. Mum and Jory didn't even tell them they were seeing each other until a year had passed, but then on New Year's Day, after a very special New Year's Eve party, Jory decided to take the bull by the horns and broach it with his grandparents.' Mum shakes her head. 'They were appalled, didn't even want to meet your gran, said if he married a shop girl he wouldn't inherit.'

The injustice of their attitude sparks a flame of anger in my gut. 'What the hell? Bloody snobs!'

'Yup.'

'So is "Auld Lang Syne" a reference to New Year's Eve?'

'Yes. Jory had been asking your gran to marry him for a few months before that, but she'd said that they should wait a while, as she guessed his grandparents would be opposed to it. She didn't want to cause a rift in the family. But she'd seen this poem in a book Jory had let her borrow from the library room at Nancarrow. It had been written on the inside of the cover, and intrigued, she'd copied it out onto that card. She'd asked Jory if he knew what it meant, and he'd told her he didn't, but that it was his mother's handwriting. Apparently, Nancarrow has a small private beach that wasn't used much. Perhaps that was the "Forgotten Beach". Because of the poem, your Gran wondered if his mother had hidden a parting glass somewhere on that beach.'

'What's a parting glass?'

'A glass that people back then used at New Year's and special occasions to drink from. You know the song "Auld Lang Syne", and the line about a cup of kindness?'

'Yes, but I never really knew what it meant.'

'Well, people would take a drink from a parting cup or

glass, to fondly remember loved ones upon parting, or to wish someone a safe journey. It was passed around at social gatherings, funerals often too. Maybe it still is in some places.'

'So that's why we raise a glass on the stroke of midnight and kiss and hug?'

'I think so. There are different interpretations – it's to bid a fond farewell to the old year too – but the poem in the book indicated that if a person found this particular glass, and took a drop of wine at New Year's Eve, it would reveal the true path of their heart. Because it was a magical glass.'

'How exciting!' I give a little laugh. 'So, Gran believed the poem?'

Mum nods, and with a twinkle in her eye she replies, 'Not only that. A few weeks before New Year's Eve, she found the glass buried in a cave on the forgotten beach and did as the old poem suggested on the night!'

'Oooh!' I'm really loving this old story now. 'Tell me what happened!'

'Well, the beach was inaccessible because of something tragic that happened to his mother. No idea what. Jory wouldn't talk about it. Anyway, Mum begged him to row her round there in his little boat. He thought she was being silly and it was all just a flight of fancy on his mother's part, but he agreed to take her. They went into a cave and the glass was in a metal box just above the tideline in a recess covered in sand. Fairly easy to find, she said.'

Mum smiles and stares out of the window at some passing clouds. 'And then what?' I prompt, desperate to know the rest.

AMANDA JAMES

'On New Year's Eve, your gran and Jory were at a party at The Old Black Bull in town. Gran asked the barman to pour some of his best wine into the glass and took a sip. Jory took one too, and they held hands and kissed at the stroke of midnight.' Mum's voice became a whisper.

'And what happened next?' I ask quickly.

'Mum told me she knew right then and there, without any of the doubts and worries she'd had previously, that Jory was her soulmate. The one she had to be with … "to walk alongside", were her exact words, for the rest of her life.' Mum turns her gaze from the window towards me, but the clouds have found a home in her eyes.

A rush of emotion pushes tears into mine too, and I have to swallow hard before I can manage, 'So what went wrong? Did Jory give in to his grandparents? Break Gran's heart?'

Mum sniffs, pulls a tissue from her sleeve and blows her nose. 'Her heart was broken, but not because of anything like that. Jory told his grandparents that they could stick their inheritance, that he loved Mum and he would marry her anyway, no matter what they thought. Mum was distraught, of course, feeling she'd come between them – she always did blame herself for things – but she knew they were meant to be together. My grandparents were a bit worried too when she told them she wanted to marry Jory, as they thought he might be too different to her because of his background. He'd been used to having pots of money, and now he'd have to make do without it. Perhaps he'd live to regret his decision. But they came round when they met

20

him. My granddad especially. He said she couldn't have picked a nicer chap.'

I can't bear to hear the conclusion to this story, as it's so full of love and hope. I can picture Gran and Jory, young, fearless, planning a life together, star-crossed lovers – them against the world. Drawing in a deep breath I say, 'Go on. Let's be having the rest.'

Mum takes my hand and gives it a squeeze. 'It's so sad.'

'I imagine it is. But I need to know.'

'Okay. About six months later, Jory went off in his plane on manoeuvres somewhere, bad weather came in and he crashed into the sea.' A chill runs the length of my spine and I squeeze Mum's hand hard. 'Nobody knows what really happened, but he was gone. A wonderful young man dead at the age of twenty, and a devastated fiancée left broken … for a long time, beyond repair.'

I grab a tissue from the night stand and dab my eyes. 'Poor, poor Gran. I had no idea about the tragedy in her past. She was always so cheerful and full of fun.' We sit in silence for a few moments lost in thought. Then I ask, 'How did she meet Granddad and were they happy? They always seemed to be.'

Mum gives me a big smile and starts to put the things back in the box. 'Oh, they were. Very. Granddad took over the bakery when old Barry Simpson retired and Mum and him hit it off. It was about five years after Jory died that they got married. He knew about Jory, but he never liked to think about her having another love before. So, she never mentioned him. People didn't talk about stuff like they do nowadays back then, anyway.'

'Except to you that time?'

'Yes. I think she was pleased she could share his story with me. Speak his name again … bring him to life.' Mum puts her head on one side, gives me a big smile. 'Your gran said she was very happy with your granddad, but she would never forget her Jory. She said she never regretted falling for Jory and finding the glass, and I should always follow my heart and only settle for the right one, no matter how hard the path might seem.'

'And you did.'

'I did.' She pats my hand and stands up. 'And you should do the same, Sennen.'

I think of Josh, and wonder if he is the right one. A pang of doubt brings a few questions with it, but I squash it. Mum's watching me carefully, so I laugh and say, 'I might need a parting glass.' I pick up the box and take it over to the wardrobe.

'Yeah. I said I'd go and look for it when I was young, but just never got round to it.'

My pulse quickens. 'Eh? What do you mean? Didn't Gran keep hold of it?'

'No. She put it back where she found it after Jory died. She was convinced the glass had a special magic or power within it and wanted others to use it. To be as happy as she had been, albeit for a short time.'

A tickle of excitement flares in my stomach. Wow! What if I could find it, just like Gran did? There are so many questions it could answer. My logical mind sniggers at this thought, and making my voice matter-of-fact, I say, 'So, it's still under the sand at the forgotten beach? Is Nancarrow House still there too?'

'As far as I know, lovely. Right. How about a nice cuppa before you go? Bet your dad is fast asleep in the armchair.'

I follow her downstairs listening to her chatting about how Dad's snoring is getting worse as he gets older, but my mind is far away thinking about Gran's story, and the hidden parting glass.

Chapter Three

Almost a week has passed since I found out about Gran's story, and the idea that the parting glass is still out there buried under the sand just waiting to be found will not leave me alone. Why, I have no idea. Yes, it's an interesting story, but the fact that an inanimate object somehow has the power to show your heart's true path is exactly that – a story. To take my mind off it, I've been busy at work, getting to the shop early to make some new pieces and firing them in the old kiln we keep in the outhouse in the yard. I must remember to ask Uncle Pete to check it over next time he pops in. It's as old as the hills. Today has been a bit quieter, and at five o'clock, I wash my hands and get ready to lock up *Sea Spray Gifts* for another day.

Uncle Pete smiles down at me from a photo above the window in the little kitchen. He's looking very happy and windswept aboard his beloved boat, *Marianne*. He looks so much like his younger sister, in that shot. Though Mum always maintains his hair doesn't have her natural curl. I'll always be grateful to him for showing me how to pot and making me a partner in the business. Poor guy was loath to retire early, but the arthritis in his fingers meant his days as a potter were done. I smile as I recall a snippet of gossip Mum had passed onto me last week. After ten years of being alone after his wife Marianne died, he's met someone. A woman who joined the choir he attends, apparently. I can't wait to ask him more about her. Possibly to do a little teasing too. We do enjoy a bit of banter.

As I'm striding up the main street through Polzeath on the way home, my phone rings. It's my oldest friend, Jasmine. 'Hey, Jas. You okay?'

'Not really, it's a bloody nightmare at work! I need a few drinks and to spill my guts.'

'Oh, that doesn't sound good,' I say, while thinking that Jasmine, much as I love her, does tend to catastrophise.

'No. That's an understatement. Work is properly doing my head in. How are you fixed for meeting up tonight for a bite and a glass or three in Padstow? You can stay over at mine.'

'Um...' Do I want to give up my Saturday night to listen to Jasmine's woes, real or imagined? Josh said he might pop over after his night out with the boys...

My pause stretches a bit too long and I hear a heavy sigh on the line. 'You got plans with Josh, I suppose. Don't worry. I know it's short notice.'

The despondency in Jasmine's tone pricks my

conscience. Maybe I should reconsider. Besides, Josh might not come over at all, and I'll be waiting home on my own like a lemon. A voice of reason adds, *like you have loads of times before, Sennen*. I put a smile in my voice and reply, 'No firm plan, so yes. I'll come to you. But I'll drive home, it's only half an hour, after all. There's something important I want to do tomorrow and I want a clear head.' Really? I had no idea I was going to say that.

'Oh, that's great. Thank you! And what's this important thing you want to do?'

'I'll tell you later.' We arrange a time and place and end the call. Then I carry on my walk up the hill by the sea, wondering if what my subconscious had just surprise-announced to Jasmine about my Sunday plans is actually something I want to do at all.

We're meeting at seven o'clock in the warm ambience of The Old Custom House on the quay. I can't wait to get inside as I hurry towards it along the side of the harbour. The fresh autumn wind pushes rainclouds before it and whips the water to a brisk chop. The array of little boats moored for the evening bob up and down, swaying this way and that, like a crowd of drunken sailors on a night out. As a soundtrack, a few halyards on masts start up a merry tune with a clatter and whistle, as if encouraging the elements to do their worst.

Despite the grumpy weather, it's uplifting. Padstow is wonderful. I might follow Jasmine's example and move here one day. Though I love Port Isaac too, the wonderful little village of Doc Martin fame, which is only another half an hour further. As I step through the pub door, I remind myself that Jasmine moved here to Padstow with her then boyfriend, Carl, so they could afford to rent with two wages coming in. I only have me, unless Josh can be persuaded, so it would be a bit tight getting somewhere as nice as Jasmine's. I know she's struggling now to meet the monthly payments after Carl dumped her for an eighteen-year-old. It knocked the stuffing out of her emotionally and financially. I smile as I recall her getting blind drunk a few days after it happened and telling me in all seriousness, 'I'm officially old at twenty-five. Nobody will want me now. Might get a boob job so I can keep up with that evil, but perfect, child-woman Carl left me for.' But it's been six months since he left and, thankfully, she is starting to feel more optimistic about meeting someone else one day.

I grab a corner table and look at the menu while I wait for Jas, but a few moments later, she bursts through the door like a firework, her flame corkscrew curls windswept and bouncing against the collar of a bright yellow puffer jacket. Pink-cheeked and out of breath, she hurries over to me and unzips the jacket, the bright green sweater underneath reflecting the hue of her eyes. 'Phew!' she exclaims, shrugging the jacket onto the back of the chair opposite me and plonking herself down on it. 'I just got here before it started pissing it down! I literally stepped through the door and the heavens opened!'

Laughing, I lean over and kiss her cheek. 'Lovely to see you. And you look incredible, so full of energy.'

'Really? I don't feel very lovely.' Jasmine rolls her eyes, but the twinkle in them tells me she's happy to receive the compliment.

'So what's the problem at work?'

'Let's get a drink and order first.' She grabs a menu from the stand to our left. 'I'm starving.'

We both go for the crab and prawn linguine in a garlic and chilli cream sauce. And the waitress brings us two large glasses of Pinot Grigio. 'Hmm,' I say to the oak beams above my head as I take a big gulp of the chilled fruity wine. 'That's hit the spot.'

Jasmine drains half her glass in one and exhales. 'It certainly does. I've been dreaming of that all day.'

She folds her arms and stares trancelike over my shoulder, saying nothing. I fiddle with the end of my plait, and then when no more is forthcoming, I ask, 'What's the problem, then?'

Jasmine twists her hair into a tight ponytail and once more lets it loose, as if she hopes it will do the same to her tongue. 'Work. Specifically, Robert Cook, my wonderful boss.'

Great, I think. He and Jas are like chalk and cheese and Robert is constantly rubbing her up the wrong way. He apparently takes the boss role literally and orders her about as if she has no clue what she's doing. 'Still being a patronising git?'

'Big time.' Jasmine sighs. 'You know I said that Jenny was leaving to have a baby and the manager's post was coming up?' I nod. 'Well, I was hoping I would be the logical choice, having worked in the bloody store for three years. I could do with the extra dosh, you know.'

I frown. 'Well, yeah. It's a no-brainer.'

'Apparently not. Though Robert certainly has no bloody brain!' She stops mid-rant as the food arrives and dives into her dish of linguine as if she's not eaten for days. 'God. This is divine,' she mumbles, through a huge mouthful.

I follow her lead and for a few moments we are too busy enjoying our food to chat. I break a bit of garlic bread and dip it into the sauce. 'Who's got the job then?' I ask, popping it into my mouth.

Jasmine wipes cream sauce from her chin. 'Nobody yet. But Robert bloody advertised it and is interviewing three people on Monday. Can you believe that?' She gives me an incredulous stare.

'I don't get it. Why bother advertising it when he knew you wanted the position?'

'Because he, apparently, has to advertise it.' She does air quotes around the word apparently. '*Atlantic Surf World*'s policy, he said.'

That makes sense. 'Right. Yeah, well, I've heard of that kind of thing before. Lots of places have to advertise widely.'

My comment is dismissed with a wave of her napkin. 'Yes, but not everyone follows it to the sodding T, do they? No. But Robert "I'm the big I am manager of three *Atlantic Surf World* shops in Cornwall" bloody Cook does. He's just doing it to get on my nerves. He hates me.' She takes another gulp of wine and bangs the glass down.

Oh dear. 'So, you didn't even get an interview?' I ask gently.

'Eh? Of course I did! I would have sodding castrated him if he didn't grant me that much. Though there's no way I'm getting the job, obviously.'

'Who says? Is it just him on the interview panel?'

'No. There'll be his boss from Exeter there too. Sally Henshaw, she's very business-like and efficient, but nice with it. I met her once at a do.'

'There you go, then. You've got as good a chance as the rest of them. Better, as you know the store!' I raise a glass to her. Though I am beginning to feel a bit irritated by her negativity. *Come on, Jas. Stop thinking the bloody worst all the time.*

'But Robert hates me.' She draws this sentence out slowly, as if I'm a two-year-old, and pushes her empty dish to one side.

Right, that's enough. It's time for some straight talking. 'Okay, you need to go to that interview on Monday and behave as if the job's yours. You're good at what you do, and what you don't know about surfing, surfboards and all the gear isn't worth knowing. You have first-hand experience too. Everyone was in awe of you when we were at school and you won junior surf champion. Remember all that on Monday, Jas. Smile sweetly at Robert and knock 'em dead.'

Jasmine's big green eyes brim and she grabs my hand across the table. 'Thanks, Sen. I needed to hear that … and yes, I will try my bloody hardest to get the job. I need it, for the money, but mainly to show that shit-head Carl and his

31

infant girlfriend that I can make something of myself. That I'm not a pathetic creature who sits at home most nights watching TV and eating chocolate biscuits, wishing Carl was still sitting next to me on the sofa.'

Jasmine blows her nose noisily on the napkin and I signal to the guy behind the bar for another two glasses of wine. 'That's the spirit. But don't do it for that loser. Do it for you.'

She stares off into the distance. 'Yeah. Yeah, I will.' Then she juts her chin out and picks up the menu. 'I'm gonna get that job. And right now, I'm gonna have a pudding to celebrate me getting that job! Start as you mean to go on, I say.'

This sounds like a plan to me too, and the sticky toffee pud here is legendary. Jasmine goes for the same and we sit back and relax. The crisis seems to have been assuaged now and hopefully the evening can mellow out a bit. 'So, what else is new?' I ask, with an encouraging smile.

'No. It's your turn now.' Jasmine leans forward and wiggles her eyebrows at me. 'What's this important thing that you have to do tomorrow, hmm?'

My heart sinks. I was hoping she'd forgotten about that, because it's not really something I want to share. It's all a bit too weird. 'Oh nothing. Just a silly idea that came up when I was looking through my gran's old stuff at Mum and Dad's last Sunday.'

Jasmine considers this, while studying my carefully constructed 'nothing to see here' expression. 'I like hearing about silly ideas.'

Shuffling in my seat, I pick up a dessert spoon and

twiddle it around in my fingers. To the table I say, 'Yeah, well, it's too silly to do anything about, so I might just go for a swim. The water is still quite warm, it said on the local weather forecast the other day, and—'

'Just tell me,' Jasmine growls, folding her arms and doing the intense thing with her eyes she's mastered since she was about twelve. Nobody fobs her off when she's got them in the death stare.

I drop the spoon and hold my hands up. 'Okay. You asked for it.' I tell her everything I found out about Gran's story, the parting glass, Nancarrow House and the forgotten beach. She listens without interrupting for once, but before she can comment, the waitress arrives with our puddings. Once she's gone, I dig my spoon into the light fluffy sponge and say, 'So there we are. Completely daft.'

Jasmine's eyebrows shoot skyward. 'Daft? No way. It is an incredible story. Sad, moving, but certainly not daft.' She pauses to savour the big spoonful of pudding she's just shovelled in her mouth. 'But you still haven't explained the "important" thing that apparently isn't now, about what you were planning tomorrow.'

I swallow and exhale. 'Important might have been the wrong word. Perhaps interesting is better. I was going to drive over to Daymer Bay and see if Nancarrow is still standing. If it is, I was going to see if I could get down to the private beach somehow...'

Jasmine's eyes grow round and sparkly. 'OMG. To see if you could find your gran's parting glass!'

A couple on the next table glance over at us in surprise because of the volume and excitement in Jasmine's tone. I frown at her. 'Shh. Yes. If the house is still inhabited, I'd have to go and ask permission from the owner.' I pause and jab my spoon at her. 'But then I'd have to explain the reason why I needed access. They'd think I'd gone bananas.'

Jasmine pulls her neck back and gives me a disparaging look. 'Well, duh. You wouldn't tell them the truth, would you? Just say you're doing a survey of all the private beaches in Cornwall for … um, a blog piece.'

My mouth drops open. 'A survey for a blog piece? Who the hell would want to know about private beaches that nobody can actually visit?' It's my turn to be disparaging. Though I must admit, the speed and inventiveness with which she came up with this idea were incredible.

Jasmine chuckles and scrapes the last bit of custard from the bottom of her dish. 'Beach nerds, obviously. It sounds plausible to me.' Replete, she sits back and pats her tummy. 'Besides, I don't hear you coming up with a feasible plan.'

While she orders coffee, I contemplate the whole venture tomorrow. The more I think about it, the more I think the survey idea isn't half bad. It's so 'out there' it works. I wouldn't ask many questions if someone came to my door with it. That aside, is it a sensible thing to do? Nosing around, digging up the past, and for what? The glass might not even be there. And if it is, what do I hope to gain from having it? The magical 'powers' the parting glass is supposed to have can't be real. But I know my curious nature wouldn't let this New Year's Eve pass without trying it out. Though once I had, if nothing happened, it would take the shine off Gran's lovely story. And I certainly don't want that. But I do really want the glass to tell me if Josh is the right one. The one I need to be with, or as Gran said to 'walk alongside for the rest of my life'. But what if he isn't the right one?

Okay, enough! I drain my glass and make a decision. No, I won't go. I can sort that out all by myself. The whole thing is ridiculous. I'm going to let sleeping glasses lie buried.

'So what time are you going tomorrow? I could try and get the afternoon off and come with you?' Jasmine's eager expression is reminiscent of a hopeful puppy desperate for a walk.

'I've decided I'm not going. It's just too crazy.'

Now she's wearing a Munch's Scream face. The Scream face with a cappuccino moustache. 'What? Why? But you must! Absolutely must!'

I tell her about my misgivings, and spoiling Gran's lovely memory. Then add, 'Besides, I can find out if Josh is the right one all by myself. I'm going to ask about us moving the relationship on when I see him. This time I won't be fobbed off either.'

'You could do both? The parting glass could just be the thing to back up your gut.'

I smile. 'You have a cappuccino moustache and a chocolate sprinkle blob on the tip of your nose.'

She looks at me deadpan. 'I know. I'm saving it for later. And don't try and change the subject.'

Feeling backed into a corner I say, 'For goodness' sake, Jas. How can an old glass actually help anyone in the love stakes? Gran was an incurable romantic. She found Jory's mother's poem and was excited when she found there was actually a glass hidden in the cave. On that New Year's Eve, she was in high spirits, had a swig of wine from the glass and convinced herself it had special powers. Logically she already knew how she felt about Jory anyway.'

'So why were you even thinking of going at all, then?' Jas wipes the moustache off and narrows her eyes at me, catlike.

Good question, Sennen. Why? I can't put it into words. I only know the idea of the parting glass has grabbed hold of my heart and won't let go. Something inside is telling me I need to find it ... that it's my destiny. Besides, Gran wants me to. How I know this, I have no idea, but I do. Maybe she's guiding me...

After a few moments' consideration I say, 'I suppose going on the same quest as Gran would have made me feel closer to her. Something we did together, even though we're apart.'

'Aw, that's lovely, but sad too.' Jas puts her hand over mine. 'But there's also the adventure of it all, and a small part of you wants it to be true, doesn't it?'

'Of course.' *If truth be told, more than a small part.* 'But how could it?'

'I don't know. I have an open mind about these kinds of things. And you should absolutely still go tomorrow. Go with your logical head on then you can't be disappointed. If you find the glass and on New Year's Eve it doesn't work, then you've honoured your gran's memory, not ruined it. Because as you say, it's something that you've done together.'

'Oh, I don't know,' I mutter into my coffee cup. Except she has almost convinced me.

'I do. It's a no-brainer. Even Robert would get it. Besides, you need to find out if the house is still there and about access and stuff. If it's not, then you will have to go by boat. Your gran and Jory did it that way.'

Is she nuts? 'A boat? Where would I get one of those? And anyway, I have no clue about how to pilot one on the bloody ocean.' Then an annoying little voice inside my head whispers. *But your Uncle Pete has a boat, doesn't he?*

Jasmine shakes her head at me. 'Dear oh dear, Sennen. You don't have much of an imagination, do you? Your grandfather was a fisherman and your dad used to go out with him all the time. I'm sure he could handle a little boat for you.'

I laugh. 'Can you imagine me telling my dad why I want him to take me to a little private beach by boat? I'd never live it down.' I keep quiet about Uncle Pete.

She heaves a sigh. 'Oh well. It's up to you in the end. But I know that if I were in your shoes, wild horses wouldn't keep me away. Something different from the same-old. A proper adventure.' A little smile. 'A last adventure with your gran.'

I swallow down the last of my coffee with a knot of emotion in my throat put there by Jasmine's words. 'Okay, enough. I will promise to consider it, but that's all. Now. Let's talk about something else.'

Chapter Four

My mind has been taken over by my body, specifically my feet, this fine Sunday morning. After I got up, had breakfast and got dressed with no particular plan for the day, my feet marched me down the path and round the back lane to my car. Then, having enlisted the help of my hands, the necessary pedals and steering wheel were manoeuvred to propel my car towards Daymer Bay, as if I had no choice in the matter. A few moments in, I considered turning around, but the tiny Cornish lanes flanked on both sides by thick hedges were having none of that. So, I decide to just allow my body to be in charge, at least until we arrive in Daymer Bay carpark. It's only a ten-minute drive anyway. Then I'll think again. Well, I'll have a go. So far, only instinct and feet have been my guide.

The car wheels bump over the rough ground in the carpark and though it's a fair autumn day, there are only about half a dozen others here. Then again, it's only just nine-thirty, so more will arrive later. Pulling the car up to the furthest point, I silence the engine and, through the windscreen, watch the waves effortlessly pulse through the Camel estuary to form a life's-blood mix of Atlantic and river. It's such a peaceful spot. A yellow sand crescent cradled in the arms of the dunes, opposite Hawkers Cove, and further along, the town of Padstow. Why I haven't been here for ages I don't know. Actually, I do. Life and work take over. Exhaling a long breath through my mouth, I wind the window down and inhale the pungent scent of seaweed and salt air. A head-clearing, soul-soothing bouquet. Then the task at hand elbows its way into my mind and interrupts my peaceful mood.

Once out of the car realisation dawns – I have absolutely no clue in which direction to walk. Why didn't I think of that before barrelling out here? Because I haven't been thinking at all this morning, probably. I sigh, take a deep breath and decide to follow my gut. But after taking a few faltering steps to the right, I stop. This is stupid. I need more information. But where from? Maybe I could go to the library to look at maps and plans, or at least ask for help … but they won't be open on Sunday. A little black cloud of defeat rolls into my chest along with a rumble of annoyance. I really wanted to find answers today. Oh well. No good crying over spilt parting glasses. May as well go for a walk and hope for the best. Then I see the little shop I drove past as I entered the carpark and think it's as good a place as any to start. In fact, it's the only place available right now.

Daymer Bay Beach Shop and Café has a welcoming

atmosphere, and the aroma of fresh coffee and croissants lifts my spirits immediately. Even if they know nothing about Nancarrow House, at least I can have a second breakfast. A plump, smiley-faced woman appears behind the counter. 'What can I get you, dear?'

'A skinny latte and a *pain au chocolat*, please.'

'Coming right up.' She goes to the coffee machine, tucks a length of grey curly hair behind her ear and nods at the window. 'Lovely day for a walk.'

I smile. 'Yes, I'll be off along the cliff path once I've fortified myself with this little treat.' And as casually as I can, above the 'shuuuush' of the coffee maker, I say, 'Have you heard of Nancarrow House? It's supposed to be round here somewhere.'

The woman pours coffee into a mug, her mouth twisted to the side in a thoughtful pout. 'Er ... Do you know, I'm not sure? It used to be. I remember walking past it when I was a kid, and that wasn't yesterday!' Her chesty bark is a log shifting on a fire. 'Nor the day before. Oh, hang on, I know the one you mean! Yeah, the owners went off to London back in the 1990s, but I have no clue about it now. I moved to Polzeath and never go up that way nowadays.' She waves her arms expansively. 'Too busy with this place.'

'Right, thanks,' I say, digging my purse out of my bag. 'So what direction is it in from here?' I notice a frown trouble her brow as she places the *pain au chocolat* on a plate and hands it to me. Maybe she thinks I'm asking too many questions, so I add, 'It's just that my gran used to deliver bread up there back in the 1950s and I just fancied having a look.'

'Oh, I see. That's nice.' The woman's smile irons out the frown and she presents me with the card reader. 'Yes, it's along the coast path to the right of the carpark. Only about five minutes or so. It's set back a bit from the cliff, must have wonderful views across the ocean. It's built of red brick and has black iron gates with a swirly letter "N" and "H" on each.'

I take my tray and give her a big smile. Thank goodness I have more to go on now. 'That's great, thank you! Should be easy enough to find.'

She purses her lips and folds her arms under her ample bosom. 'Hmm. If it's still there. I wouldn't be surprised if they've turned it into a jazzy health spa or flattened it and built holiday cottages on the land. Money talks.'

This is not what I want to hear. 'Yeah. But let's hope not,' I say. I thank her again and take a seat by the window.

Second breakfast finished, I hurry across the carpark and take the sandy path to the right alongside the beach and water. Once I'm clear of some high bushes, the wind blows hard salt kisses on my cheeks, and much as I appreciate the affection, it does make walking all the more arduous. As I round a bend, my back is to the elements so the onslaught is calmed a little, and I notice a few houses set back along the path, dotted here and there like chunky charms on a thin bracelet. None are extraordinarily grand or red-brick though, so I hurry on to the next bend ... and we have lift-off! Or at least there's a red-brick wall peeping through some tall trees.

Nearing the trees, I see a chimney and slate roof, and below, around the perimeter, there's a impenetrable natural barrier of tangled brambles and foliage. I skirt around it and arrive at what seem to be the front gateposts, though the grand gates marked with an 'N' and 'H' that the lady in the café talked of are no longer hanging there. The posts are crumbling and the whole entrance and path are obscured by more brambles. However, on closer inspection and as I wiggle through the gap, I can see there is work going on – or has been. Around the edge of the garden is the remains of an old stone wall through which a makeshift gravel path has been laid. On the path stands a redundant digger, and beyond that the west wall of the house has a frame of scaffolding climbing up it like a metal spider, one leg resting under the broken window pane of an upstairs room. More interesting information reveals itself, to the right of the path. The shaft and notice of a broken *For Sale* sign lie half hidden in rubble and weeds. Why didn't it sell? Or maybe it did, and the new owners ran out of money?

Moments later, my eye is taken by two structures propped up against what's left of the wall further on. If I was in any doubt that this is the Nancarrow House my gran spoke of, I'm not now. Stepping towards them over some overgrown boulders I run my fingers across the rusty edges of the letters 'N' and 'H' clinging grimly to the old gates like children to a parent on the first day of school. It all feels so desolate here. I listen for sounds of life, but all that whispers in my ears is the wind, shushed by the ocean beyond. The house is sad. I can sense the neglect and loneliness. Its huge bay windows on the ground floor are half shuttered like eyelids lowered in grief. It's obvious nobody is living here, because of the jungle garden and broken window, but will there be in the future? Evidence seems to suggest it, because of the scaffolding and digger. And what about the *For Sale* sign? Hmm. More to the point, what about the forgotten beach? That's why I'm here, after all.

I look behind me and listen again. Nobody and nothing. If I'm quick, I can be up past the side of the house and round the back before any walkers pass by to see me snooping. Setting off at a run, I'm soon around the corner of the house and on the sweep of a gravel drive, it too riddled with weeds and foliage. The ocean can be glimpsed through the trees and a paved path weaves towards it through what I think used to be a flower bed, or vegetable patch. Picking my way around nettles, I arrive at the edge of the land. The ocean bashes itself against the foot of the cliff and, if I lean forward slightly, I can see a spit of a beach below. My heart rattles about a bit in my chest as I realise what I'm looking at. The forgotten beach, and on it, somewhere, is the parting glass, with any luck! Despite my excitement, my legs tremble with trepidation and I step quickly back to safety. A few feet away, I notice two huge rusting metal poles driven into the ground with a thick padlocked chain wrapped between and around them. From the chain, a dirty white sign gently squeaks as the wind plays with it. Though the red writing is a bit faded, the message is still loud and clear: 'DANGER – KEEP OUT!'

I don't need shouting at twice. There's no way I'm

venturing over that gateway, even if I could climb through the chains. Time to go before I'm caught, I think. Considering I had no clue this morning if the house was still here, it's not been such a bad few hours' work. At least it's still here, broken, battered, lonely – but here. Maybe if I can find out who owns the place, they would give me permission to access the beach somehow. I could sneak there on a boat and they would be none the wiser, I suppose, but I'd rather be upfront about it. Besides, I'm curious to see what's going to happen to the old place and who the owner is. I shake my head. This house is in danger of getting under my skin.

Back at the car, I have one final look at the waves and think about what to do next. I don't have to think very hard, because a new plan is delivered to my brain on the white horse surf. Maybe they are brainwaves. I chuckle to myself at that hilarious joke and then get behind the wheel. At least I know what I'm doing in my lunch hour tomorrow.

My old school chum Claire looks like she might be some time with the couple seated opposite her desk, so I idly look through the *For Sale* lists on the wall of Miniver and Gordon, Estate Agents. She gave me a little wave as I came in and as I waved back, I did wonder if this was a wild-goose chase. But right now, I don't really have another option if I want to find out more about Nancarrow House. My God, these houses are expensive. It's a wonder any local people are left. Such a shame. Houses are being snapped up by people from elsewhere and rented as holiday homes or sold as second homes. Many young locals are having to leave Cornwall if they want to get on the property ladder, or even rent. In disgust, I flick my finger at a photo of a three-bed semi-detached needing updating for an eye-watering price, and catch Claire's glance and puzzled frown. The couple are just leaving and she's clearly wondering why the hell I'm stood there, flicking my fingers at her sales board.

Sitting down opposite her, I pull the chair up to the desk and hope my pink cheeks soon fade. 'Hi, Claire. Sorry about the flicky thing, it's just that I got a bit fed up seeing the prices of everything. People our age can't afford to buy locally.'

Claire gives me a wry smile and shoves her tortoiseshell-rimmed glasses up along her retroussé nose. 'Tell me about it. Me and my boyfriend are struggling to rent a one-bed apartment in town, and we both work full-time.'

'No discount on these lovely houses, then?' I laugh.

'Chance would be a fine thing.' Claire tucks her dark shiny bob behind each ear and then asks, 'So what kind of place are you looking for?'

Now I feel even more embarrassed. 'Um, I'm not actually here to look at anything. I just wanted some information on a house in Daymer Bay. You might not know anything, as it's not up for sale. But I think it was at some point ... not sure when though...' My voice tails off as the interested expression slides from her face.

'I need more to go on than that.'

'It was a grand old place my gran used to deliver bread to years ago. She loved the house and I thought I'd go and get a look at it. It's called Nancarrow House, or was. When I went up there yesterday it was in need of some TLC and a good gardener. There was scaffolding up and a digger there, but no sign of life. I noticed a broken *For Sale* sign stuck in the grass and wondered if you knew anything about it?'

The uninterested expression is replaced by a slightly more animated one, but Claire's one-eye-on-the-door gaze lets me know she thinks I'm wasting her valuable time. Which I suppose I am. Perhaps she wanted to grab a coffee while the place was empty. 'Yeah, I remember that place. It was put up for sale about eighteen months ago, then the guy who owns it took it back off the market a few weeks later.'

'Oh really? Why?'

'Said he'd had second thoughts and that he ought to keep it in the family.' Claire shoved her glasses up her nose again and stared at the desk. 'If I remember rightly, he said he was going to do it up and use it for when he and his friends wanted a bolthole from city life.'

'Which city? And do you remember his name?'

Claire raises her eyebrows. 'Are you interested in the house or the owner?'

'Both. If I know who the owner is, I could ask him if I could…' *If you could what, Sennen? Go down to a forgotten beach and look for a magical glass?* '…Um, go inside and imagine what it was like when my gran visited,' I finish lamely.

'Hmm. That kind of information is confidential, Sennen.'

'But we've known each other since primary school. There's no way I would say I got his name from you.' I'm aware I sound desperate, but that's because I am.

Claire heaves a sigh and looks at the door again. 'Okay, but you'd better not. And the chances of him letting you in there are pretty slim, I'd say. Not sure he's the chummy type. In fact, he's a bit snotty to be honest. He's a lawyer, barrister or something, from London. Very up himself because he's "as fit as" and has more money than sense. His family moved from Cornwall to London in the 1990s, I think, and the house was left to rot.'

I smile. That was an awful lot considering it was confidential. 'And his name?'

'Tremaine Nancarrow. Now I really must get on, Sennen.'

'Yes. Yes, of course!' I jump up, thrilled to have a name and to know the house is still owned by a Nancarrow. 'I'll leave you to it. And thank you.'

Chapter Five

My little kitchen is full of the delicious aroma of chicken casserole, roast potatoes and chocolate pudding. A rumble in my tummy has me glancing at the clock. Six-forty-five. I hope Josh won't be late as I'm bloody starving. I can't help smiling as thoughts of rushing into his loving arms fill my head. It's been over a week since I went over to his, as he's been so busy with surfing lessons and competitions. Thankfully, he will have a bit more time for us now winter's coming, though I expect he'll have to take a delivery driver job again to tide him over like he did last year.

Taking a sip of a nicely chilled Sauvignon Blanc, I take it and my thoughts into the living room and plop down on the sofa. It's been a good day all round. The shop was fairly busy, I found out about Tremaine Nancarrow, and tonight I'll broach the subject of Josh and me getting a place together. I've decided not to wait for his birthday, because I need answers. The idea of all that adds a roll of trepidation to the grumble in my tummy. What if he says the usual? Do I just accept it, or push for some kind of plan? How long will it be, for example? One year, two? When?

An image of him tanned, bare-chested and long-legged striding up the beach, his long white-blond curls lifting on the breeze like some latter-day Viking, comes to mind. And I love the way his sea-green eyes crinkle at the edges when he smiles at me, but will he be smiling later when he's heard what I have to say? My phone ringing cuts into my thoughts and I pick it up. Jasmine. Oh, my goodness, I forgot to ask how her interview went!

'Hi, Jasmine, I was just about to ring you,' I lie.

'Ask me.' The excitement in her voice is palpable.

'Ask you what?'

'Ask me if I got the job.'

'Did you get—'

'Yeeeeees!!! I bloody did! Robert was actually nice to me and Sally Henshaw said I would be an asset to the Newquay store!'

'Newquay? But that's about forty minutes south of us. I thought you wanted to manage the store here?'

'I did, and yes, it's more travelling every day, but this store is bigger and I get more dosh!' The squeal at the end of 'dosh' makes me hold the phone away from my ear.

'That's brilliant! I'm over the moon for you.'

'Me too. Do you fancy coming out for a celebratory drink?'

'I'd love to, but Josh is coming over. I've cooked a meal.'

'What is it?' I tell her. 'God, I could just eat that! I've

been on the phone to Mum for the last hour and haven't got round to eating anything.'

'Sorry. Only enough for two.'

'Just joking! I'll order a pizza. Fancy having that drink on Thursday? I'm gonna be in the Newquay shop Wednesday and Thursday, so will have lots to tell you.'

'Sounds good to me! I'll look forward to it!' We end the call and my phone tells me it's almost ten past seven. I must turn the oven off – the casserole will be dried up. As I'm taking the dish out of the oven to check on it, my phone rings again. Kicking the oven door shut with my foot, I pop the dish on the stove and see the caller ID.

'Hey, babe,' Josh says, and then for the second time this evening I have to hold the phone from my ear as a hacking cough barks down the line.

'You okay?' I reply once the coughing stops.

'No. I've been feeling rough all week, then this fricking cough started. Kept me awake all night. I hoped I'd feel better if I had a nap after work, but I'm worse, if anything.'

My heart sinks. Looks like the cosy dinner for two and a chat about the future won't be happening. Then a glimmer of hope rises along with a wisp of steam from the dish. I take the lid off and give the chicken a stir. 'Oh, poor baby! Do you want me to come over? I've made your favourite casserole; I could bring some to you?'

More hacking coughs deafen me. 'I'm not that hungry to be honest, sweet. Think I'll get my head down again. I'll be better in a couple of days – sorry you went to all that trouble for nothing.'

So am I crosses my mind, then I tell myself off. 'Hey, you can't help it. Just wish I could do something to help. I miss you.'

'Me too. But with rest I'll be fine by the end of the week.'

Didn't he just say a couple of days, now it's the end of the week? 'Yeah. Hope so.'

'Right, see ya, then, Sen.'

'See you, Josh. I love y—' I'm left talking to thin air.

Great. Disappointment like a lead weight drags my mood down. I take out the roast potatoes and stick them on the hob next to the casserole. Dinner for one then… Why do I get the feeling that Josh and I have hit a bump in the road? A bigger bump than the wheels on this thing we have can roll over. Okay he's poorly, but there's been a distance between us, if I'm honest, and I don't mean in miles. Maybe I'm not interesting or exciting enough for him. He could have his pick of any girl after all. I let out a long sigh and take a plate out of the cupboard. Then I grab my phone again.

'Hey, Jas. You ordered that pizza yet?'

'Just about to. Why?'

'Fancy a casserole instead?'

It's Thursday afternoon and rain is firing horizontal bullets at the shop window. There must be an invisible weather machine-gun trained on me from the butcher's opposite. I stare at it across the rain-soaked street. The shop, not the invisible machine-gun, because how could I? It being invisible. Oh God. I'm losing my marbles. I'm in danger of going stir-crazy, and can count on one hand the customers who have been in today – actually, no. On one finger. But it's unsurprising, given the monsoon out there.

For the last half-hour I've been googling Tremaine Nancarrow. The results are interesting. He's a swanky London barrister, but I knew that. And from the very few photos available to me on Facebook because I'm not a friend, he looks to be fond of the finer things in life. Climbing in the Himalayas, at a black-tie event in some posh banqueting hall surrounded by guys raising glasses and pretty women hung with diamonds. Oh, and not forgetting the one of him thundering along the beach on a magnificent black horse as if he's in a TV commercial for a bank.

Claire's description of him being up himself as the result of being 'as fit as' is totally believable too. The fit thing *and* the up himself bit. How fortunate can one person be? All that, and the looks of a Greek god? But then instead of choosing to be pleasant to others, he decides instead to be snotty. Entitled snob. I'm not looking forward to getting in touch with him at all. Still, needs must.

I close the cover on my iPad and walk away from the window. Might as well close up fifteen minutes early. A bubble bath and a glass of wine before I meet Jasmine for a drink seem like great ideas. Josh is still unwell and didn't sound any better at all when I spoke to him at lunchtime. If he's no better on Monday, I made him promise to get a doctor's appointment. Knowing him he won't though. He said he's just got to ride the storm. I look back at the torrential rain. Yup, so will I if this keeps up on the walk home.

I'm greeted by laughter and song as I walk through the door of the Golden Lion pub. Someone is having a birthday party and the place is busier than usual on a Thursday night out of season. As I thread my way through the crowd, I glance at the red-haired woman sitting at a table surrounded by people, cake and presents. She's glowing with happiness, her sparkly green eyes dancing under the low lights. I'm surprised to see Jasmine amongst the woman's friends and she gives me a wave and points to a table at the other side of the room.

I follow her towards it and we sit down. 'Who's the birthday girl?' I ask, slipping my coat off and wishing I'd changed out of my faded jeans and old burgundy woollen top. I know it's only a drink at the local pub, but I should try to make more of an effort with my appearance if I'm to keep Josh interested.

'Nancy Cornish. She lives next door but one to my mum. Lovely woman, full of energy and always ready to help. She's a PI no less!' Jas plays with a button on her black and white polka-dot shirt and crosses her legs.

'Really! Not sure what I expected from a private investigator, but the image I have leans more towards a balding man in his mid-fifties, with a tired expression and jaded view of life.'

Jasmine laughs. 'She's a psychic investigator, not a

private one. And bloody good at it she is too. Nancy helps her husband Charlie to solve crimes – he's a copper. But she mainly helps people solve their own little mysteries. She once helped my great-auntie find some medals belonging to my great-uncle that she'd sent to the charity shop by mistake. And that led to her meeting a long-lost friend.' Jas puts her head on one side and gives me a wink. 'Well, they are more than friends nowadays, if you know what I mean.'

Gobsmacked, I look at Nancy and back to Jas. 'Really? That's amazing. I'm not sure I believe in all that stuff, but—'

'You would if you met her. I'll introduce you later if she comes past. She's busy thanking everyone for the surprise birthday meal right now.'

I'm not sure I want to be introduced to a psychic – it's all a bit out there for me – but I keep quiet and change the subject. 'Okay, let's order and then you can tell me all about your new job.'

The burgers are fantastic here, and as we munch our way through, Jas tells me how much she's enjoying the new job. 'I love Newquay. It's got such a beach-bum vibe going on, even at this time of year. And the people in the store are lovely. Even though I'm the boss now.' Jasmine preens a bit and takes a swallow of cider.

It's great to see her confidence returning since her boyfriend left, and I'm certain this new job will be the making of her. 'Your fears about Robert scuppering your chances were unfounded then?'

'Yeah. He was really nice to me after the interview. He was the one to tell me I'd got the job and he looked genuinely pleased that I had. Weird.'

'Maybe you were wrong about him all this time?' I wonder, dipping a chip into ketchup.

'Mm. No clue. I only know that for the last year, every time he's seen me, he's been snappy and rude. So, your guess is as good as mine. I'll never understand men.' Jasmine stares into the distance for a moment and then fixes her gaze on mine. 'Oh! I forgot to ask, have you made a decision about going over to try and find Nancarrow House?'

I wiggle my eyebrows at her. 'I might have already been.'

'You sly dog. Tell me all!'

I tell her all about my visit and my conversation with Claire and then show her the photos I found of Tremaine Nancarrow.

'Oh my God, he's bloody gorgeous. Good enough to eat! Look at those eyes! Turquoise blue, I'd call them, and all that tawny-coloured floppy hair,' she gushes. 'It's in a little ponytail in that one. Nice. And those pouty lips…'

I hold my hands up. 'Okay, I get the impression you think he's a bit good-looking.'

'A bit? Are you blind?'

'Skin deep, I'm afraid.'

'You don't know that.'

'Claire said.'

'Yeah, but that was just her opinion. You have to keep an open mind when you meet him.'

'Yeah. Not sure I will do though. If Claire's right, he might not be very welcoming.'

'But then again he might be absolutely fine.' Jas leans forward, rests her chin on interlaced fingers and gives me an impish look. 'Can I come if you do meet him?'

'No. You'll drool all over him and ruin his designer clothes.'

'Oh, very funny.' Jas sits back, raises her pint and regards me over the top of it. 'How are you going to get in contact?'

I shrug. 'I've got a work email and phone number. I'll ring and ask to speak to him.'

'You'd better get on with it then. I need to know everything there is to know about TT.'

'TT?'

'Tasty Tremaine.' Jasmine's eyes sparkle with humour.

'Oh dear, what are you like? Now, tell me more about the new job.'

Jas smiles and rummages in her bag. She puts a pen, comb, purse and phone on the table and then in triumph brandishes an ID badge with 'Jasmine Thomas – Manager' written on it. 'I can't stop looking at this,' she says with a little laugh.

I look at her cheeks, pink with pride, and want to hug her. 'I'm so pleased that you're happy in your job now, Jas.'

She's about to answer when the PI, Nancy Cornish, walks past our table, presumably on her way to the Ladies. 'Hey, Nancy! Meet my bestest friend, Sennen.'

Nancy gives me a big smile and sits in the empty chair at

the end of the table. 'Hi, Sennen, love the name. After Sennen Cove?'

'Yeah. It's where my mum grew up.'

'You enjoying your birthday?' Jas asks, fiddling with her badge as if she wants Nancy to notice it.

'Yes. It was a lovely surprise. Charlie organised it and invited the whole of Padstow, I think!' She nods at the badge. 'Your mum told me you got the promotion, well done!'

Jasmine's cheeks glow pink again. 'Thank you! I'm so pleased.' As she says this, she plonks the badge down and it nudges the pen. Nancy just manages to grab it before it rolls off the table onto the floor.

Then her whole demeanour changes. She loses the smile and her eyes focus on something only she can see at the other side of the pub. Jas and I shoot each other puzzled glances and then, after a few moments, Nancy turns to Jas. 'The person who owns this pen has very strong feelings for you, Jasmine. I think he will become very important to you if you let him,' she says, with a smile.

Jasmine's mouth drops open. 'Eh? You have got to be joking!'

Nancy put the pen on the table and shrugs. 'Nope. Very serious.'

'But … but that's weird. Until recently he's been a proper pig…' Jasmine says, bewildered.

The penny drops in my head and I realise who the pen belongs to. 'Robert?'

Jasmine nods. 'Yeah. I borrowed it from him the other day and forgot to give it back.'

Nancy stands up and smooths her skirt. 'If he's been a pig, I'm guessing it's because he wanted to keep you at arm's length. No idea why. Now, if you'll excuse me, ladies. I must go to the Ladies!' She waves goodbye and hurries off.

'Oh, my word. I need another drink!' Jasmine says, jumping up. 'Same again?'

Ten minutes later we still are no wiser about Robert's odd behaviour. He has been horrid to Jas for the last year. Why the sudden change? Then a thought occurs. I take a sip of cider and say, 'Anyway, never mind about why he might have feelings for you all of a sudden. I've not heard you say what you think of him.'

She wrinkles her nose. 'His personality? I think he's a pompous, arrogant arse. But that's because of his behaviour towards me. Well, until after the interview, when he was really very sweet. His looks? Extremely attractive.' Jas lifts a cautionary finger. 'Not on TT's scale, but then who is? Short dark hair, a little goatee, bright blue eyes, muscular physique, just under six foot, I'd say.'

'Hm, sounds like this might go somewhere.'

Jas twists her mouth to the side and shakes her head dismissively. 'No chance.'

'So, Nancy isn't such a brilliant psychic, then?'

Jasmine shifts in her seat obviously uncomfortable with this question. 'Er … well, yes. Normally. She must be having an off day.'

I laugh out loud. 'Yeah, okay. If you say so.'

'Look, there's no way Robert and I would work. He's about five years older than me anyway.'

I raise my eyebrows at her. 'Thirty? Yeah, such an old man.'

The corner of her mouth twitches into a half-smile then it irons out. 'Anyway, I don't want to talk about it.'

'You sound like Josh.' I'd not meant to say that, but Josh's behaviour has been tying knots of tension in my gut all week.

'What doesn't he want to talk about?' Jas says, absently, as she once again rummages in her bag.

'Getting a place together. Moving things on. But then I don't know how he feels right now, because I haven't seen him for nearly two weeks.' I'm talking to the top of her head. She's more interested in what's at the bottom of her bag than anything I'm saying, but I carry on, nevertheless. 'Yes, he's had a bad cold and chest infection or whatever it is, but I have the feeling he's avoiding me, somehow. I can't put my finger on it.'

'Hmm.' More rummaging.

'"Hmm"? Is that it?'

'Sorry, can't find something.'

'What are you looking for?'

'Oh. It's er … a thingy, you know?'

'Thingy?'

'Hmm.'

She still hasn't looked up from her bag and her couldn't-care-less attitude is verging on the rude. 'Right. So, what do you think about Josh?'

'Do you fancy a pudding?'

There's something not right about her voice. It's gone all squeaky and the tips of her ears have gone redder than her hair. 'A pudding? Jas, look at me.'

Releasing a deep sigh, she raises her head but her eyes flick off towards the door as if she's longing to walk through it. Her face is on fire and she puts a shaking hand to her mouth. God. What's wrong with her?

'Look at me,' I insist. There's a jittery feeling growing in my gut and I shove my hands under my armpits to stop them trembling. Something is very wrong and it involves Josh. I just know it.

Jasmine turns her head, holds my gaze, and two big teardrops brim from her eyes and roll down her cheeks. 'I'm so sorry, Sen. I was going to tell you over the phone, but I bottled it. Thought it would be better face-to-face. But then we were having such a nice time tonight ... and ... I'm rubbish at giving crap news.'

Nausea rolls into the jittery feeling and I take a few deep breaths. 'Please. Just tell me.'

Lowering her gaze, Jas takes a long swallow from her glass and blurts, 'The other day when I was in Newquay, I went for a walk in my lunch break as it was such a lovely day. As I walked along Fistral Beach, I passed a café. A couple were sitting on the outside deck and I took a double-take, because I thought I recognised the guy.' She stops and dabs a tissue under each eye. 'The woman was about our age, or a bit younger. Long blonde hair – surfer type.'

My own eyes mist over as I know what's coming. This is what I've been dreading. Red flags have been waving at me for weeks now, though I chose to ignore them. Became deaf, dumb and blind. An ostrich. I dig my nails into my palms as if I'm clinging desperately to a lifeline, but I know I can't be saved. I decide instead to save Jas any more discomfort and ask, 'It was Josh, wasn't it?'

She sniffs, nods and touches my arm, her eyes brimming with fresh tears. 'Yeah. At first, I thought he might be with just a friend or his sister. But I put my hood up to hide my hair – it's not hard to spot – put my sunglasses on and walked past again a bit further away to sit on the sand so I could keep watch. They were talking and laughing' – she slides her eyes from mine – 'and then it became obvious she wasn't his sister.'

These words punch me in the gut. My imagination is doing a great job of providing all kinds of scenarios and I lean forward, wrap my arms around my chest to protect myself from further blows. Even though I know what she says is true, I hear myself groan, 'Oh no… not my Josh. Please no.' Then a question escapes, intent on torturing me further. 'Were they kissing?'

'Yeah.' Jas gives me a watery smile, takes my hand. 'I'm so, so sorry, Sen. I knew I had to tell you, but it was really hard. I know how much you love him and—'

I cut her off – I can't stand to hear more, or the pitying looks any longer.

'Don't apologise. I would have done the same if the boot were on the other foot.' Withdrawing my hand, I sit back in my seat, stare at a moving picture reel of Josh and some faceless surfer chick all over each other. His hands in her hair, hers in his, snogging the face off each other in full view of people in the café. The café we've been to together, many times. A surge of anger bubbles up from my depths, sending my heart-rate into overdrive. 'That bastard!' I hiss. 'He told me he was ill. Cancelled at the very last minute the meal I'd got ready for him... All a pack of fucking lies so he could go and be with her. I bet they had a right old laugh at my expense.' My voice catches in my throat and I down the rest of my drink in one, then slam it down on the table.

Amongst those nearby, the conversation falters and a few look over at me. I'm so close to yelling at them, asking them what the hell they are staring at, but I manage to keep a lid on it. And rush off to the loo. Inside the cubicle, I sit biting my knuckles to stem the escape of the multitude of sobs lining up at the back of my throat. I hear the door open and Jas say, 'Sennen? You okay, mate?'

'Ha! Yeah. Yeah, Jas. Absolutely fab-u-lous, darling!' I snap, then immediately regret it. None of this is her fault. 'Sorry...'

Jasmine taps on the door. 'Hey, don't apologise. I would be the same. Open the door and let me hug you.'

'No. If I do that, I'll be a mess. I need to get out of here, go back to yours.' I wish I'd not agreed to stay over. All I want is my own bed and a vat of wine to drown in. Oh, and a shotgun to blow that cheating bastard's head off.

'Okay. I'll get a taxi.'

'You got wine at yours?'

'Yeah. I always have wine.'

I take some calming breaths while I listen to her order a taxi. Then I come out and walk straight past her, through the pub and into the cool night air. Jasmine follows me out and tries to make me feel better by saying how I must be in shock and it will seem a bit more bearable in the morning, but all I can think about is stopping myself from crying. I mustn't cry. Because if I start…

Once the taxi has driven off Jasmine opens her door, chattering on about this and that in a desperate and futile attempt to lighten the atmosphere. 'Now we have red, white, gin, vodka … oh, and tequila!' She pulls a bottle from the cupboard and does a fake smile. 'Which do you fancy?'

'All of them!' Then my bravado crumbles like the ridiculous clown smile I've just painted on. 'I just want to be numb. Blank out the images of … of…' Then to my annoyance, the tears that I've been holding back overwhelm me and I sink down on her sofa sobbing my heart out.

Jasmine puts her arms around me and gives me a big squeeze. 'Just let it out, Sen. Let it all out, sweetheart.'

So I do. Because I haven't the strength to keep it in.

Chapter Six

Last night I resolved to cut all ties with Josh, remove his number from my phone, his toothbrush from my bathroom, and all the love I had for him from my heart. This afternoon, after my stomach has finally finished evacuating the last vestiges of the ocean of booze I put away at Jasmine's, I snatch my phone from my bag, get back under the duvet and look at his name on my contact list. Since Jas dropped me home a few hours ago, I crawled between bed and bathroom like some demented creature. Swearing, ranting, vomiting and repeating. A yoyo of misery wrapped in a tangled string of self-pity and regret. I kept reiterating to myself that I must remove Josh from my life like the disgusting splat of seagull shit I'd scrubbed from my windscreen the other day.

That was then. Now I'm feeling more human, an angry voice is telling me to ring him. Ring him and demand an explanation. Why should he be allowed off the hook so easily? To get away without having to see or speak to me again? Sail off into the sunset with his bit on the surfboard? He owes me an apology at the very least! How bloody dare he treat me like this! Then a different voice whispers a few pertinent questions in my ear. Isn't all this indignant fierceness just bluster? Isn't it really hope, in a kick-ass disguise, sneaking in at three a.m. by the back door, like a teenager on her last warning? Isn't this phone call nothing but a way of hearing his voice again, even though the conversation will crucify me? Am I expecting a miracle? Do I want Josh to say he's made a terrible mistake, to say he's sorry and beg me to marry him or something? Pathetic.

My weary head flops back onto the pillows like a punchbag under an invisible fist. What the hell should I do? To phone, or not to phone? That is the question. Or one of them. Many others are packing a suitcase and queuing up on my tongue's runway. I swallow them and make a decision. Sod it. I'm phoning him. I can't just cut him out without a word. I need closure. A bloody stupid phrase, but it fits my reasoning. Before I can talk myself out of it, I jab my finger at his number so hard my nail bends. Ouch.

'Hello, Sen. How are you doing?' A cough follows, but this time I know it's false.

'No better then?'

'Getting there… Still not up to working though.'

'Or seeing me?'

'Not really, hon. I would hate you to catch it.'

'You don't mind Surfer Girl catching it though, eh?'

'Who?'

'The girl that you were snogging the face off in the café at Fistral a few days back. You know, the one that Jasmine saw you with. Unless she's one of many women you're seeing?'

The silence between us is wide and deep. Echoing around inside it, I can hear my heartbeat thudding in my ears, and hope throwing me ridiculous scenarios. This is the bit where he denies it, asks me if I've lost my mind, says Jas was mistaken, says he has a long-lost twin he didn't know about until last week. This is the bit where I wake up from a nightmare, sans hangover, in a sun-drenched room, with happy little bluebirds tweeting at me from my windowsill. The bit where all the red flags I've ignored ostrich-like have been figments of my imagination. This is the bit where I get to carry on with my life and live happily ever after.

Josh blows the silence away with long heavy breath. 'No. No, she isn't one of many. I didn't want you to find out like this, Sennen. But at least it's done now. I was going to tell you soon. Real soon. But I think I'm a bit of a coward.'

The birds fly from the windowsill into a thunderstorm and the phone trembles in my fingers. No denial, no excuses, no apology… Nausea rolls again, but this time it has nothing to do with the booze. Tremors rack my whole body, and I can't find my voice for a moment. When I do, it's loud and angry and injured. 'You think? YOU THINK! How long have you been cheating on me, you spineless bastard!'

'Not long. It wasn't planned, just happened.' Josh's tone is calm. Collected. Detached.

'Bet she's a client.'

'Yup.'

'Your eyes met across a surfboard, hm?' Hot, angry tears

stream down my face. I wipe them away with the duvet. There's no way I'm breaking down in front of him.

'Something like that.'

His detached, almost bored tone pushes my buttons. 'So, what happened, Josh, eh? Just fancied a change after two years?'

'As I said, it wasn't planned. Erm … think I was beginning to feel pushed into a corner, if I'm honest.' A sigh. 'You know, with you always wanting to talk about moving things on, settling down. All that domestic stuff. It's not me.'

'No. We all know you're a free spirit, a rebel, an inspired-by-nature boy,' I mimic the wistful way his voice sounds when outlining the description of himself he's so fond of sharing with me. And I fell for it, didn't I? Made excuses for him to my parents, told myself I loved his free spirt, his refusal to be tamed and tied down. I had to admit to myself that the truth had been filtering through my blindfold for some time though, growing brighter and brighter, until I was blinded by it. So, what did I do? Shoved my head in the sand where it was nice and dark – blotted it out.

His reply is bitter and sharp. 'Nice to know what you really think of me.'

'Oh please. Don't make *me* out to be the bad guy.'

'Well, I'm not the bad guy either, Sen. I just follow my heart. Life's too short to be doing stuff—'

'That you don't have to. Yeah. You *have* mentioned that a few times!' I thump my fist down on the pillow, wishing it was his smug face.

'Okay. I think we're done here. You're bringing me down, big time.'

'Ha! I'm bringing YOU down?' I'm incredulous. 'After what you've just pulled! You haven't even had the decency to apologise!'

'Okay. I'm sorry you're upset. But it's for the best. You need some family guy – a pipe and slippers dude – and that's not me.'

'You condescending bastard! You don't have the first clue about what I need! In fact, you don't care about anyone but yourself. It's all about you, isn't it, Josh!' Realisation strikes home like a hammer blow and I add quietly, 'It's only ever really been about you.'

'Bye, Sen. It was good while it lasted. You'll meet someone else and—'

I cut him off. A range of emotions – rage, sadness, humiliation and bewilderment – twist themselves into a tornado and surge through me, bashing around my insides like a trapped demon. I howl, thump my fists into the pillow some more, throw stuff, swear, cry and then fall silent as numbness creeps across me like shadows at twilight. Staring at a crack in the ceiling, my thoughts idle, my gut hollow, I let my body float. Leaden eyelids plunge me into welcome darkness and, totally exhausted, I give myself to sleep.

Another missed call from Jasmine. I consider switching it from silent, but instead, shove the phone back under the cushion on the sofa and dig a spoon deeper into the tub of chocolate-chip ice-cream as big as my head. Really? What a cliché. Girl gets dumped. Girl sits on sofa stuffing herself with ice-cream and crisps while watching mindless rubbish on TV for three hours. Guilt, don't forget that, Sennen. Guilt has added to the self-pity fest. Poor Uncle Pete. I think again about how I worried the hell out of him by not opening the shop today. He'd popped round to *Sea Spray* to see how things were going, only to find it closed, so he'd phoned me. I'd explained the situation and made him promise not to tell my parents. I couldn't cope with Mum racing over here demanding to know all the ins and outs.

Licking the spoon, I consider Jasmine. I really ought to ring her or she'll be round too. I've missed four of her calls since switching the phone off after the Uncle Pete conversation. I shovel three or four more spoonfuls of ice-cream into my mouth and pull the phone from behind the cushion. This is not a call I want to make. Not what I want to be doing at all – reliving the horrible truth of what happened today – when I've so nicely hidden it under a pile of junk food. But needs must.

'Thank God! I was just putting my coat on to come over. You okay?'

'Um, yeah. Kind of.'

'Did you contact Josh?'

I tell her as quickly as possible about what happened and pretend I'm someone else. Someone in a play reciting rehearsed lines to a faceless audience. Detaching myself from reality, so I can stop myself from weeping and wailing down the phone. 'So, time to move on. I'm not wasting any more time over that shithead.'

'Oh, mate, I feel for you. I've been there.'

'Yeah. I know. Thanks.'

'I must say, you seem remarkably calm. Must be the shock.'

'Nah. I was really upset earlier, but I've cried my last tears over him. He doesn't deserve them.'

'That's for damned sure.' Jas sighs. 'Didn't you have any suspicions about him at all?'

'Um, if I'm honest, I did…' My mind replays scenes of Josh saying he had to go here, there and everywhere whenever I suggested he came round to my parents, or I go to his. Or the way he'd always changed the subject when I'd talked about the future, or the one time when he said he'd been out with his mate Nathan, but then Nathan had seemed surprised when I'd seen him in the street the next day and mentioned it. He'd covered well, but the guilty lie was written all over his face.

'Oh, right… Why didn't you say anything to him?' Jasmine's question is loaded with pity and I have to swallow hard before answering.

'Because I was doing the ostrich. Sticking my head in the sand, pretending I was imagining things. Making excuses, blaming myself for not being interesting enough or attractive enough to make him want to see me more, and move in with me. I was so in love with him, Jas. I couldn't bear to think of life without him. Pathetic, I know.' This being strong act is falling apart, and I press my fists into my eyes to stop tears forming.

'Now listen to me, young lady. You are not pathetic! He's the pathetic one. Look, are you sure you don't want me to come over?'

I close my eyes and release a calming breath. 'No. Thanks for offering, but I'm going to ring our Ruan, he will be furious at Josh, and want to rehash it all. But me and my little bro have always confided in each other, as you know, no matter how painful the subject is. Then I'll be ready for my bed and then off to the shop early tomorrow morning to make up for today. I'll make a few pots too.'

'Okay. Well, we'll catch up in a few days.'

'Yeah.' And then to end on an upbeat note, I say, 'By then I'll expect lots of juicy information about your first date with the delectable Rob.'

'Ha! There won't be one. I haven't seen nor heard from him.'

'You will if Nancy's right.'

'Hmm. And I expect news of TT and the mysterious Nancarrow House.'

Surprised, I say, 'What? There's no point in finding out about all that now, is there? I wanted the parting glass to help me decide if' – I twist my fist into my eyes again and clear my throat – 'if Josh was the one.'

'I know, love … but you also wanted to find it because you thought you'd feel close to your gran. The last thing you did together – a way of honouring her memory.'

Thoughts of Gran wrap around me like a hug and before I can stop them, tears form and fall silently down my cheeks. 'Hmm. I'll see. Night, Jas.'

Ending the call, I close my eyes and let memories of

sunny days with Gran on the beach act like a soothing balm on my tired, sad heart. I open my eyes and say to the ceiling, 'What do you think I should do, Gran? Look for the parting glass, or leave it alone?' I picture her face. She doesn't answer, but there's a wistful smile playing across her lips. I think that tells me all I need to know.

Chapter Seven

W here has the time gone? The calendar tells me it's the fifteenth of October. Weeks have run into each other, and I've got through them by putting one foot in front of the other. Each step I've taken into the future has been easier than the one before, and Josh has been left further behind in the past. I'd be lying if I said I was over him, or that I don't sometimes lie awake at night allowing memories of us together to torture me, but the proverbial corner has been turned. I think. I hope.

One day at a time, as my mum said to me when I broke the news, weeping and wailing on her shoulder and then collapsing in a snotty heap. I smile as I grab my car keys and leave my flat. Dear Mum, I'm lucky to have her. Since then, she's been very supportive and clearly secretly glad Josh is off the scene, though she's never spelled it out. Her feelings on some things I can read plainly. Undetectable and unspoken to others, to me they flash like neon signs on a dark night. My brother Ruan was more explicit. I know he's never really liked Josh because he told me, said he was up himself and false. But would I listen? No. Ruan said he was sorry I was hurting, but relieved that I was free of the lying, conniving, cheating pile of horseshit. And Dad? Dad is Dad. Nothing really fazes him. He gave me a quick hug and said, 'What will be, will be.' And how could I argue with that sound philosophy? Laughing at the thought of him having a fit recently because one of his assistants had forgotten to order some shrimps, his face as pink as a cooked one, I get behind the wheel and start the car.

A crisp blue autumn sky stretches a smile across Daymer Bay, and under the direction of an offshore breeze, a host of red and yellow leaves dance the Twist around the carpark. Out of the car, I have an urge to join in the dance, as the scent of autumn mingles with the salty air and a couple of oystercatchers swoop down to the shoreline. Once I've immersed myself in the scene and my senses have had their fill, I zip up my fur-lined parka, pull my yellow wellies on and set off up the coastal path to see what's happened to Nancarrow House in my absence. I'm glad I decided not to contact Tremaine Nancarrow. I'll wait until there's some activity up at the house before I ask to see inside the old place. And if all fails, despite wanting to be above board and ask permission to explore the forgotten beach, I can ask Uncle Pete to ferry me over one day. The parting glass is the most important thing on my agenda, and nobody's going to know, are they? For now, I'm just here to enjoy a walk and look at the house again. It's daft, but I have to admit to myself that there's a fascination with it – I'm drawn towards it. Towards this area. Maybe Gran's got a hand in it, somehow. She'd be thrilled that I'm interested in her past, and in the place where she met the one she wanted to 'walk alongside'.

Nancarrow House is a run-down hulk of a thing, clinging to the clifftop like a novice climber who has lost their footing. As I draw nearer, an unexpected rush of sadness for the building swells in my chest, coupled with irritation that the owners had let it come to this. If they didn't use it, why not sell it on? Thankfully, this poor old thing is set to be restored to its former glory, according to Mum's text message this morning. She'd heard it from Bob Simmonds, the local builder and next-door neighbour but two. Bob is a jovial type who'd never got fed up with me singing Bob the Builder to him when I was a kid. Apparently, he and his crew have been given the job by, presumably, Tremaine Nancarrow. I take a deep breath of sea air and turn my face to the wind.

On it comes the unmistakable sound of construction. Banging, hammering, the rumble of a digger. So, they have begun already. Quickening my pace, I arrive at the gateposts just as the digger coughs out a mouthful of soil onto the path at my feet.

'Oops! Good job I saw you, there!' Bob says, with a surprised smile, his weather-beaten face reminiscent of an old leather handbag. 'What brings you up here, Sennen?'

I briefly consider telling him I'm doing a survey of private beaches as Jasmine suggested, but then realise it's easier to tell a partial truth. 'My gran used to deliver bread here years back and Mum said she loved this old place. Just wanted to have a look round.' I smile and look over to where his workmates are cutting back some foliage. 'What exactly are you doing to it?'

Bob gets down from the cab and turns the engine off. 'We're clearing the grounds a bit so we can get to the brickwork properly.' He reaches in a rucksack and pulls out a flask. 'Then we're going to repair the mortar and various other bits and bobs, maybe a new roof, or at least half a one.' He pours what looks like a cup of sludge and takes a swallow. 'Want a coffee?' He points at the flask.

'No thanks, Bob. And what about inside? Does it need much doing to it?'

The old handbag face rearranges itself into a thoughtful expression. 'Only decorating and refurbishment, really. Definitely needs a new bathroom. It's not been used much since the 1990s. And the decor is at least ten years older than that. Very outdated.'

'Hmm. I suppose it would be,' I say, looking up at the house.

'Could do with a dampcourse too.' He takes more coffee and points a meaty finger towards the grounds. 'Garden needs an overhaul, as you can see. There's even talk of a swimming pool being put out the back.' Bob says this as if he thinks the money could be used in better ways.

'So, who's going to live in it after all that?'

'Mr Nancarrow. Tremaine. He's the son of Julian Nancarrow, the one who upped and left to go to London in the 1990s. Seems like Tremaine wants to have a bolthole, as he put it, for weekends and stuff.'

I know the answer already, but it seems as if Bob has a mine of information ready to tap into. 'This Tremaine's from

London, then?' Bob nods and pulls a sandwich from a Tupperware box. 'Has he got a family?'

Bob takes a huge bite of what looks to be ham and cheese and the handbag manoeuvres around it. 'No idea,' he mumbles from the side of his mouth. 'He said his parents are still in London, I think he's the only son.'

'And he's not married?'

Bob's dark eyebrows knit over his deep-set brown eyes. 'How come you're so interested in Mr Nancarrow then, Sennen?'

'I'm not really,' I say in a small voice, and turn away so he won't see that I might possibly be fibbing. 'Just curious.'

'Well, he's in there right now if you want to go and ask more questions.' Bob gestures at the house with what's left of the sandwich. 'He might even make you a cup of tea.' The twinkle in his eye tells me that's never going to happen.

I manage a little laugh and turn my back to the house. 'Yeah, as if.' Then to cover my tracks I tell Bob all about how my gran used to walk over from Polzeath with fresh bread every day and how things were all so different back in the 1950s, and could he imagine anyone doing that nowadays? I don't tell him about her and Jory, but I tell him about her box of memories and some of the things we found in there. I'm rambling on purpose, and Bob's eyes start to glaze over, and his polite expression looks fixed on with concrete.

'Well, that's all really interesting, Sennen, but I better get on before Mr Nancarrow—'

'Before Mr Nancarrow what?'

Bob and I give a start and turn to face the owner of the voice. I'm looking up at a pair of turquoise blue eyes in a ruggedly handsome face, across which the breeze is tugging a tangle of dark blond curls – or tawny, as Jas described them. He lifts a hand to tug it back and secures his hair behind his ear. My goodness. This is obviously TT, as Jasmine has dubbed him. I have to admit, she wasn't wrong. He's certainly a looker. He's a look of Gran's Jory too. I get a quick sweep of the turquoise blues and then he turns his attention to Bob, who gives a sheepish grin and answers, 'Before you moan at me for slacking on the job.'

'Moan? I never moan, Bob.' Tremaine Nancarrow's eyes crinkle at the corners as his mouth lifts at the edges slightly. He turns his attention back to me. 'And aren't you going to introduce us?'

Bob nods and places a hand on my shoulder. 'This is Sennen Kellow. Her family have lived practically next door to me and mine for years. Her parents still do, don't they, Sen? Lovely people your mum and dad.'

'Nice to meet you, Sennen, I'm Tremaine Nancarrow.'

Under Tremaine's direct gaze and strong handshake, I'm completely lost for words. Mainly because I don't know what to say next, in explanation for my just appearing at his house, but also because of my surprise attraction to him. Aren't I supposed to be in mourning for my lost love? Heat flares in my cheeks and I manage, 'You too.' Then there's an awkward silence and Tremaine's questioning expression prompts me to add, 'My gran used to deliver bread here years ago, and I wanted to come and look at the place.'

His dark eyebrows add a furrow to the questioning expression. 'I see,' he says. Though the tone implies he doesn't.

To clarify, I burble, 'You know, to see a bit of history I suppose. But then it won't be the same inside as it would have been in the 1950s, will it? Well, unless you have kept all the same decor since then.' I hear myself give a ridiculous chuckle. A chuckle that wouldn't seem out of place coming from the mouth of a cartoon character. Then I toss my plait over my shoulder and flash Bob a 'rescue me' sign with my eyes.

Bob isn't very good at reading signs, apparently as he says, 'No. As I told you earlier, the decor is 1980s. But when Mr Tremaine here has it sorted it will be a little palace.'

Mr Tremaine here? For goodness' sake, Bob. I wonder if we have somehow been transported back to the nineteenth century. Bob just needs a cap to tug, and he'll have the peasant-and-master vibe down pat. 'Yes, I forgot,' I mumble and look at the house. Mainly so I don't have to look at Tremaine and Bob.

'So you came to look at a place your grandmother delivered to? Did she have some connection with the place? Apart from just delivering bread?' Tremaine's cultured voice holds a note of incredulity.

Can I blame him? I mean, who the heck rocks up to someone's house out of the blue just because her gran used to deliver bread there? There must have been dozens of houses she delivered to, after all. There's no way I'm spilling the beans about Gran and Jory right now to Jory's … what? I don't really know. Probably his great-nephew? Especially as the great-nephew is looking down his aquiline nose me at the moment. 'Um, not really. But she loved architecture. She was always banging on to me about how beautiful Nancarrow House was and that they don't build them like that these days … and … so forth.'

And so forth? I never say, 'and so forth'. It's probably because I'm telling fibs.

'Right, yeah.' Tremaine shoves his hand through his windswept hair and nods at the house. 'I'll give you a quick look around the grounds if you like, but I won't ask you in today. I have work to do. Maybe another time?' He stifles a yawn.

Oh dear. How boring for him having to talk to a local peasant. I'm about to tell him to forget it when pride is elbowed out of the way by an image of Gran with the parting glass. If I can ask him about access to the beach, I won't have to ask Uncle Pete, and therefore keep my treasure hunting expedition to myself. Well, and Jas. There's no way I can keep it from her. 'That would be lovely, thank you.'

Tremaine looks less than thrilled, but says, 'Right. Follow me.' And to Bob, 'Hope to see you've managed to do what we planned by this evening.'

Bob nods and smiles. 'Oh yes. I'm on it, boss.'

I want to tell Bob to grow a pair and stop being so obsequious, but of course I don't. I give him a wave and hurry after Tremaine who's striding towards the house on his long legs.

Five minutes later, we're round the back of the house and he's waving his hands about as he explains his plans for the grounds. The pompous lecturing tone is probably how he sounds in court when giving evidence. In fact, his whole demeanour is that of a lawyer as he struts about with his hands behind his back, droning on. 'The old stable will be made into a garden room of some sort. Then over by the trees will be the swimming pool,' he's saying now, as he bends to grab a rotten branch and chucks it into the undergrowth. 'I've always wanted a full-size one, not one of these horrid little plunge pools.'

Is he for real? How many people can afford to have *any* kind of pool in their back garden? 'I see. Not a hot tub man, either, I suppose?'

Tremaine's sensuous mouth twists itself into a tiny pout as if he's tasted something sour. 'God no. Those things are full of germs and other people's sweat.' I notice him glance at my yellow wellies and a smirk twitches one side of his mouth.

Okay. Maybe they aren't the kind of footwear that would grace a Paris catwalk, but so what? I need to get my question asked and leave. He's such an obnoxious toad I can hardly bear to be near him a moment longer. 'Is the beach at the end of that path?' I point and hurry towards it.

Following me, he says, 'Yes, but it's far too dangerous to get to.'

At the squeaky 'Danger – Keep Out' sign, I fold my arms and affect a puzzled expression. 'Blimey. How come you can't get to it?'

Tremaine shoots me a 'duh' glance and mirrors my pose. 'Because as I said, it's too dangerous.'

This sparks a snappy, 'Well, yeah. But *why* is it

dangerous?' I point under the chain. 'There look to be some steps, no?'

He walks to the edge of the cliff and stares out over the lazy blue ocean. 'Only a few. There was a full set many years ago, but after a family tragedy they were left to crumble.'

'Oh? What happened?' I hope I'm going to find out from Tremaine what Gran couldn't from Jory.

The blue of the sea is reflected in his eyes as he turns his gaze to mine. Tremaine looks as if he's not going to tell me, then he sighs and says quietly, 'As a young woman, my great-grandmother Victoria fell down them and broke her neck.' Then he looks away again.

A chill runs down my spine as an unwelcome picture of the woman's demise is presented, courtesy of my vivid imagination. My 'That's awful' hangs in the air between us, small and inadequate.

He nods at the horizon. 'Yes, she'd had tragedy in her life already. Her husband, my great-grandfather Alexander Nancarrow, had died in a riding accident, leaving her with two young sons. They all lived here with Alexander's parents, and when she died, they brought the boys up.'

A level of understanding dawns. So, these are the grandparents of Jory. The ones who forbade him to marry Gran. Maybe they were affected so much by the death of their son and, later, daughter-in-law that it had made them bitter and set in their ways. 'Your great-great-grandparents must have been devastated.'

Tremaine kicks a stone across the grass, shrugs. 'Hmm. Not too sure. My father said they were a bit stand-offish, according to my Granddad Edward. Of another time. His brother, my great-uncle Jory, came up against them as a young man and came off worst. Something about a local girl. Can't remember an awful lot of the story now, as I asked my dad about it all when I was little.'

Excitement jumps in my chest and I'm torn. Do I say what I know and show my hand about why I'm really here? Or do I let him talk? I must admit, I'm surprised he's being so forthcoming and easy, given Claire's description of him. Okay, he did seem a bit snooty and pompous at first, obnoxious over the swimming pool, but he's certainly relaxed and chatty now. Something tells me to leave what I know alone for now, nevertheless. 'I see. Why do you think they didn't have the steps repaired?'

'Again, can't remember. Granddad Edward apparently told my father that his grandparents chained it off and put up a sign forbidding anyone to repair the steps after they were gone. He respected their wishes.' Tremaine rattles the chain and frowns at the sign, seemingly lost in thought.

'And will you?' I ask.

'Will I what?' he replies over his shoulder, still miles away.

'Respect their wishes. Or will you build the steps again as part of the restoration, and make use of the beach?'

Turning to face me, he strokes a hand over his stubbly chin as he considers this. 'Not really thought about it. But I don't see why not.' Then he gives me a broad smile that brightens up his serious face like sunshine on a moody ocean. It blows me away and shoots a spark of electricity through my stomach. 'Might be cool to have a swim in summer and a barbeque on the beach when my friends are down from London, hey?'

I shift my eyes from his. 'Yeah. Then you'll have a choice of the pool or ocean. What could be better?' My words are unexpectedly laced with sarcasm. Why? Loyalty to my broken heart, because I'm supposed to be devastated about Josh, but here I am drooling over this guy's smile?

Tremaine doesn't seem to notice but shakes himself and looks at his watch. 'Anyway, must get on. Pop back again sometime.' I get a quick dismissive nod and then he waves his arm, indicating we should go back to the house.

As I lead the way, my heart sinks as I'm unsure what to do or say next. Do I take him up on his offer to return, or was he just being polite? Tremaine Nancarrow is a bit of an enigma. One minute he seems relaxed and friendly, the next he's cold, distant and pompous. Rounding the corner, I see Bob's busy with the digger so I don't interrupt, and at the gateposts I turn to thank Tremaine for showing me around, but there's no sign of him. Nice. He can't even be bothered to say goodbye. How rude! Well, sod him. I stomp off along the coastal path with no plans to ever come back.

Chapter Eight

Madonna's 'Holiday' is almost drowned out by the thump of feet on ancient floorboards, clapping hands and a number of groans. The latter are the result of the exertion required of the participants in the keep-fit class at the local church. It's proving a bit too much for some, including me. I give side eyes to Jasmine as we're asked to do three more squats in time to the beat, and she mouths at me, 'I'm dying.' I nod my agreement and look to my left to see how Mum is coping. Better than me and Jasmine by the look of grim determination on her face, and the energy with which she's approaching the squats.

'Slow down, Ma, you're putting me and Jas to shame,' I pant, and attempt a lunge to the side.

Mum runs a sweatband across her brow and grins. 'Put your back into it, girl, and stop whining.'

'Why did we let her talk us into this?' Jas hisses. 'I'm gonna collapse any second.'

I'm about to answer when Gloria, the sixty-something

instructor – resplendent in a pink leotard – changes to some contemplative flute music and says, 'Okay, ladies. Time to wind it down. Slow steps on the spot and let's have some nice relaxing stretches.'

'Thank God. Any more of that and I'd need a nice relaxing stretcher!' Jasmine says with a giggle.

This sets me off and I cover my mouth to prevent a guffaw bursting from it and shake my head at Jasmine. But she looks so comical with her pink face and mass of crazy red curls trying to escape from her headband that laughter bursts out anyway. Mum gives me daggers and Gloria furrows her perfectly shaped eyebrows at me. I look at my feet and try to channel the thoughts of calm and peace that Gloria's urging us to let flow through our beings.

'Deep breaths, ladies. In … and hold for four … and out for eight. In for four…' Gloria says, wandering round the class and coming to a halt in front of me. 'And out for eight.' When I hear Jasmine snort as she tries to hold in another giggle, I keep my eyes fixed on the floorboards.

'Sorry, Gloria. I thought my daughter and her friend would have grown out of their teenage behaviour. Them being twenty-five,' Mum says with a sigh.

Embarrassed, I look up into Gloria's icy glare. 'Not to worry, Jenna.' She gives Mum a ghost of a smile. 'But you only get out of these classes what you put in.'

Jasmine coughs and shuffles her feet as if she's a naughty schoolgirl in front of the headmistress. 'Yeah, sorry. Just got a bit giddy. But we did enjoy the class, didn't we, Sen?'

'We did, yes. Um, thanks.'

Gloria nods and glides elegantly to the front of the class. Mum gives us an eye-roll and Jas whispers in my ear, 'Thank fuck that's over.' I have to bite the inside of my cheek and do some of Gloria's deep breathing to keep a straight face.

In the coffee shop across from the church, Mum is still going on about how mortified she was about our behaviour and it's getting old. 'Okay, let's change the subject now, Mum.'

'Okay. But poor Gloria hasn't a very well-developed sense of humour. I think she was wondering what she said that was so funny. I'll have to explain it was nothing to do with her before you come next time.'

I nearly choke on my latte. 'Er, I'm not sure there will be a next time. We only came along to stop you going on at us.'

Mum pulls her neck back and folds her arms. 'That's a shame. I thought it would be a nice thing for us to do. You know, all the girls together.'

'It nearly killed me, Jenna,' Jasmine says. 'You middle-aged ladies are so much fitter than us two.'

Mum harrumphs. 'Yes. So, what better reason for you to come to the classes?'

'If it's something you want all us girls to do together, I have some weightlifting activities for you.' Jasmine winks at me. 'We tend to do it on weekends, don't we, Sennen?'

I frown. 'We do?'

Jasmine mimics lifting a glass and makes noisy gulping

sounds. 'Nothing like lifting a pint or two after a hard week's work, eh?'

'Oh, very funny,' Mum says and takes a sip of coffee.

'Talking of work,' I say to change the subject. Mum's not really upset, but I can tell she'd hoped the keep-fit class would be a regular thing. Maybe she gets a bit lonely sometimes with only Dad for company? Then I remember she has the choir, the Post Office job and baking for the residents of the care home, so maybe not. 'How's the new job going?' I ask Jasmine.

'Fantastic!' Jasmine licks cake crumbs from her lips and dusts more off her white T-shirt. 'There's so much more freedom in this new post. I can use my initiative and don't have to ask the manager if I can do this, that and the other. Because I *am* the bloody manager!'

Even Mum has to smile at the exuberant note of glee in Jasmine's tone. 'Well, that's nice. And how's working in Newquay?' she asks.

'Great. I organised some flyers, and a colleague and I handed them out to the surfers on Fistral during our break the other day. Robert said it was a genius idea and thought it would really help to boost trade. He organised a load more for the other stores.' Jasmine's eyes sparkle like emeralds and her cheeks turn into hamster pouches as she beams a hundred-watt smile at us.

'Hmm. Robert, eh? Has he asked you out yet?' I say with a cheeky wink.

Jasmine's eyes dance away and she does a high-pitched little laugh. 'Not happening. Told you.'

'Robert? Does he work with you?' Mum asks.

'He's the manager for the area. Your daughter has a silly idea that he likes me.'

'And you think he doesn't?' I ask.

Jasmine sighs and puts her head on one side. 'There's as much chance of me and Robert getting together as there is of you and TT.'

Mum pounces on this titbit like a ravenous lioness, her tan and orange fluffy jumper adding to the image. 'Oooh. Who's TT?'

I glare at Jasmine. Great. Mum's boyfriend detector is up and running, so now I'm going to have to tell her everything. Maybe I can hold back about wanting to find the parting glass? But if I keep quiet, I'll bet that Jasmine will jump in with it. I sit back and look at their expectant faces and sigh. Nothing but the truth will do when Mum's on the scent like a tenacious bloodhound. A bloodhound and a lion – what chance do I have against those two?

'His name is Tremaine Nancarrow. Jasmine has dubbed him Tasty Tremaine because of his good looks.'

'Good looks? He's a god,' Jasmine tells Mum, with a dopey smile on her chops.

I get a knowing look from Mum. 'Hmm. So that's why you were so interested in the information I got from Bob the builder then? It wasn't any interest in the house because of your gran at all, it was its gorgeous owner.'

'No. I really am interested in the house, well, the beach mostly...'

'She's been up there already,' Jas informs Mum, her eyes sparkling with mischief as she ignores my death stare. 'It's all overgrown and neglected. So, I told her to contact this

TT and ask him if he's going to do it up. Our old friend Claire from our schooldays says he's an entitled snob, but I reckon Sennen should try and see past that. If I had an opportunity to meet such a hot guy ... well, nothing would hold me back. But not Sennen, she's done bugger all about it.'

Mum shakes her head at me and I can tell she's about to launch into some lengthy advice, so I say to Jas, 'Well that's where you're wrong, miss bloody know-it-all. I went up there a couple of weeks ago and he was there.'

Jasmine's eyes nearly pop out of her head and her mouth drops open. 'OMG. Why the hell didn't you tell me? And what was he like? Is he just as hot as his photos?'

'He's not bad,' I say, and pay close attention to swirling the contents of my coffee cup.

'Not bad! I can tell you think he was stunning by the way you can't look me and your mum in the eye!'

'Oh, for goodness' sake, keep it down, will you?' I drain my cup and wish myself far away.

'Come on, let's be knowing. What was he like, this Tremaine?' Mum says, leaning her elbows on the table, neck thrust forward.

I'm beginning to feel like a prisoner, caught in the pincer movement of two experienced interrogators. 'He was a bit odd, actually. Snooty to start, then friendly for about five minutes, then stand-offish and pompous. Never even bothered to say a proper goodbye.'

Jasmine flaps her hand at me. 'But did you ask him about going down to the beach to find the cave and—'

'The parting glass!' Mum interrupts, her face lit with

excitement. 'How lovely! I can't believe you actually want to find it!'

I shrug. 'It seemed like a nice way of feeling close to Gran. One last adventure together, as you put it, Jas.'

Mum's eyes mist over. 'It would be.' Then she frowns. 'How come you kept all this a secret?'

'Because the glass might not be there after all this time. Maybe the cave got bashed about with the tide and it was washed out to sea. I didn't want to raise your expectations before I knew for sure.'

'Well, my expectations are raised for a romance between you and TT now you've met him and he was friendly.' Jasmine's ear-to-ear grin earns her an eye-roll from me.

'I told you he was pompous and brusque too. You only hear what you want to.'

'What exactly did he say about the parting glass, Sen?' Mum asks.

'I didn't mention that.' Then I give them a brief precis of the conversation I had with Tremaine.

Jasmine shoves both palms at me as if she's pushing an imaginary door closed. 'Whoa, hold on just a cotton-pickin' minute here. Are you telling us that he said you were welcome to go back and look round the house another time, but you didn't take him up on it?'

I unzip my pale blue fleece right down and roll my sleeves up. All this grilling is frying me to a crisp. 'Yeah, because he's such an obnoxious git. And what's the actual point of looking around the old place and getting permission to go to the beach in the end, anyway? I could ask Uncle Pete to take me on the boat … Just don't want to tell him what the hell I'm going there for. He'll think I'm crazy. And I know it's silly, but that's not the main problem…'

Mum reaches her hand across the table and covers my own. 'Do you mean the main problem is you're worried the glass might not be there?'

She gets straight to the heart of the matter as usual. This idea has been flitting in and out of my thoughts for weeks. I've felt closer to Gran the whole time I've been planning the treasure hunt … and if it's not there, neither will she be. 'I guess it is,' I reply in a small voice.

'It's not silly, lovely. Imagine how wonderful it would be if it was there, just waiting for you like it was for my mum? You could bring it home, clean it up and on New Year's Eve fill it with the best wine.' She gives me a little smile. 'Magic does happen if you believe in it.'

'Listen to your mum, Sennen. We could all do with a bit of magic in our lives. It's three weeks ago since you were there. He might have built the steps up and everything!'

Despite her wearing her enthusiastic-child face, I give her a withering look. 'As if. I think it would take a bit longer than three weeks.'

'No harm in popping up there though, eh?' Mum says.

The hope in her eyes and Jasmine's expectant face take my legs out from under me more effectively than the bloodhound and lion. Heaving a sigh I answer, 'Okay. Anything to keep you off my back. I'll go over on Sunday.'

Jasmine wraps her arms around her body in delight. 'Yesss! Try and get a photo of TT too. I want to see how he measures up in real life.' Then she narrows her eyes. 'Well, when I say real life, I mean a recent photo. At least we will know that he's not touched it up.'

'No way. And spilling all my business was a nice swerve, Jas. You think you've thrown me off the scent about Rob.' I narrow my eyes and wag a finger at her. 'You can think again, mate. Nancy Cornish wasn't wrong. Mark my words.'

'Who's Nancy Cornish?' Mum becomes a lion again and starts the Spanish Inquisition on Jasmine. Jas gives me a pleading look, but I just throw back my head and laugh.

Chapter Nine

Sea Spray Gifts' display in the window is looking mighty fine, even though I do say so myself. The new pots I've made over the last few weeks sit centre stage. Their autumnal colours of yellow, russet and orange nestle like beach fires amongst driftwood, dried seaweed and shells. The dinner-plate images are bold and shouty like the seagulls wheeling across their fiery sunsets, while the mugs are understated. Around their rims, tendrils of ochre and crimson wrap around lilac skies, and through their middles, boats sail across calm seas. Customers love them and I might have to make some more if they keep selling so well.

Uncle Pete said they were some of my best pieces when he popped in yesterday, which gave me a boost. He was one of the finest potters in Cornwall until arthritis robbed him of his skill, so coming from him it really meant a lot. I rearrange a piece of driftwood and think about how I nearly gave in and asked him to take me to the cave by boat. It would save an awful lot of fuss going up to Nancarrow

House tomorrow and speaking to TT – Terrible Tremaine as I think of him. Something stopped me though, and it wasn't because I thought my uncle would think I was silly. Gran was his mum after all. It was because I wanted to do it alone. Actually, not alone, with Gran. If Uncle Pete had to take me in his rowing boat and faff about wading through the shallows, dragging the boat up the beach and then waiting for me, it would seem less special, more ordinary, less of an adventure. Me and Gran need to do it together and under our own steam. It just feels right.

In the kitchen, I run water into the kettle and hope to get a quick lunch before the next customer arrives, while tomorrow's visit to Nancarrow settles in my mind like an agitated butterfly. What if Tremaine didn't mean it when he said I could go and look round? Maybe he was just saying that to be polite. The image of him smiling broadly at the thought of having a barbeque on the beach comes to me now, as it has over the last few weeks. Sunshine on a moody ocean. Jasmine would be hopeless if he smiled like that at her. She'd probably faint clean away like the heroine in some ill-researched novel set in the nineteenth-century. I grab my tea and prawn, cucumber, and mayo sandwich and put it on a plate. It's made with lovely granary bread from the local bakery, Da Bara. I'm drooling already.

To keep my eye on the door, I sit on a little stool behind the counter and take a big bite of the sandwich. It's pretty full, and I just catch a prawn in a dollop of mayonnaise before it hits my new multicoloured velvet top. Phew. That wouldn't look or smell good to the customers, would it? There're a few potential ones now – a couple of women looking in through the window and pointing to my new display. They look animated, impressed. Perhaps they'll come in. I lower the sandwich; it doesn't look good to be stuffing my face when I'm supposed to be working. The women nod, laugh, then link arms and walk away. Oh well. Maybe they will be back another time.

I take a sip of tea, duck down and wrap my mouth round the sandwich, then as I sit back up, I see there's someone else at the window. A guy – tall, tousled-haired and stupidly handsome – is staring at a large plate of a seagull and lighthouse. A guy with turquoise-blue eyes and a half-smile. Oh my God. Surprise makes my reactions slow, and this time my fingers only jab ineffectually at a blob of mayonnaise as it escapes my very full mouth, splats into my cleavage and slides down my top. No! I scrabble around for tissues, which I keep under the counter, but find an empty box. Shit. I was going to put a new box out the other day and forgot. Did he see me, I wonder? Hopefully not. If I keep crouched, I can scuttle into the kitchen, get a damp cloth and get rid of the evidence. Then the shop bell tinkles and my heart plummets. Footsteps sound on the tiles. Damn it. Will I be able to make the kitchen before he gets to the counter? It might not be him. Hopefully he's walked on, and someone else has come in. Crab-like, I make my way to the kitchen door…

'Sennen? I was right, it *is* you.' Tremaine's voice holds a note of amusement.

No. No, it isn't. It isn't. Go away! a voice yells inside my head, as I stand upright and run to the kitchen, grab a tea towel and scrape the mayo off. 'Won't be long!' I call over my shoulder.

'No rush, I could see you were enjoying your lunch. I'll just have a look round the shop.'

Enjoying my lunch. Stuffing my face, he meant. Mortified, I check my make-up – and for any sign of mayonnaise – in the tiny mirror above the fridge. My fringe is sticking up for some reason and I smooth it down with the flat of my hand. Then I stop. What am I doing this for? It's not as if I want to impress him, is it? Releasing a long breath, I go back to stand behind the counter and see that Tremaine's twirling the birthday-card stand round. He's in dark jeans and a sea-green hoodie and his shoulder-length curls show evidence of a battle with the wind. Apparently finding nothing to his taste, he wanders over to a low table, which has a similar display to the one in the window, and crouches down to examine a fruit bowl. Why the hell is he frowning? Miserable git.

'Need any help with anything?' I say, in my polite shop assistant voice.

He straightens up, a tentative smile banishing the frown, and walks over to me holding the bowl. 'I couldn't find the price on this, but I want it no matter what it costs.' Tremaine gazes in admiration at the blue fishing boat sailing across a serene ocean, traces of dawn breaking overhead in splashes of red and yellow. 'Simply stunning.'

Ah, he was frowning because he was looking for the price. I soften a little. It's always nice to have your work appreciated. 'Sorry, the tag must have fallen behind the table. It's £45.'

Tremaine's thick eyebrows shoot up to his hairline. 'Is that all? For this hand-crafted piece of art.' He shakes his head in wonder. 'Who's the artist? A local person, I bet. You can see the affinity with the ocean in every brushstroke.'

He's an art lover. Who knew? The comment is accurate, and the compliment welcome. I say, 'Yes, a local. It's me. I'm the artist. I made the bowl too.' I wave my hand at the various ceramics in the shop. 'I made all of them.'

The eyebrows go up again. 'Wow! You are so talented. I bet you sell hundreds of these.'

I smile, heat kissing my cheeks at his compliments. 'Not hundreds. I couldn't physically make hundreds. But yes. They are popular.' I take the bowl and start to wrap it in tissue paper.

Tremaine pulls a wallet out of his pocket and flips it open. 'I hope the owner of the shop pays you well.'

Hm. He assumes I'm the shop assistant. Disappointing, but typical. Even in this day and age. I mean, a young woman behind the counter couldn't possibly be her own boss, could she? I stick Sellotape along the tissue paper and smile sweetly. 'I *am* the owner, or part owner. My uncle owns the lion's share. He was a wonderful artist and potter in his day, but he's taken early retirement.'

A thoughtful cock of the head as he puts his payment card in the machine. 'What's his name? I used to follow all the local artists years ago.'

'Pete Williams.'

'Really? I have one of his hanging plaques in my London home! It's sunset over Godrevy Lighthouse.' Tremaine's 'sunshine on a moody ocean' smile is back and it's bigger and brighter than before. Good job Jasmine's not here.

'How lovely,' I say, popping the bowl in a bag and handing him the receipt.

'It is.' I get the big smile again. 'I love the bold strokes. You and he have a similar style.'

'Yes. He taught me everything I know.'

Tremaine sighs and the smile becomes wistful. 'Lucky you. I once had hopes of…' A brief shake of the head as if he's ridding himself of unwelcome thoughts. 'Never mind.' He looks into my eyes with an intensity that feels as if he's searching for an answer. Then he abruptly turns and makes as if to leave. 'Goodbye, Sennen. Perhaps we'll meet again,' he tosses over his shoulder as he walks away.

What the hell? This guy changes his mood with the wind. I think about tomorrow's visit to Daymer Bay and before I can stop myself, I say in a rush, 'Does the offer to have a look inside Nancarrow House still stand? Because if it does, I was thinking of popping over on my day off tomorrow.'

The frown's back as he turns at the door. 'Offer? Hmm … tomorrow…' He ponders. Then a brief nod. 'Yes, should be okay. Come over early afternoon.' Then he opens the door and raises a finger at me. 'Oh, I meant to say. You might want to get rid of the cucumber slice stuck to the side of your left breast.' Tremaine gives a mischievous chuckle. 'Unless it's just an extension of your artistic expression.' A second later, he's gone.

I look down. Oh my God. I'm left with a face as red as a

November sunset and a crusty bit of cucumber to peel from my top.

———————

After yesterday's cucumber incident, the idea of popping over to Nancarrow House is about as appealing as shoving a wasp's nest down my knickers. Apart from feeling embarrassed about that, Mr Nancarrow is so hard to fathom and uncomfortable to be around. I'd love to find out why he's so moody. Unpick the threads of the mask of misery he pulls over his gorgeous smile. Why does he wear it so often, where does it come from and why the hell do I even care? I don't know anything about his life, nor should I want to, really. Naturally curious, I suppose. Torn between staying home in my PJs and eating a chocolate bar as big as my head, or getting dressed, doing my make-up and driving out to see TT, I begin to pace the kitchen.

Pacing is always useful when I can't decide what to do next. Though you're going nowhere, the movement makes you feel like you actually have some direction and purpose, even though you really haven't and your thought patterns resemble a bowl of cold spaghetti. If I can only find the end of the spaghetti then I can follow it to its logical conclusion. The big meatball of logical reasoning. Logical reasoning will have the answer to my dilemma. The end remains elusive though. I think I see it, but then after a few seconds it becomes squashed and sticky, tangling around itself and other strands of spaghetti like an anaemic worm.

Mid-pace, a voice in my head says, *Go to the bloody house*

for goodness' sake! The voice sounds a lot like Gran's and I know she's right. Jasmine might be right too, about Tremaine having built the steps back up, and then I can skip down to the beach and find out if the parting glass is still there. Simple, no? Before counter arguments can fuel my pacing again, I rush upstairs to get dressed.

———

A little while later I'm standing in my bra and pants next to a heap of clothes on the bed and floor. Why does nothing feel right? I don't normally worry so much about what I'm wearing, do I? I'm only going to visit an old ruin and hopefully the beach, after all. I tell myself it's because of the cucumber incident yesterday. Looking a bit smart today will be one in the eye for Mr Nancarrow. But then shouldn't I wear what I feel comfortable in? Glancing outside helps me decide. It's the end of October. The sun is being mugged by a huddle of clouds and a fresh wind is whipping along the hedgerows. Black jeans, salmon-pink jumper and green Doc Martens. I stand in front of the mirror, apply subtle eye-make up, pink lip-gloss and divide my hair into two plaits instead of my usual one. I give my reflection a satisfied nod. Okay, that'll do.

———

The transformation of the garden and front of the house is nothing short of miraculous. Sunshine has broken through the clouds, bathing the scene in a halo of golden light. The red brick walls, once dulled from years of attack by salt air and sand, are now clean and glowing, and the lawns and shrubs are well tended and sit green and lush either side of the new gravel drive. Front of house, literally, hang the old iron gates, now as good as new, with the initials 'N' and 'H' proudly displayed at the top of each. Lifting the latch on the gate I give it a little push and it swings open on well-oiled hinges.

As I walk up the path, I note the scaffolding to the side, and see the roof is yet to be finished, but it's well on the way. The windows wink at me as the sun finds them and it makes my heart glad to see the old place looking happy again. There's a different atmosphere here to the first time I saw it. It's as if the house has found a new lease of life, a reason to start again. There's a movement by the curtain at the downstairs bay window and I see it's Tremaine, a cloth in his hand against the pane. When he notices me, he waves and disappears, only to come around the side of the house a few moments later.

Today he's an upmarket aftershave advert with his slow, long stride, tawny curls blowing in the wind and his eyes accentuated by his light blue shirt and the warmth of his smile. 'Hello!' he calls, waving the cloth at me. 'I'm about to put the kettle on and I made scones earlier, come in!' Then he turns and hurries back round the side of the house. I'm stunned by his greeting and my feet stay put. Tremaine Nancarrow – the entitled snob as Claire called him – has welcomed me like an old friend and actually made scones with his own fair hands. What the hell?

Before I go in the back door, I cast my eye over a skip on

the gravel driveway. It's full of broken furniture, an old sink and various black plastic bags. There's also a long rectangle made of string tied to posts near the trees and the little path leading to the sea. Marking out a swimming pool perhaps?

'Sennen? Are you coming in, or what?' Tremaine's disembodied voice floats through the door, pulling me from my ponderings and inside the house.

'Yeah, I'm here,' I answer, standing in a large hallway unsure where to go. There are tins of white paint lined up along the skirting board and some have been used on the panelling by the look and smell of it. Like a row of teeth, some panels look as if they've had a professional polish at the dentist, while others are still yellow with the build-up of tartar. Tremaine's head pops round a door along the hallway. 'Tea or coffee?'

'Tea, please.'

'Okay. Mind that paint splat by the door here, it dropped off my brush earlier and it's still a bit sticky.'

He does his own decorating too? Hovering in the doorway, I watch him moving around a huge kitchen newly painted in lemon and white. It has all new sage-green units and light wood work surfaces as well as a massive fridge and range. It's the kind of kitchen I would have, if I'd a house like this to put it in. My poky flat is magnolia city with a red blind and curtains to 'liven it up a bit' as Mum says. Liven it up? Sadly, the soulless box would need a shock from a defibrillator, more like. The open-plan design means the kitchen is basically a breakfast bar, with a line of creaky cupboards that have seen better days.

Such a contrast to this place. Over a Belfast sink and

drainer, the big kitchen window looks across the driveway at the ocean playing peekaboo through the branches of the trees. Wow. 'What a wonderful view,' I say, walking across the red ceramic tiles to the big pinewood table and chairs in the centre of the room.

Tremaine pours boiling water into two mugs and spreads a scone with butter. 'It is. This place has sea views on three sides. My ancestors knew what they were doing when they instructed their architect.'

I smile at him and run my fingers over the back of a chair. 'How old is this house?'

'Mid-nineteenth century. My great-great-grandparents built it.' He brings a plate of scones over and puts them on the table. 'Sit down and help yourself. Scones are my speciality.' His smile is almost shy, as if he's a child waiting for praise.

'They look delicious,' I reply, sitting down and picking one up, but with him staring at me I feel self-conscious, particularly after the cucumber incident.

Tremaine points at the scone. 'Try it, then.'

Taking the smallest bite possible, I nod and smile while I chew. Tasty. He raises his eyebrows in question. 'Mm. It's really good.'

A brief nod. 'Not made a bad batch yet.'

Nothing like modesty.

He goes to get the tea and pulls up a chair opposite me. 'What do you think of the place so far?'

'You have made such headway outside already. And this kitchen is stunning.'

'Yes, I do love it. I'll show you the rest of the place when we've had our tea.' I'm treated to another of his big smiles, then, as he demolishes half the scone in one bite, a blob of butter lands on his expensive shirt.

A hand flies to my mouth to stop a guffaw and the remains of scone bursting out. I'm successful with the latter only. Tremaine scowls at me, grabs some kitchen roll and scrubs at the stain seeping into the material, but only succeeds in spreading it across his chest. 'Might be as well to get some hot soapy water on that,' I offer, realising my merriment isn't particularly helpful, but it is unavoidable, given yesterday's cucumber.

He waves an imperious hand. 'It's fine. I have other shirts if it doesn't come out.' The rest of the scone is gobbled up as if it has angered him and washed down with a slurp of tea.

Sense of humour bypass then? Trying to make light of the situation I say, 'What are we like? Me with my sandwich yesterday, and now you with the scone.'

'Hmm.' His mouth twitches briefly at the corners as if it can't make up its mind whether to smile or not. Then he points out of the window. 'Did you notice the markings-out for the pool?'

Not so subtle change of subject, Tremaine. I wonder why he's so bothered about dropping the butter? I finish chewing a mouthful of scone before I answer. 'I did wonder if it was the pool. You've got on very quickly with putting your plans in motion since I was last here. It's only been three weeks.'

The frown lines between his eyes soften and I get a more of a smile this time. 'Almost three and a half, but yes, once I get the bit between my teeth on a project, I have to complete it.'

'How about the steps to the beach? Did you decide to repair them?' I cross my fingers under the table.

Tremaine pushes his plate away and leans back in his chair. 'Yup. They are underway, the builder man says another week or so.'

Yes! 'That's brilliant! Totally fantastic!' Images fill my head of me scraping back a heap of sand from the parting glass and holding it aloft in triumph.

'It is?' he asks, a question in his eyes.

And no wonder. My unexpected burst of enthusiasm sounded weird even to my own ears. Now what do I say? 'Erm.' Then my words tumble out one after the other in a hurry. 'Yeah, I mean it will be wonderful for you to pop down to the beach first thing in the morning. Or evening, or whenever you like … and have the picnic you talked about.'

'Picnic?'

The frown's back and why wouldn't it be? Me burbling on like a fast stream. 'Not picnic. No, I meant barbeque. You said you could have a beach barbeque when your friends are down from London.' The excitement over the steps, my waffling evasion, plus the intense way he's looking at me have started a fire under my skin. I hope he can't see the flush seeping up my neck.

Realisation dawns and a light comes on in those turquoise blues. 'Ah yes. So I did!' He gives me his broad smile, transforming his face from moody ocean to sun-drenched beaches. 'Not had a barbeque for years. Since I was a boy really…' A faraway expression finds him and he stares past me, lost in thought.

'Where did you have it?'

His eyes refocus and he says, 'Here in Cornwall at my aunt and uncle's house. I was at boarding school but spent most of the holidays with them.' A sigh. 'All of them, actually.' His last words sound like they taste bitter in his mouth. Then he brightens. 'Thankfully I loved staying with them and my cousins. There was always something going on and we had such fun.'

Interested to find out why he didn't spend the time with his parents, I almost ask the question but my instinct tells me to leave it alone. If he wants to share it, he will. Instead, I say, 'Whereabouts do your aunt and uncle live in Cornwall?'

'Near St Agnes. My uncle is Mother's brother. They grew up there and Mother met my father at some function or other. Father lived here with his parents, and when they married, they moved in for a while. When my grandparents died in the late 1990s my parents decided to move to London, where Father spent most of his time anyway.'

Surprised at the amount of information he's divulged, and at the formal title given to his parents, I decide to ask more questions while his door is open. 'You were born in London?'

'You flatter me.' He gives a little laugh. 'I was born in ninety-two, but we moved when I was around five. London has been my base for most of my life. I don't really remember my grandparents very well, but I do have fond memories of Cornwall, and love this house. I'd be here more often if work didn't demand me.'

Tremaine puts jam on another scone and pushes the plate my way. I decline and sip my tea, wondering again about the formality he adopts when talking about his parents. There's something about the way he talks about them that makes me think there's a distance between them. Who calls their parents Mother and Father nowadays? What's wrong with Mum and Dad? And why would a child be sent from boarding school to his aunt and uncle in the school holidays? Being in boarding school is harsh enough. The poor kid wouldn't see his parents at all, really. Juxtaposing my loving upbringing at the village school and local comprehensive with an image of a lonely kid in some loveless institution makes my heart go out to him. Is that why he's such a prickly character at times?

He looks at me and dabs his mouth with kitchen paper. 'You seem far away,' he says, head on one side.

'Just wondering about the house.' A bit of a fib, but I'm not sure he'd like the truth. 'Do your parents still own this place, or is it yours?'

'Mine. I came down here a while back after Father was banging on about selling it and I became rather fond of the old place. I persuaded him to take it off the open market and he let me have it for a song. He'd been meaning to do something with it but kept forgetting and was glad to be rid of it.'

Forgetting? 'More money than sense' springs to mind, but I say, 'He had no attachment to his childhood home?'

'Father?' Tremaine snorts in derision. 'God, no. He has

little attachment to anything. Not what you call a sentimental kind of man, to say the least.'

His eyes look like ice pools and his lips turn down at the corners. Poor guy. Dredging up my sunniest smile, I say, 'Well, I'm glad it's in your hands now. It will be much happier.'

He gives me a withering look. 'Houses don't have emotions, Sennen. They're just bricks and—'

'Mortar. Yes, that's what my dad says, and yes, they are made of building materials, not flesh and blood, but perhaps the emotions of the people who lived in them over the years have been left behind in their foundations.' Ignoring the fact he's looking at me as if I've just announced I'm here on holiday from Mars, I continue, 'You might not see it, but this house definitely feels happier now than it did last time I was here.'

Tremaine gives me a wry smile and spreads his hands. 'I'm not convinced, but would you like to look around the rest of it now?'

I drain my cup and push my chair back. 'Can't wait!' I say, with an answering smile. 'Lead on.'

Chapter Ten

The afternoon has gone by in a flash and I can't believe how much I've enjoyed Tremaine's company. The tour of the house was interesting, and I was happy to see he's leaving many of the old features. The bathroom is a shambles though. It looks like it's been there since the house was new, but he showed me plans for its transformation. They are nothing short of spectacular. There's to be a wet room as well as an old-fashioned claw-foot bath with a high back, the kind you see maids filling with buckets of water for their lord and master to bathe in. The way Tremaine sometimes behaves, I can quite imagine him as a member of the landed gentry living in the nineteenth century. The work's due to be started and completed in the next few weeks and amazingly, I've already been invited back to see it when it's finished.

Transformed also is Tremaine. Happily, there've been no moody oceans at all since the butter incident, only sunshine smiles and laughter. His laughter, though rare, is deep and throaty, the kind of laugh that you can tell is genuine. One that comes from the belly and is infectious. Out in the garden now, sitting in some old chairs looking out over the ocean, I heave a contented sigh. The sun has lost what little strength it had, though with our coats on it's pleasant to sit here and watch the evening arrive. A mist is drawing a veil over the headland and a few seagulls give mournful cries as they come in to roost along the clifftop.

The rusty sign is still up warning people not to venture further, but I can hardly contain my excitement as I think about being able to go down to the forgotten beach very soon. It's been very hard keeping my reasons for wanting to go there from Tremaine, as he's been so open and easy to talk to. But instinctively I know he'd think the whole idea preposterous. Best to bide my time and then slip down to the cave, just me and Gran. I'm desperate for the parting glass to be still there. I know I have to prepare myself for disappointment, but I would be beyond thrilled if it was just waiting for me under the sand.

'Can I interest you in a gin and tonic?' Tremaine gestures to the sinking sun. 'It's over the yardarm, so it's allowed.'

I look into his smiling turquoise eyes, the sea matching the darker blue rim around the iris. Do I want a G&T? Is it wise on an empty stomach, and then driving on the little windy Cornish lanes? His smile deepens and little laughter lines crinkle at the sides of his eyes. My heart squeezes. Be strong, Sennen. You've just been dumped. You're vulnerable, needy.

'Um, I'd love to stay and have a drink with you, but I do have the car.'

'One won't hurt, surely.' Tremaine places his hand briefly on my arm. 'I'll bring snacks too?'

Though he comes across as the 'big I am' sometimes, I can tell there's a vulnerable side to him. A side that feels like a child at a new school wanting to be liked, seeking praise. 'Okay, but make it a weak one, please.'

He jumps up, obviously delighted, and hurries off in the direction of the house. Alone with my thoughts and the soothing shush of the ocean, I ponder on how I feel about Josh now. It's ridiculous, given what he did to me, but being here with Tremaine, even though we aren't romantically involved, I feel guilty. Guilty for feeling attracted to him (there, I've admitted it), and enjoying his company. Inside my chest, a fist of pain clenches whenever I think of what Josh did, what we lost. Despite ignoring some of the warning signs, I'd thought my future was set – ready to take the next step. To walk alongside him, always. Settle down, have children at some point. Who'd have thought a few short months ago I'd be without him, and here with TT at the house where my grandma fell in love?

Tremaine's voice and the tinkle of ice against glass snap me out of my thoughts. 'Here we are,' he says, setting a small silver tray on an old rusty table. On the tray are two half-full cut-glass tumblers, each with a good handful of ice and a slice of lemon. In little floral bowls are a selection of nuts, crisps and crackers, and on a matching plate are a few mini-sausage rolls.

'My goodness, this looks like a proper feast,' I say, reaching for my drink.

The lonely child asking for praise gives a bashful smile. 'Only a few snacks and some sausage rolls I made earlier.'

Blimey. Wait 'til I tell Jas, she'll never believe it. 'Scones *and* sausage rolls. Amazing.'

Tremaine nods and offers me the plate of rolls. 'Yes, I try to bake when I'm not working. My job can be very stressful, so it's nice to unwind and think of nothing while creating something tasty.'

Jasmine's 'Tasty Tremaine' pops into my head and I hide a smirk in a sip of G&T. 'Hm. Perfect, not too strong and the tonic is so refreshing.' Tremaine's face lights up in a smile. 'And these are truly delicious.' I swallow a mouthful of light flaky pastry and perfectly seasoned sausage meat. 'Lovely crockery too.' I nod at the bowls.

'Yeah. They've been here in the cupboard since my father was a boy, I think. Not a patch on yours though.' He licks a bit of pastry from his lips and I try not to stare at his perfect mouth. But my imagination allows me to trace a finger over it and bring my lips to his. 'I'm going to put the bowl in pride of place in the hallway once the house is finished. Then every visitor will see it as soon as they come in.'

A flush of pride heats my cheeks because of the compliment, but more because of my imaginings, and through an ear-to-ear smile I say, 'That's such a lovely thing to say. Thank you.'

'It's the truth,' he replies simply. 'It's rare, your kind of artistic skill.' He looks like he's about to say more, but instead he clears his throat, takes a drink and stares off over the darkening ocean.

'Thank you.' We sit in companionable silence sipping our drinks, eating nibbles, and something I want to say nags at me, but I don't know whether I can allow it out into this peaceful chilled atmosphere. My words might ruin things, make the pompous entitled snob return. Maybe it's the gin that gives me a nudge, but I say, 'I hope you don't mind me saying, but you're so much nicer now than you were the first time we met.'

Tremaine raises his eyebrows but gives little away. 'I am?'

'Yes. You were a bit pompous and stand-offish most of my first visit. You were okay now and then, but overall, I got the impression you found me a bit of a nuisance.' His expression is unreadable so I press on. 'But today you have been such lovely company, and I've really enjoyed spending the afternoon with you.' Inwardly cringing at the last bit, I take a big gulp of my drink. Why did I have to say all that? It sounds as if I'm coming on to him.

I'm relieved and a bit surprised when he does one of his deep belly laughs, his head thrown back, the breeze tangling his curls. 'It's refreshing to find someone so honest, Sennen. Most of the people in my world are anything but.'

I look at his eyes, sparkling in merriment, and wonder if he's making fun of me. 'I'm sorry if I went too far. My mum says I can be a bit blunt.'

'Not at all.' The light touch on my arm again. 'It's true, I can be a moody bastard – it's been said before.' He drains his glass and exhales. 'If we're being honest, I think it's because I find it very hard to trust people. I'm always wondering what their agenda is, you know?'

I nod. Since Josh, I feel similar, sadly.

'Too many people I know are shallow and only out for what they can get.' He turns to me and says earnestly, 'But since yesterday when I saw you in the shop, I knew you weren't like that. Your work spoke to me and I knew you had a good heart, and an artistic soul.'

Whether it's because of the whole Josh debacle, or simply because of the lovely things Tremaine said, I feel hot fingers of emotion reach up from my chest and flick on a tap behind my eyes. I blink and look away, dabbing at the corners with a napkin. 'That is one of the sweetest things' – I clear my throat and swallow tears – 'anyone has ever said to me.'

Tremaine pats my knee awkwardly. 'Hey, I didn't mean to upset you.'

'You didn't. These are happy tears.'

'Well, good. I think.' He gives a little chuckle and shuffles in the chair. He's clearly embarrassed and doesn't know what to say next.

A change of subject might be needed. 'How do you know so much about art then?'

'It's been a thing of mine, from when I was little. I always painted, asked my uncle and aunt to take me to an art gallery in the holidays. My cousins weren't too happy about it though. They preferred to go to the beach, or theme parks. I did enjoy all that too, of course.'

'It's a wonder you didn't want to make a career out of your art, if you loved it so much.'

'Oh, believe me, I did. I'd made some ceramics at an afterschool club near the boarding school. They weren't perfect, but they were good and I was proud of them.' Tremaine looks at me and then away. He's wearing the melancholy distant expression again. 'Father saw them and said they were childlike and crude. We argued and I said I wanted to take it further once I'd left school. I said I wanted to paint too. He said over his dead body. I would be getting a career befitting a Nancarrow and would make something of myself.'

Indignance flares in my chest on his behalf. 'That's awful! I'm no expert but trashing a child's dreams could really affect their self-esteem.' Tremaine shrugs but says nothing and I worry he's feeling embarrassed that he didn't follow his dream, so I add, 'I expect you didn't feel able to go against him when you got older? Your father sounds a bit controlling.'

'A bit? He's the most controlling person I know.' The bitterness in his tone is sharp. Acidic. 'I would have gone against him, but I knew trying to make it with no money, nowhere to live and no family to support me would be almost impossible.'

'Why wouldn't you have money or support?

'Because he said he would cut me off without a penny. Disown me. I would be unwelcome in his house.'

Bloody hell! Julian Nancarrow sounds like a carbon copy of his miserable grandparents. They threatened to cut Jory off in exactly the same way. Thankfully Jory stood up to them. I think about that and why Tremaine didn't feel able to do the same. Perhaps his lonely childhood had affected his self-esteem like I just said. A wave of empathy prompts me to say, 'What an awful cruel thing to do. Did your mum go along with it all?'

'My mother goes along with everything he says. She's never been what you call very maternal. Prefers the finer things in life. Parties, jewellery, clothes, houses abroad … you name it.'

'I see.' I don't, but what else can you say when someone tells you his mother doesn't give a toss about them? 'So, do you have siblings?'

'No. Just me. That made it so much worse. I was – am – the sole heir to the fortune. Father couldn't be doing with some bloody artist as a son. No. I needed to be a fancy London lawyer, even though I don't like the job – bores me to tears.'

Poor guy. This just gets worse. 'Really? What kind of law do you practise?'

'Corporate.' My blank look receives a sigh. 'It involves me helping people buy and sell businesses, checking outstanding debts, legal claims et cetera. Lots of Father's fat cat friends are my clients. Father is a property developer and knows lots of rich people.'

Yup. Boring as hell. A job like that would rip my soul out. 'Hm. It doesn't sound the best. Is there any way you could maybe leave after a few years? You know, now you have money of your own?'

'Possibly. But I think a career change at this stage is a bit late. The job is tedious but it pays very well and I know it inside out. Because it does pay so well, and I have the old man's money to dip into, I'm able to spend more time in Cornwall. And right now, that's very important to me.' He slaps both thighs and stands up. 'Anyway, let's go inside, it's getting chilly and I can feel the damp from this chair seeping into my arse.' Tremaine gives me a brief smile, grabs the tray and sets off for the house.

Following on behind, I wonder if the abrupt way he ended our conversation means I've opened old wounds. Maybe I shouldn't have asked so many bloody questions. Or perhaps it was simply because it's almost dark and too cold to be sitting outside. The idea that the poor guy has had little love in his life won't leave me alone though, and I wish I could give him a friendly hug. An image of him in my arms makes me feel more than friendly towards him and I remind myself that I need to take a step back. The Josh debacle is still festering and there's no way I should be thinking like this about Tremaine. I've only known him five seconds and we are too dissimilar. We belong to different worlds. Corporate law, boarding schools, inheritances? What do I know of those?

As I pass the skip just outside the back door, the wind catches a black bag, and the rustling next to my ear makes me jump. On closer inspection, and in the light from the kitchen window, I see a pile of books poking out of the top. In fact, quite a few books. They're old, battered, leather-bound, and some are mildewed. The wind rustles the bag again and puffs a damp musty breath out into the salt air. I select a book entitled *Poems of Summer*, open the old green cover and gasp as I read:

On the forgotten beach at the edge of the land,
lies a forgotten treasure beneath the sand.

A cup of kindness for Auld Lang Syne,
Sweeter than the finest wine.
In a parting glass from years gone by,
Dwells a magic strange to you and I.
Sup it down before you part,
to find the truth within your heart.

My fingers tremble with excitement as I trace the poem inscribed inside the cover. This must be the very book that Gran had borrowed from the library here and copied the poem from all those years ago! My heart's racing as I flick through the pages for more clues. But there is just a selection of old poems. As I'm reading the inscription again, Tremaine pops back out of the house, hugging himself against the chill night air.

'There you are. What are you doing? It's freezing out here.'

Not wanting him to see it, I quickly shove the book inside the bag and heave the whole thing from the skip. 'Just looking at these lovely old books. Surely, you're not chucking them out?'

'Yes, they're disgusting and stink of mould. I found them jammed into corners on shelves, and in chests. I scooped them all up and plonked them in there. No self-respecting second-hand bookshop would want them in that state. Most are falling apart.'

'So, you never even looked at them?'

'God, no.'

'What a shame. I love old books.'

He rubs his arms vigorously. 'Come inside by the fire,

for goodness' sake. Bring the stinking books if you like – you're welcome to them.'

Result! There's no telling what treasures I might find between the pages. But then I realise the bag is too heavy to carry down the coast path to the carpark.

Inside on a comfy old leather sofa while he stokes the fire, I mention my dilemma to Tremaine. 'So, can I leave them here until tomorrow? I could pick them up before work?'

I get an incredulous look. 'Your car is down in the carpark?' I nod. 'Well, yes, I suppose it would be, or I would have seen it. Blimey. How the heck can you see to walk the cliff path in the dark? You could fall.' He shakes his head. 'I'll pop you down to the car to save you making an unnecessary trip tomorrow – and make sure you drive up to the house next time.'

I'm glad that he seems so concerned for my safety and ridiculously pleased he's mentioned a next time. Feeling nonetheless a bit foolish for not thinking ahead, I say, 'If you're sure? I don't want to put you out.'

'You aren't.' Tremaine rubs his hands and stretches them to the lovely dancing flames of the open fire. 'And if you have no plans for the rest of the evening, do you want to join me for dinner? I'll make lasagne.'

Oh. This is a surprise. He can't be so put out by my questioning then … but should I stay, given what I was just telling myself about Josh, and Tremaine and me being from different worlds? He turns from the fire and raises a questioning eyebrow, his smile slow and sensuous, the planes of his face softened by the low lights and leaping flames. My heart joins them 'Yes, that would be lovely,' I hear myself say. Dear God. There's no hope for me.

At 10.30 pm I'm still telling myself off, but myself isn't listening, and the telling-off voice is very quiet and doesn't mean what it says. We had a wonderful dinner, chatted about my family, friends, everything and nothing, and in the process put away the best part of a bottle of wine and an after-dinner brandy. Now I'm standing in the kitchen waiting for a taxi. Tremaine's insisting on paying for it, and the one tomorrow that I'll need to collect my car from the carpark. I'm telling him that won't be necessary and he's saying he won't hear of it. Suddenly we're laughing for no apparent reason, and then he takes a step closer to me.

'Thank you so much for spending this afternoon and evening with me, Sennen. I've had the best time.' Tremaine strokes a finger along my cheek and follows it with a little peck.

The touch of his lips and brush of stubble on my skin send a tingle down my neck and shoulders and I look up into those eyes the colour of the ocean on a sunny day. They hold my gaze as his arms slip around my waist and pull me close, the heat of his body and pressure from his well-defined chest muscles against my breasts set my heart racing. Then, as he tips my chin up and lowers his lips to mine, the doorbell rings! Damn it! The little quiet voice from earlier says it's just as well, because no good will come of it, but it's flattened pretty sharpish under a fist of frustration.

'That's my taxi!' I say unnecessarily and move away to collect my bag and the bag of books.

'Yes.' Tremaine does a rueful smile. 'Great timing.'

I laugh and hurry to the door. 'Well, there's always next time.' The quiet voice starts to protest, but I tell it to shut the hell up.

'Yes, on that subject,' he says, putting a hand on my arm as I open the door. 'I know we said you'd come back and look at the bathroom, the steps to the beach and stuff, but they won't be done for a few weeks. Would you like to come to a party I'm throwing next weekend? It's a kind of housewarming. Though as you know, I live in London most of the week, unfortunately.'

'Sounds like fun. I'd love to.'

'Don't bring the car. I'll send a taxi.'

'Okay, that's kind of you.' I hover in the doorway, mindful of the taxi driver's grumpy face through the screen. 'I'd best be off.'

'Yes. I'll text you the time to be ready and stuff in the week. Goodnight, Sennen. It's been fantastic.' He gives me a quick peck on the cheek and I give a wave over my shoulder as I hurry to the taxi.

The taxi driver talks incessantly all the way home, but despite trying to concentrate, I hardly take in what he's saying, because my head is too full of Tremaine Nancarrow.

Chapter Eleven

M y little flat feels even smaller this evening as I think of the wonderful meal Tremaine and I shared last night in his huge kitchen. I sit down on the couch to a meal for one and a glass of orange juice, and think about Tremaine. Again. He's been in my thoughts all day at work, even though I've tried to shut him out. The way he laughs, his sparkling eyes the colour of the ocean on sunny days, his vulnerability, his sense of humour, the way he set my pulse racing and my skin tingling when he leant in for that kiss, just before the taxi came. Any friendship between us, which is what would be safest, looks like it's been left at the starting block and overtaken by something else. Or could be, if I let it.

My feelings are like juggling balls in the hands of an amateur. Up and down, up and down, never landing where they are supposed to, dropping, rolling, bouncing off at a tangent, just when I think they've come to rest. I sigh and shove a forkful of chicken curry into my mouth as I ponder my next move. I need another opinion. Jasmine might be a good sounding board, because I don't know what to do for the best. Perhaps I'll phone her when I've finished this. Though on second thought, this kind of conversation is better face-to-face and I'm a little too tired to go out. Maybe a nice relaxing bath and an early night with a book would be the best thing. My eye falls on the black plastic bag of books in the corner I brought back from Tremaine's. I'll have a sort through those. There's sure to be something of interest.

The bath did the trick. I'm much more relaxed now, and the juggling balls have been put away in a box labelled *'not to be opened before tomorrow at the earliest'*. The bag of books is open on my bedroom floor and I put the one with the poem in pride of place on my shelf. I won't keep it beside my bed until I've had time to give it a clean. Mildew, dust and mould are not the kind of smells conducive to a good night's sleep. I'll need to wash my hands too after searching through the other ten or so books in the bag. There're a few Shakespeare plays, a *The Hound of the Baskervilles*, a *Tess of the d'Urbervilles*, a *Frankenstein* and various obscure ones that look a bit dry and boring.

Underneath all of them is a slim black book, quite narrow and without marking or title. It has patches of mildew like the others and a bit of red ribbon hanging out of the pages as a bookmark. I open the cover and realise it's a notebook. There's a black and white photograph tucked in next to the bookmark of a striking woman dressed in tweed, her pale hair styled into a 1930s bob. Her eyes stare out at me, confident, as if daring me to look away, and she's standing in front of Nancarrow House. On the back, long sloping letters in blue ink tell me who she is, and on the top of the first page of the notebook, who it belongs to:

Song of Joy – Victoria Nancarrow

A jolt of realisation goes through me. This is Tremaine's great-grandmother, the one who fell down the steps to her death on the forgotten beach. And if I'm not mistaken, the handwriting's the same as in the poem Gran copied. I quickly grab the book from the shelf and compare them. Yes, Victoria is the one who inscribed the poem inside the cover. Wow! Though only a handful of pages have been written on, it looks like I just found my bedtime reading. I jump into bed, get comfortable, then turn the first page...

This notebook contains my love, my life, my song of joy. It's an exposition, a declaration, and lastly, an explanation to my sons of why I uprooted them from their home, wealth and privilege and took them away from everything they ever knew. I will tell them in words they can understand as children, of course. But as men, they will read this and know why their mother acted in the way she did all those years ago.

My marriage to Alexander Nancarrow was short, and often sweet. He was a good man, though not one of my choosing, as we were matched by our respective parents. Perhaps now, in the 1930s, there is the scent of change in the air for some women, though I fear it will still be many years before women of my class and background will be able to choose a real love match. A match that's above class, occupation, religion or creed. A match that unites two hearts and cannot be divided.

I am happy to say I have found that match in Callum Penhallow. He is the gardener at Nancarrow House, and from the first day I saw him tending the roses, I knew he was a gentle soul. Kindness to nature and everyone he meets is his first concern, and though I didn't want to, because I knew a union between us would never be allowed, I couldn't help myself falling very much in love with him. Callum came to Nancarrow about a year after my poor Alexander died in a riding accident. I was lonely and shiftless, because though I had two small children to tend, my mother-in-law Helena insisted on employing a nanny. I was friendless too, rarely leaving the house and grounds. Helena was fond of telling me that widows aren't wanted in social circles, especially by those with flighty husbands. So, when I met Callum, my stifled existence was given a welcome breath of fresh air.

Callum talked to me about gardening, the sea, farming, anything really, and he wrote poems. Good poems. Poems of love and derring-do. Poems of home, hearth, and contentment too. There, my last words rhyme, how funny! Perhaps I'm picking up Callum's knack. At first, we were just friends. He was my solace, my refuge, someone to look forward to seeing. As I explained, I had little else in my life, apart from my darling boys, of course. But children of six, and one and a half years old are not good conversationalists. Well, my Edward is now not far away from seven, and quite articulate, but there's a limit to our discussions.

Callum and I love to discuss the growing habits of various

plants and he's taught me so much. He's such a learned botanist, impressive for someone so young – twenty-eight, just a few years older than I. His knowledge about most things is impressive, actually. One of his dreams is to be a teacher, but for someone of lowly birth, that is a pipe dream. Unless a miracle happens. Miracles seem a little thin on the ground, alas. Though as I told him, dreams are the things that give us wings. Oh look – another rhyme!

As the months went by and winter turned to spring, we began to realise there was more than friendship growing between us in the garden. Brazen it might seem, but I was the first to voice what I was feeling. Callum was far too aware of the social gulf between us to ever say anything I might deem 'forward.' But once I had shared my thoughts with him, he told me his heart was glad, because he'd loved me from the first time he had seen me, walking amongst the roses. Our first kiss under the shadows of the oak tree was chaste and quick, but the song of joy in my heart at his touch was loud and all consuming.

We have met every day without fail ever after. Sometimes in the shadows of the oak at dusk. Often on the forgotten beach, as I think of it, because of a poem I found about it. More on this later. It's a small beach at the foot of the cliff beyond the garden. It has remained unused for as long as anyone can remember. Helena has deemed the ancient stone steps dangerous and impossible to negotiate. When I once asked Alexander about it, he said as a child he was forbidden to go down there. Thus, over time, I suppose it became forgotten. However, not by Callum and I. Because it is 'forgotten', it's the perfect place for a forbidden lovers' moonlight walk. The steps are a little worn and tricky in places, but once one knows where to place one's feet, there is little problem.

One day soon we will no longer have to meet clandestinely. One day soon, we will be able to walk with our heads held high as man and wife. Plans are afoot.

It's three months since I wrote the above and plans are at last in place for our escape. In that time, Edward has turned seven and little Jory is almost two. Christmas and New Year have come and gone, and Callum and I have chosen tomorrow, Jory's 2nd birthday to make our new life, as there will be a full-moon and a low tide. We will leave by boat, as it's safest. There is every chance we will be seen if we left by road, not least because the children might wake their grandparents, as they will be excited at going on an 'adventure' in the dead of night.

Once the children have been woken, we will run to the steps where our belongings will be waiting. Edward will be instructed to stay at the top with Jory, while I hurry the belongings down to Callum. Then we'll leave this place. You might be forgiven for thinking us reckless, but we are not, because Callum and I have a house waiting in the village! His great uncle Neville passed away recently and left a farmhouse house and ten acres of land to him. Callum was always his favourite and he learned many things from Neville. Callum will work the land and I will help him. My heart is full at the thought of being a farmer's wife, instead of a lonely widow waiting here for old age and death. Who says miracles don't happen!

If Helena, and my father-in-law, Tremaine, forgive me for leaving in this way and making a life with Callum, they will be allowed to visit their grandchildren. Though I fear they will not.

In fact, I know they will not. Helena made a comment about the amount of time I spend with Callum last week. She noted the way we always seem to be laughing and talking together and said it was unseemly. Upon asking why it was unseemly to have such a friendship, she answered, 'because he is no gentleman. He is a village boy, a worker. Ladies bearing the Nancarrow name do not have friendships with workers.' She forbade me to see him and said she'd be watching us. Thankfully, she will not be able to watch us after tomorrow, as we will be gone.

Sometimes I used to wonder if we could be truly happy, as we are from very different worlds, but since New Year's Eve, I wonder no longer. Without a shadow of a doubt, I know Callum is the right man for me, the one with whom I want to spend my life. I mentioned earlier, a poem I found. It was on a scrap of paper and fell from the pages of an old book belonging to my father-in-law's grandmother. The paper was torn and yellowing at the edges. It was handwritten, possibly by her, I have no idea. But it excited and intrigued me. I copied it down on the inside cover of the book. I shall write it here again now:

On the forgotten beach at the edge of the land,
lies a forgotten treasure beneath the sand.
A cup of kindness for Auld Lang Syne,
Sweeter than the finest wine.
In a parting glass from years gone by,
Dwells a magic strange to you and I.
Sup it down before you part,
to find the truth within your heart.

Could the forgotten beach be the little Nancarrow beach where Callum and I had been meeting? Could there really be a magical parting glass hidden under the sand, that would tell my heart's truth?

As soon as I could, I went down to the beach one sunny afternoon, and as always when I am there, a feeling of calm and peace descended on me. There was also a feeling of anticipation and excitement running through my veins and I laughed to myself as I stood at the edge of the water looking out into the blue. I decided to come alone, as I wondered if Callum would think it a little silly, going in search of magic. The beach is small, yet far too big to look under every grain of sand and I wondered where to start. After an hour of digging little holes all over the place at random with one of Callum's trowels, seeds of doubt started to grow in my excitement. I wondered if this was a fool's errand, after all.

About to give up, I noticed the little cave at the base of the cliff near the end of the beach. Could the magic glass be in there? I didn't know, but what had I to lose by looking? Hurrying over to it, I found it to be shallow, damp at the entrance, and dry at the rear. The tide obviously never came up past the opening, judging by the seaweed line and the barnacle encrusted forewalls. Lowering my head I went inside, tracing my fingers along the rough, bumpy wall, until no more than ten long strides brought me to the back of the cave. A natural recess at eye-level covered in sand was the only place anything might be buried, as everywhere else was rough rock.

My heart was racing as I gently inserted the trowel until the tip met with resistance. Quickly scraping away the sand, I soon saw a metal box, rusted and old, and inside was the most beautiful glass! I took it from the box and hurried back to the house. Then, on New Year's Eve, in the light of the full moon at my window, I did as the poem suggested. And as the wine slipped down my throat, my heart whispered its truth. Callum. Callum was the one. My only one, forever and always. Such joy I felt! I wanted to dance, sing, shout my love from the rooftops. Alas, I could not. But I knew very soon, my hand would be joined with Callum's and my life would be complete.

We were married last week in the small village church with two of Callum's friends as our only witnesses. I am now Mrs Penhallow, and we spent our 'wedding night' in the afternoon in our little farmhouse. Though we only had a few short hours before I would be looked for, those were amongst the happiest moments of my entire life. The others being the birth of my two boys. Tomorrow we will be free of this place and the control of my in-laws. Free to live, laugh and most of all, free to love. I took the parting glass back to the cave and placed it in its box under the sand. One day I hope it will be found by another and bring them the same joy it has brough to me.

To my wonderful sons, I will show you this notebook when you are men. I will, of course, have talked to you about why I left Nancarrow House before then, but I wanted to preserve my exact emotions and reasons for my actions at this precise moment in time. Years pass, and take with them the sharpness of our memories, fade the way we felt and thought. My words written here will allow you to know the strength of my love for you both, for Callum, and my hopes for the future for us all. I want to watch you grow into men, be present in your lives, give you the love and guidance you both need without the intervention of others. My greatest hope it that you will be successful, independent, but most of all happy. Without it, what do we have? What are we? Happiness is everything. And at last, I can say, I truly am.

I can hardly see the last few words, because an ocean of tears push behind my eyes and though I put my hand over my mouth, a huge sob breaks free. Poor, poor Victoria! Just as she found the love of her life, it was cut cruelly short the very next day! It's heart-breaking. I can't bear it. Cannot. I close the book, hug the book and a pillow to my chest and cry like a baby. I cry for her, for Callum, for her children, for the waste of a young life, and for the sheer bloody unfairness of it all.

When my eyes are dry again, I think about her sons. Poor Jory was so little. The thought of him and his brother, waiting at the top of the cliff in the moonlight for a new adventure, only to end up motherless, starts me off again. Did Edward and Jory ever get to see the words in this notebook? My guess is not. After she was killed, her belongings would probably have been taken back to the house and dumped in disgust. I'm surprised they weren't burnt. Maybe her in-laws didn't realise what was in the book, just shoved it somewhere and forgot about it.

I get out of bed and put the notebook next to the book of poems on the shelf, wash my hands and face and then slip back under the duvet. I heave a juddering sigh, stare at the ceiling and wonder about the parting glass. So what if it finds the truth within your heart, there's little comfort in that when everything ends in tragedy. Why would I even want to find it now? Seems to me as if it's cursed. In the silence, Victoria's words ring loud and clear. *We are from very different worlds*. These are more or less the exact words I said to myself yesterday when I was with Tremaine. Gran and Jory were from different worlds too and look what happened to him after they drank from the cursed glass.

The juggling balls are back and my thoughts go round and round, along with my churning stomach. Should I still go to Tremaine's party now? Yes, it was lovely spending time at Nancarrow House yesterday and getting to know more about him. It's clear we both feel something beyond friendship for each other, but it's all too difficult right now. Isn't it? There's the hurt from Josh, the different world thing, and now the history of death and destruction associated with the parting glass. Yes ... but there's also the way his gorgeous eyes light up when he gives me the big broad smile and... This has to stop. I slam my hand on the light switch and plunge the room into darkness.

Chapter Twelve

J asmine wipes her eyes with a tissue and hands Victoria's notebook back to me. 'Thanks for such a fun time so far, Sen.' She sniffs. 'Just the thing to cheer me up on a rainy Wednesday evening in November.'

'Hey, that's not fair. You asked me to let you read it, even after I told you it was heart-breaking.'

'I know.' She pats my hand, puts her feet up on my sofa and points at the cheesecake on the coffee table. 'I might need more of that to fortify myself.'

I laugh and cut her another slice. We've had real comfort food this evening. A fish and chips take-away from The Atlantic Café Bar and M&S cheesecake. As I hand her a plate I say, 'You know what got me most of all about Victoria's notebook?'

'The fact that her children probably never read it?'

'Yes! We are so on the same wavelength – maybe we share a brain cell.'

'It kills me to think that their little minds were poisoned

by their grandparents. God knows what they were told. Probably a pack of lies about how their mother didn't care about them.'

'Hmm. Judging how Tremaine's father is nowadays, I think that's true. All he cares about is making money and the family name. Lies passed down the line mixed with ridiculous and outdated standards. So sad.'

We eat our cheesecake lost in our own thoughts and I wonder about Tremaine again. I wasn't going to tell Jas anything about Tremaine and my woes when she phoned yesterday, as what good would it do? I've made my mind up not to go to the party and to leave the parting glass where it is, if it's there at all. But because we've been friends for a hundred years, she could tell there was something bothering me, even over the phone, and it didn't take her long to wheedle it out of me. Well, the gist, not the whole thing. Judging by the Spanish Inquisition expression she's suddenly wearing, borrowed from my mum, I expect that's the next topic of conversation.

'More coffee?' I ask.

'Or a glass of wine?'

I raise an eyebrow. 'One glass. You're driving.'

'Yes, Mum.'

As I busy myself in the kitchen, she calls, 'Okay, let's have it then. All of it. Chapter and verse. Why, if you had such a good time with TT, aren't you going to see him again, or go to his fancy-pants party? And before you start, can I say I think you must be clinically insane to even consider giving him the brush-off? I'd be there like a shot. Unless he's an axe murderer.'

I hand her a glass of red, take a sip of my own and sit opposite in my old comfy armchair. The well-worn leather wraps around me like a hug. With a smirk I say, 'Who'd want to murder an axe, eh?'

Jasmine puts her hands on her stomach and fakes a belly laugh. 'Oh stop, you're killing me.'

'It wasn't that bad.'

'It wasn't that good. Anyway, get on with it. Why are you dumping TT?'

'Hardly dumping. Nothing much has really happened between us.'

'Oooh. Nothing "much" means that "something" has, then.' Jasmine leans forward and gives me the stare. Her intense emerald eyes feel like they're drawing all the truths from my heart like a magician draws scarves from a hat. 'You kissed him when you were at his, the other day, didn't you?'

'No, actually,' I answer truthfully, but the heat travelling up my neck signals she's not far off the mark.

'He kissed you?' She rolls up the sleeves of her stripy blue and white jumper, obviously meaning business.

'No.'

I get the jabby finger through the air. 'Well, I know there's more to tell. Come on.'

'Okay, he was about to kiss me … and I was about to let him … when the taxi driver rang the doorbell.'

'Ooh!' Jasmine's eyes grow round with excitement. 'Bet that pissed you both off.' I shrug and slide my gaze away. 'So, what the hell has gone wrong? You haven't seen him since then, have you? Nor texted?'

'No. But surely, having read Victoria's notebook, you can see why it would never work between us.'

Her mouth drops open as if it's on a hinge like a ventriloquist dummy's. 'I don't see that at all. Yes, her story was bloody heart-breaking, but why should it stop you making a go of things with Tremaine?'

Do I really have to spell it all out? The puzzle in her face deepens. Looks like it. I go ahead and tell her everything that I've been thinking and worrying about. When I'm done, I'm not sure what is largest, her eyes or the O of her mouth.

'That's crazy!' she says, putting her glass down on the coffee table and gesticulating like there's a swarm of invisible mosquitoes around her head. 'Just because your gran and Victoria had a bad things happen, doesn't mean to say that *you* will. It's all bloody coincidence.' More gesticulation. 'And the thing about different worlds, it doesn't matter so much nowadays as it did then.' She does another few mosquito swipes. 'I know you, Sennen. If you don't go and look for the parting glass, you'll never forgive yourself.'

'Ha!' I retort, sending my own mosquitoes flying for cover. 'I'll bloody regret it if I find it and tragedy happens, won't I? Mum said there were different interpretations of what the parting glass is used for. I googled it and it said it's been used as far back as Anglo-Saxon times, as a final act of hospitality – to send people on their way with joy in their hearts. But it was used at funerals too! There's no wonder it's a bad omen!'

'Oh, for goodness' sake! Why are you being so negative?

What about Robbie Burns and his cup of kindness, eh? It's in the poem, remember? A cup of kindness for Auld Lang Syne. And don't you remember the joy and happiness your gran and Victoria spoke about? Victoria said if we don't have happiness, what are we?' Jas shoved her hand through her curls. 'Or something like that. Hang on, give me the book back and I'll look it up.'

As usual she's getting to me, but I don't want to be got to. I'm fed up with making decisions and then going back on them. I want my emotions under control and direction. Lately I feel like a cork on the ocean, tossed about in a storm, never knowing where I'm going to end up. I can't risk being hurt again. Humiliated again. I yank my woolly green polo neck up over my chin and mumble into it. 'No. There's no need. I get what you mean, but there's the Josh thing too.'

'The Josh thing? The bloody Josh thing! What the hell has that little weasel got to do with anything? Has he been trying to get you back?'

'No. But I'm still hurting because of the way he dumped me. I'm obviously on the rebound, which will affect the way I am with Tremaine. But most important, I'm not sure my heart could take being ripped out and trampled all over, if the same happened again.'

Jasmine's expression softens as she swallows a big mouthful of cheesecake. I'm not sure if it's because she's enjoying the cake, or because she's taken what I've just said on board. 'Hmm. I can see that, but only to an extent.' She wipes her mouth and takes a swig of wine. 'Tremaine and Josh are very different men. You can't assume Tremaine will do the dirty on you just because Surfer Boy couldn't keep it in his wetsuit.'

Despite everything, this brings a little smile to my lips as I conjure with the image. 'I know. But once bitten...'

'Right, yeah. Best to be safe, not sorry. Best to never go near another man again and live the rest of your life alone, wandering the beaches, howling at the moon, lamenting your youth and lost love.' Jasmine puts her tongue out at me and grins.

I heave a sigh. 'I'm not saying never, I'm saying not now. I need time to let things settle. Tremaine is lovely, but he's all caught up with the parting glass and the past. That damned thing must be cursed, I'm convinced of it. It's not a cup of kindness but a cup of cruelty.'

We sit in silence for a while sipping our wine, studiously avoiding each other's gaze. Jasmine keeps ruffling her hair and frowning into her glass, and I can tell she's building up to say something to convince me to change my mind. It won't work though. 'Coffee?' I ask, mainly for something to say.

'Yes, but not now. Right, lady, I want you to listen.' Jasmine folds her arms and flops back against the floral sofa cushions. 'Okay, I reckon your gran and Victoria were the happiest they had ever been when they drank from that cursed glass, as you call it. Your gran told your mum she never regretted falling in love with Jory, didn't she?'

'Um, yes, but—'

'Never mind "yes, but"s. And most importantly, after Jory died, she put the glass back under the sand because she wanted others to find it. To find their own happiness.

Victoria did the same.' Jasmine knits her eyebrows and does the death stare. 'Are you going to ignore all that? Ignore both your gran *and* Victoria? Just because of that little shit-for-brains Josh?'

A squirm of discomfort in my gut shifts the barrier of opposition I've been constructing in my mind to whatever Jasmine came up with. She *does* make a very convincing argument. I'd forgotten that Gran had said that to Mum. Jasmine's got a very good memory. Then, before the barrier disintegrates altogether, I say, 'Okay, maybe. But there's still the different worlds thing. We don't have much in common, and I'm guessing that will eventually come between us.' That sounds feeble, even to my own ears, and Jas pounces on it.

'Oh please! You've only known him five minutes. You might find you have lots in common. You both love art and stuff. Poor Tremaine was bullied by his dad and could never take up his dream. You could help him make some pots and shit.'

'I don't think making shit would be very pleasant,' I offer, deadpan.

'Stop hiding behind humour,' Jas says, equally straight-faced, through her eyes are twinkling. 'You know I'm right, but just can't bring yourself to say so and go for it, can you?'

I think of the cork on the ocean's storm again. 'Oh, I don't know, Jas. It's a big step, and I really *am* scared about getting hurt again.' There's a tremor in my voice and I wash it down with some wine.

'Of course you are! Anything worth having isn't easy.' She sits forward, elbows on knees. 'But you have to think of the present. Not the yesterday or the tomorrow. It's no good to dwell on stuff – go forward with hope and you won't go far wrong. Happiness is worth fighting for – Victoria said so. Or if she didn't, that's what she meant.'

I look at her earnest little face surrounded by a tumble of red curls, her eyes beseeching, her smile tentative. And just like that, the barrier is gone. The cork is floating on calmer waters and the sun's coming out. I nod and smile. 'Okay, you got me.'

She jumps up. 'So, you'll look for the glass and go to the ball?'

'I'm not Cinderella.'

'Answer the question.'

I sigh. 'Yep, okay.'

Jasmine punches the air, bounds over like an excited puppy and launches herself at me. 'Yes!! I am so pleased. You won't regret it; I can feel it in my water.'

I'm suffocated under a cloud of curls. I spit a few strands of her hair out and push her off. 'Hey, that's enough; you're strangling me!'

Jas laughs and does as I ask, flopping back down on the sofa, her face beaming like a harvest moon. Sometimes she infuriates me, because we are too alike, but I don't know what I'd do without her. She's always there for me, whether I need her or not, and mostly I do. The relationship is reciprocal, both of us trying our best for the other. Talking about happiness, it's about time she found her own, and as we sip our wine, I remember what the psychic Nancy Cornish said in the pub.

'All this talk about finding your happiness and fighting for it malarkey? How about you?' I say.

'How about me what?'

'How about you find yours? You had a similar experience with Carl as I had with Josh, and it's time to let Rob make you happy.' Expecting Jasmine to dismiss this as usual, I'm intrigued to see heat flare in her cheeks. She shuffles on the sofa, puts her glass down and then picks it up again, obviously flustered. 'Something's happened between you, hasn't it?' I say with glee, leaning forward, trying to perfect my own expression of inquisition.

'Not yet. But he has asked me out,' she says in a shy, non-Jasmine-like way.

'Oh my God! And you said yes?'

'Er … yeah.'

It's my turn to punch the air. 'Whoop! Why the hell didn't you tell me?'

The shuffling again. ''Cos I wanted to keep it quiet until I knew it was going somewhere. There was no point in getting your hopes up if he turns out to be just a player.'

'Nancy Cornish didn't seem to think he is. She said he had strong feelings for you.'

'Hm. That's what made me say yes, to be honest. The whole thing makes me nervous.'

'Why?'

Jasmine starts to say something, then her eyes slide away from mine and she shrugs.

I can tell she feels embarrassed to say what it is, so I prompt, 'Because you have been hurt once recently and don't want to get hurt again? Because you're not sure if you have enough in common and that might come between you?'

I get a half-death stare. 'Okay, yes, touché.'

'See! It's not easy, is it?'

'Never said it was.' Jasmine lifts her chin and draws her lips into a tight pucker. 'I think you'll find that I actually said something like: nothing worth having is easy, and happiness is worth fighting for.'

I bite back a giggle and say, 'No. The fighting for happiness bit you are referring to, I think you'll find, was Victoria.'

She flings her arms up. 'Oh, for goodness' sake, can we change the subject?'

'No. I want to know how it all happened – him asking you out, I mean.' I count my questions off on my fingers. 'One, where were you when he asked you? Two, were you surprised and what did you say? Three, where are you going on the date? And four, did you find out why he'd been horrible to you in the past? Nancy said he'd done it to keep you at arm's length for some reason.'

Jasmine sighs. 'Any more questions before I begin?'

I pretend to think. 'Um, no. No, that's it for now.'

'Right. We were walking on the beach handing out flyers to surfers. Think I told you he was impressed by this idea – said it was inspired.' Jasmine gives a proud smile. 'Anyway, we got talking and he just asked me, out of the blue. To answer another of your questions, yes, I was bloody gobsmacked! Okay, I know what Nancy said, but sometimes psychics get things wrong, don't they?'

I shrug. 'No clue about side-kicks.'

'Oh, ha-ha.' She smiles. 'I said I didn't know, as it was all a bit sudden, and I brought up the way he'd been with me until recently.'

'Oooh. What exactly did you say?' I pop in the kitchen to make a cuppa and she follows me in.

'I don't know *exactly*, but something like: "How come you couldn't stand me all last year then? Whenever you came in the shop, you'd criticise me and snap at me when I asked questions. I could hardly believe it when I got the job and you were actually nice to me on the day of the interview."'

'Good. Best to get it all out in the open before you fall in love and get married.'

One of Jasmine's best withering looks come my way. If I'd been a plum, I'd now be a prune. 'Anyway, Rob didn't beat about the bush, he stopped at the top of the slope overlooking Fistral Beach and led me to a table at the café. We sat down, ordered coffee and then he told me exactly why he'd been the biggest shit in Cornwall – his words – with me over the past year.'

'Well, at least he was honest, didn't try to deny the way he'd acted.' We go back to the living room with our drinks.

'Yes. He does seem very honest.' Jasmine smiles and I can tell by the warmth in her eyes that she already likes him, a lot. 'Turns out he was in a relationship when he first met me. The girlfriend, Louise, was very controlling, apparently. He didn't go into too much detail, but she was always checking up on him, demanding he call her four times a day. Stuff like that. Rob said she was killing any love he had for her, but he was scared of leaving her, as he was worried she might harm herself.'

'Oh, no. Did she say she would?'

'Think so. As I say, he didn't elaborate.' Jasmine takes a sip of tea and stares into space.

'And?'

'And he said he was very attracted to me from the first day we met but found out from general conversation that I was with someone. Then when he heard on the grapevine that Carl and I split up, he was going to pluck up courage and make a clean break with Louise, despite the worry, as everything was going from bad to worse with her. But a friend of his said it might be inappropriate for him to ask me out as he was my boss. The power relationship thing, you know? I might only say yes to him as I would feel under pressure.'

'Honest *and* moral. You have a good one there.'

Jasmine raises an eyebrow. 'I'll remind you that I don't have him at all, yet. We haven't even been out on a date.'

'Yeah, but you will and it will all be wonderful,' I say with a giggle and take a sip of tea. 'Anyway, you haven't said why he was horrible to you, or what happened with Louise.'

She folds her arms. 'That's because you keep interrupting.' Making herself more comfortable on the sofa, she continues. 'Rob was horrible because he was pushing me away – keeping me at arm's length. He didn't set out to do it, it just happened. He reckons it was the only way he could stop himself from telling me how he felt. It made him totally miserable. But then out of the blue a few weeks back,

Louise said it wasn't working between them anymore and she'd met someone else!'

'Excellent! And when you got the manager's post, the last hurdle fell. There wouldn't be the unequal power relationship there, so he pounced on you!'

Jasmine laughs. 'Hardly pounced, but yes.'

'So where are you going on your date, and when?'

'Out for a meal at the Golden Lion, and it's tomorrow.' Jasmine puffs her cheeks out and pretends to retch. 'I'm SO nervous. I can't decide what to wear, for a start.'

'You'll be fine. I'll help you decide, and you can message me if you like in between courses when you pop to the loo. I'll be there for moral support.'

The confident Jasmine that is present the majority of the time has fled the room leaving a worried child in her place. 'Oh God, Sen. What if it all goes wrong? I'll still have to work with him and it will be so awkward … but I really like him already too.'

'Look, just be yourself. Stop worrying about what you're wearing, if it's going to work and stuff, and remember what Nancy the side-kick said. So far, she's been bang on.' I finish my tea. 'We're in the same boat, aren't we? You and Rob, me and Tremaine. Both got tons of baggage round our necks and fears of rejection. But let's channel the spirit of Victoria and my gran, Morwenna, and we won't go far wrong.'

Jasmine nods. 'Okay. And you'll be there for me tomorrow on WhatsApp if I need you?'

'I will. You must do the same for me on Saturday when I'm at this bloody party with loads of people I don't know. Well, apart from Tremaine, and I don't know him very well, do I?' The thought of it makes my stomach turn over, and doubts start gnawing at the edges of my confidence.

Jasmine's looking thoughtful again and nods slowly a couple of times. 'Unless Rob and I come with you? I could do with having a closer look at this Tremaine fellow. You're my best and oldest friend and I need to know if his intentions are honourable.'

This idea sends a rescue package of relief and comfort to my mind, and I say, 'Yes! That would be the perfect solution. I'm sure Tremaine won't mind, as it's a party. It's not as if there'll be just the two of us. I'll phone him tomorrow and ask.'

Chapter Thirteen

A seagull swoops down for the remains of my sandwich, and I send it away with a yell and a swipe. Cheeky bugger nearly took my finger with it. It sits on a rock and gulps down the mouthful of ham and mustard on rye it managed to steal, while I shove the crust that's left back into my lunchbox. Having lived in Polzeath all my life, I should have known better than to sit on the beach with food on show. It's a cold bright day and the tourists have long gone, taking their easy pickings with them. I would have known better if I'd not been stewing over the phone call with Tremaine I had earlier, and decided to eat my lunch on the beach to blow the cobwebs away. Or blow my frustrations away, more like.

Stuffing the lunchbox into my rucksack I set off along the beach as fast as the deep sand will allow, determined to leave behind the memory of the lacklustre and, at times, rude response Tremaine had to my request. The memory tags along however, quickly overtakes me and slips into the forefront of my thoughts, just as I stop to get my breath and watch the waves on the sun-dappled ocean rolling to shore.

Tremaine had been all sweetness and light when he'd first answered the phone, delighted that I'd called and he told me I'd been in his thoughts often. This encouraged me, so I'd told the truth and asked him if it was okay for Jasmine and Rob to tag along to the party as I was a bit nervous not knowing anyone. There was an awkward silence and then he'd said, 'Of course. But there really isn't anything to fear. My friends aren't ogres, you know.' That threw me. It wasn't really what he said, but the tone of his voice could have kept a trawler's catch fresh on a July day.

I'd replied with something like, 'Oh, I know. It's just that I would feel less like a spare part.'

'A spare part? You must think little of me if you'd think I would leave you on your own, for goodness' sake.' He'd tempered this short shrift with a little laugh, but it had sounded forced, reluctant.

I suck in a big breath of salt air, shove my hands into the pockets of my parka and consider not going at all, for the umpteenth time. A breeze picks up a few waves and drops them with a splash at my feet, and as it passes by, it nips my cheeks with icy fingers. A laughing dog lollops into the sea without a care for the temperature, or the commands from its owner – a round lady splashing towards it in red wellies and bundled in a hat and scarf. I decide to move on before the dog includes me in an impromptu shower once it returns to shore.

Frustration lands a few kicks at sand and pebbles as I march back up the beach. To go to the party or not? That's the question. Tremaine and I had ended the call amicably enough, once I'd reassured him that I knew he wouldn't leave me alone all evening, and if it were a problem, I'd tell Jas and Rob not to come. He'd waved that aside, told me he was very much looking forward to seeing me and changed the subject. Even so, there was an awkwardness underlying the conversation, unwelcome as a stone stuck in a shoe. If I go, I risk the whole thing being a disaster if his friends are a lot of entitled snobs who spend the evening looking down their snouts at me. Even if I have Jas and Robert to fall back on, I'm not a great actress, so won't be able to pretend convincingly, and Tremaine will see through it.

If I don't go, I'm giving in to my insecurities, placed there in part by Josh dumping me. I have to admit that I've never been the most confident person in the world, and the little I did have has taken a knock. Then, as I leave the beach and set off along the street to the shop, Morwenna and Victoria appear in my mind's eye and give me encouraging smiles. Two strong women who were unafraid to take risks to find happiness, who stood up to be counted. It's time I took a leaf out of their books – Victoria's quite literally. She and Callum were worlds apart, just as much as me and Tremaine. Maybe even more, given the time she was living in. Did it stop her? No. Was she determined to do what her heart told her to, and bugger the consequences? Yes. I sigh and start off up the beach again. I'm a bloody wimp who needs to grow a backbone. In that moment, I make a decision to go to the damned party, and nothing is going to change it.

Why didn't I ask Tremaine about dress code? I sit on the edge of my bed and look at the mountain of clothes and discarded tangle of hangers sticking out from under it, like the legs of an alien spider. I could ring and ask him now, but that would make me look incompetent. The taxi will be here in half an hour and I should be ready by now. Besides, he might laugh and say there is no dress code, then I'd feel stupid for asking. Damn it. I want to look nice, but not as if I've tried too hard. There's no way I want to turn up in an evening dress only to find it's smart-casual, or even just casual. How do I know what these city types wear to housewarming parties? The words 'different worlds' have been popping into my mind quite a lot lately when I've thought of this evening, and now they are in my head again.

When I'd helped Jasmine chose her outfit for her first date with Robert the other night, she'd asked what I would be wearing this evening, and I'd been blasé and cool about it. I cringe now as I remember telling her that I'll decide at the last minute and it is no biggie. She'd tried to hide a wry smile and a 'yeah right' expression. Jasmine knows me so well. At least her date went really well. They'd had a wonderful time and really hit it off, apparently. I'm over the moon for her, because it's about time she had someone nice in her life. I'm also over the moon they will both be there tonight too because I'm not sure I'd cope on my own. I mean, look at me, I can't even dress myself, for God's sake.

I release a long sigh, look at the mountain again and

decapitate the summit by removing a sparkly navy top and a pair of black trousers. They will be a halfway house between evening dress and smart-casual. I'll pair the trousers with my high-heeled red boots – it's not as if I have to run for a bus, after all – and I'll leave my hair loose for once. The plait it's been in since I washed it this morning will have put some nice waves in it. Then I add some smoky eye-liner, pink lip-gloss, my favourite dangly turquoise earrings and I'm done.

———————

By the time the taxi crunches up the gravel drive at Nancarrow House and pulls up under the floodlights, my stomach is on fast spin. Excitement is outstripping anxiety at the moment, and I'm looking forward to seeing Tremaine. As the taxi pulls away, he appears in the doorway, and my excitement accelerates, along with my attraction to him. Dark trousers, an open-necked light blue shirt, his hair almost golden under the lights, and those eyes, turquoise as the ocean's shallows on a summer's day. A slow smile lights up his face and he hurries forward to greet me.

'You look absolutely beautiful,' he says as he kisses me on both cheeks. His cologne hints at bergamot and cinnamon and his eyes sweep my face in an appreciative gaze. I want him to try and kiss me again.

'You look very handsome yourself, Tremaine.'

'Thank you.' He runs a hand gently down the waves in my hair. 'Your hair out of its plait is incredible, and your eyes are –' Tremaine strokes a finger down my cheek – 'simply stunning.'

My stomach is no longer on a spin cycle, but in a tight knot as heat floods through me. When his forearm brushes mine as he links arms with me, every hair stands on end and a wave of electric energy crackles along my skin. Tremaine leads me inside where a gaggle of guests are in the kitchen laughing and drinking. They all have very plummy accents and exude the kind of confidence associated with their class, but I notice a couple of women are in evening dress, though most are smart-casual like me, and I feel instantly better. He introduces me in passing, and they lift a hand in a wave, or nod and smile as we walk through into the living area. It's empty in here and Tremaine closes the double doors behind him and leans his back against them.

'I want you to myself before more people arrive,' he says with a slow, sexy smile and pulls me into his arms.

My heart thumps in my chest, and, a little surprised, I say, 'What if someone wants to come in?'

He kisses my cheek gently and I feel his breath in my hair as he whispers in my ear, 'They'll have to wait until I've done what I've wanted to do all week.'

Though he's sending my senses into the stratosphere, I'm a bit unsure and ask, 'Which is?'

'This,' he murmurs and kisses me full on the lips. As the kiss deepens and his hands roam my body, any misgivings I had about someone trying to open the door are swept away on a tide of passion, my arms clasping him tightly, my fingers winding through his hair.

A rattle of the door handles makes us both jump and I reluctantly step away from him. Breathless, I straighten my top and say, 'Looks like we've been found.'

'Yes, and more's the pity. We'll pick up where we left off later, yes?' I nod and slip my hand in his. Tremaine kisses the tip of my nose and steps away from the door. 'Okay, let's go and meet my friends.'

Most of his friends seem okay, but it's hard to judge, as we only have time to share a few words as Tremaine whisks me round them one after the other. I pull him to one side as he's about to drag me into the hallway to meet 'Rupert the GP', and say, 'Can we slow down a bit? How am I to get to know people when you pull me away mid-sentence?'

A frown creases his forehead. 'Oh, sorry. I was worried that you might feel uncomfortable because of what you said about inviting your friends as you won't know anyone.' He shrugs and looks sheepish. 'I was just trying to get you to say hello to as many people as possible then you wouldn't feel awkward.'

Oh, bless him. How sweet. Without thinking, I give him a warm hug and whisper in his ear, 'That's lovely. Thanks for looking after me. But let's take our time now, okay?'

He looks down at me and his mouth curves into a smile. 'Of course. And you can give me another hug if you like.'

'I might do in a while … if you're good.'

Tremaine laughs and we step into the hallway just as Jasmine and Robert come in the front door. She looks lovely in a midnight blue shift dress and dark jacket; he's in black jeans and a tan shirt, and just as handsome as Jasmine described. I go over to hug Jasmine and say hello to Robert. When I tell Tremaine who they are, he steps forward and extends his hand. 'Hello, very pleased to meet you both. I'm Tremaine Nancarrow.'

Although she has the tall dark and handsome Robert by her side, the sunshine-over-a-moody-ocean smile Tremaine's wearing has a strange effect on Jasmine. 'Wonderful to meet you too!' she says in a high-pitched squeak, and does a weird duck of her head as if she's going to curtsy but thinks better of it. 'I've heard so much about you.' Jasmine rolls her eyes and giggles. 'That was such a cliché, why do people always say it? I've not heard that much about you, but enough.' She flaps a hand at him. 'And of course, it is all good!'

Robert and Tremaine are both wearing slightly puzzled expressions with fixed smiles on their lips, and a tide of crimson flares in Jasmine's cheeks. Her eyes plead with mine and I slip an arm through hers. 'Come on, let's get you a drink.'

She leans in as we enter the kitchen. 'Jeez, what the hell was I doing babbling away like that? Tremaine must think I'm a complete fruit-loop.'

'That's because you have just had the full force of the TT effect.' I laugh and hand her a glass of red. 'Some women have fainted clean away on the spot under such a charm offensive.'

Jasmine takes a gulp of wine and lowers her voice, 'All joking apart, he is totally beautiful. Even better than his photos.' She shakes her head at me and smirks. 'You lucky, lucky cow.'

Affecting a scowl I reply, 'I can see I'm going to have to watch you, madam. And I'd make sure Robert doesn't hear that kind of talk.'

A big smile lights up her face. 'He's so lovely, isn't he? What do you think of him?'

'Give me a chance, I've only said hello! But he does seem nice, and not too shabby looking either.'

Tremaine and Robert come into the kitchen chatting and laughing and Jas and I share a look of pleasant surprise. 'Now, Rob. What can I get you?' Tremaine sweeps a hand across the array of booze on the countertop. 'We have beer in the fridge too.'

As Tremaine gets the drink and they continue to chat, a tall woman with Titian hair swept up into a chignon and wearing a bold black and white patterned dress catches my eye from across the room. Dressed like that with her black winged eyeliner and knee-length white boots, she looks like a 1960s catwalk model. I'm surprised when she makes a beeline for me, and glance round to see if she's actually looking at someone else.

'Sennen, isn't it?' she asks in a cultured but growly voice. The growly bit sounds added for effect. I nod and smile as she extends her hand. 'Phillipa, one of Trem's university buddies.' She narrows her deep brown eyes. 'I was reading English, not stuffy old law of course.' Her tinkly laugh sounds like a sprinkling of fairy dust. 'He told me you own the dear little art shop in town.' She touches my arm briefly. 'Adore the pots, darling – so cute.'

Patronising or what? 'Thanks, glad you like them,' I say in my polite 'shop voice'. Though if she's just down here for the party I have no idea when she's seen my stuff.

'I came down yesterday and had a wander,' she says, answering my unasked question. 'Trem tells me you make all your own things?'

'Not everything in the shop, but certainly the pottery, and some of the paintings are mine.'

The brown eyes widen. 'The paintings too. Aren't you clever?' Phillipa takes a sip of her champagne and regards me over the rim of the glass. 'I bet the place is a little gold mine in the tourist season.' She gives me a wide smile, her teeth the colour of fresh snowfall, her eyes alight with keen interest.

For some reason I'm beginning to feel uncomfortable. A bit like a spider under the gaze of a cruel child with a pair of tweezers. This conversation is more than just small talk... 'Yes, it does well. But then Polzeath is a very popular—'

'I won't beat about the bush, Sennen. I'm a bit of an art buff. My boyfriend is a talented artist – he makes pots too, and I think his stuff would sell very well in your shop.'

A wave of irritation breaks over me. So that's her game, cheeky mare. 'Right. Well, I don't usually sell other artists' pieces in my shop—'

Phillipa interrupts by holding up a finger, her long sparkly nail catching the light. 'That's the thing, Sennen,' she growls, and produces an ice-chip smile. 'It wouldn't be your shop ... because I want to buy it. It will make a fabulous gift for my boyfriend.'

Luckily, I've just swallowed a mouthful of wine,

otherwise it would have been all down my top as my jaw drops. 'Eh? But my shop isn't for sale.'

'I know. But it will be once you hear how much I'm prepared to pay for it.' There's a glint in her eye and an assurance in her voice of someone used to getting their own way.

Struggling to keep polite, I reply, 'No. It's not for sale. Sixty per cent of it belongs to my Uncle Pete and there's no way he'd sell, even if I wanted to. And I don't. So, I'm afraid you'll have to buy another shop.'

I'm about to make my excuses and walk away, when she says, 'Hmm. That's a shame. I've set my heart on it and I'm prepared to make a serious offer.' Phillipa twitches her mouth up at the side and shoves a card into my hand. 'My number's on there. Ring me when you've changed your mind, darling.' She gives a brief nod and stalks off.

Bloody arrogant, stuck up, cheeky fuc—

'Another drink, Sennen?' Tremaine's cheery voice in my ear interrupts my internal raging.

'Yes, a bucketful please,' I snap, and explain to him what's just happened.

He laughs, which doesn't help my mood, and replies, 'Don't mind Phillipa, she's a little spoilt, but normally means well. Her dad owns a diamond mine, and there's an endless pot of money for her to play with.'

I can hardly speak. Who owns a sodding diamond mine? Then anger finds my voice for me. 'Right. Well, it's about time Miss Moneybags realises wealth can't buy everything. That shop isn't just my living, it's part of me, of Uncle Pete. Part of our family and the community. I make my pieces with love, and hope people will feel something when they see them. No amount of money can buy that.' There's a lump in my throat, a wobble in my voice and I'm willing myself not to cry in front of everyone.

'Hey, I know that.' Tremaine slips an arm around me and kisses my cheek. 'I told you last week that I saw your heart and soul in your work. Please don't let silly Flipper upset you. Come on, put her out of your mind and I'll introduce you to more people.'

Flipper? How sweet. Not. The nagging worry about the two of us being too different that I'd tried to lock away is out of jail and grumbling in my ear. It gets louder too, as I'm introduced to more people. Tremaine has a variety of friends, corporate lawyers in the main, but also Rupert the GP, a magician and a banker. The lawyers were polite, but I noted a reserved indifference in the somewhat strained conversation between us. Rupert was extremely pompous and Oliver the magician was eccentric and full of fun, doing endless magic tricks as if he were on stage. He was the only one I really warmed to. The banker, Gabby, talked about how she smashed through glass ceilings and now is the boss of fifty bank managers. I'm all for equality, but I get the feeling that Gabby is only interested in making lots of money and lording it over everyone else. Male or female. There's no common ground between me and almost all of the people here, even though I've looked for it. Prejudice is an ugly thing, top down or bottom up, but it seems I was right, sadly. Different worlds... But can we overcome it? Build a bridge? Or is the gap too wide to span?

On my way back from the loo I decide to see how Jas and Robert are getting along. The last time I saw them they were chatting to Oliver the magician. Jasmine had her eyes closed and was standing on one leg, obviously involved in some magic trick, while Robert had his hand over his mouth trying not to laugh. Can't wait to hear what Jas will say when I tell her about the sheer audacity of Phillipa. I still can't get over it. Absolutely unbelievable how the woman assumed she could buy my shop just like that and ... a hand on my arm stops me in my tracks, and I look into the cool blue eyes of an attractive brunette with a warm smile.

'Sennen, isn't it?'

My heart plummets to ground level. Great. Here we go again. 'Yes, it is.' I shake her hand and try to return her smile, but it feels a bit forced.

'I'm Miranda, Tremaine's cousin. And I know it's a cliché, but I've heard a lot about you.'

Jasmine would smile at that one. 'Sorry I can't say the same. I know he has cousins, but he hasn't mentioned you by name.'

'That's because he's only just getting to know you. He can take a while to open up.' She laughs and holds my gaze. But unlike Phillipa, I can't detect an underlying ulterior motive lurking.

'Right. He did tell me quite a bit about his parents the other day though, so...' I let my words trail off as I'm not sure I should be revealing this information.

Miranda raises her eyebrows. 'I'm impressed. The boy must be truly smitten.'

I laugh. 'Not sure about that, it's early days,' I say, returning Tremaine's wave from across the room. Though I'm actually quite pleased that she thinks so.

Tremaine threads his way through the huddle around the drinks table and gives Miranda a big hug and kiss on the cheek. 'I see you've met the gorgeous Sennen, then? Hope you're saying nice things about me.' He slips his arm around my shoulder and pulls me to his side.

'Oh please. You think we have no other topic of conversation apart from you?' Miranda says with a wink at me.

He tilts his head to the side and says to her, 'So what *were* you talking about?'

'Okay, I'll admit it. It was you, my favourite cousin. Obviously.' Miranda gives a wry smile and I smile back. There's something about her that puts me at ease, makes me feel more comfortable than I have all evening.

'Favourite cousin? I'm your only cousin,' he says with a sigh.

'Exactly.'

'Do you live in Cornwall, Miranda?' I ask, genuinely interested to know more about her.

'Yes. In St Ives. I'm newly married to the most gorgeous man on the planet, and we live in a house not dissimilar to this one overlooking the bay.'

'That's where she gets her inspiration for her books,' Tremaine says with a hint of pride in his voice.

'Oh, what kind of stuff do you write?' I ask.

'Uplifting stories set in Cornwall with just a hint of magic,' she says with a twinkle in her eye.

'My cus is quite famous, Sennen. You'll have heard of her. Probably seen her books in all the local bookshops,' Tremaine says. 'Under her pseudonym of course.'

'Stop it, Tremaine.' Miranda shakes her head at him and tucks her sleek bob behind each ear. 'You know I don't like all that showy-offy stuff.'

Intrigued, I say to Tremaine, 'Come on, spill the beans. What's her pseudonym?' He tells me and for the second time tonight I'm glad I've just swallowed a mouthful of wine. 'Wow!' I say to Miranda. 'Didn't you write that TV series set in Cornwall last year?'

Miranda's gone a bit pink and looks like she'd rather be anywhere but here. 'Yeah, that's where I met my husband, Harry. He was the director. But seriously, I'd much rather talk about you.' She stops and shoots me a thoughtful look. 'Actually, how would you fancy meeting for lunch next week? I've a feeling we'd get on.'

'I'm in London Tuesday to Friday, but maybe the week after?' Tremaine replies.

Miranda pulls a face and pokes Tremaine in the chest. 'Did I invite you, Mr Sticky Beak? I think not.'

'Charming.'

To me she says, 'Sorry. I'm putting you on the spot, aren't I? I'll give you my number and you can give me a call if you'd like to.'

Because she's so lovely and the most down to earth person here, I say, 'No need. I'd love to.'

Tremaine smiles at me. 'My, you're going to be busy this

next week then. What with lunching with Miranda and surfing next Sunday...' Mischief dances in his eyes and he gives a throaty laugh when I goggle at him.

'Surfing? I can't surf!'

'That's why we're all going together. Jasmine and I will teach you and Rob, and then we're back here for a roast.' About to protest, he puts a finger to my lips. 'It's all arranged. Resistance is futile.'

Chapter Fourteen

Since the party three days ago, my brain has felt like an overstuffed pumpkin. Before I found out about the parting glass and met Tremaine, there was plenty of room inside it. I did ordinary things. I went to work, made pots, came home, went out for a drink with Jasmine, did the shopping, went to my parents' for Sunday lunch, all nothing much to concern my grey matter with. Now there is so much information in my brain, it is literally mind-boggling. Firstly, it's boggling about going to lunch in an hour with a famous author; secondly, that I almost suggested to Tremaine that I stay over on Saturday, instead of sharing a taxi with Jasmine and Rob; thirdly, I'm thinking about Tremaine every waking second and spending lots of time with him in my dreams too; and lastly, I'm boggling over Surfers' Sunday, as Jasmine has dubbed our forthcoming outing.

I switch the hairdryer on, tip my head upside down and

give my damp hair a good blast. It would be good if I could do that to my boggled brain. Clear it out, start afresh. I mean, what was I thinking when we were standing in the doorway of Nancarrow House as the taxi pulled up? Tremaine gave me a last lingering kiss, and I whispered in his ear, 'It's been fun. It's a shame I have to…' I was about to say the word 'go' when Jasmine almost yanked my arm out of my socket as she grabbed my hand and pulled me toward the taxi. And thank goodness she did! Okay, to set things in context, Tremaine and I *had* recently been on the upstairs landing in a particular steamy embrace, and I'd had a few glasses of wine, but that's no excuse. I have never in my life thrown myself at a man like I was about to, before Jas rescued me.

It's as if I'm living someone else's life. My old one got misplaced. Maybe two lives got packed into identical suitcases, chucked on the carousel of time, and I picked up the wrong one. This new life is unpredictable, uncertain, magical, daunting, exciting, exhilarating and so many other 'ings'. Oh, yeah, mind-boggling. Let's not forget that. I need to take a breath, remember my misgivings about being on the rebound and the different world thing. I need to be a bit more grounded, instead of feeling like I'm being swept away like a cork on the tide again. A cork in a storm on the tide, at that. Maybe I should Velcro my feet to the floor. Maybe Miranda will have some in her handbag.

The restaurant Miranda has picked for lunch is *the* swankiest in Padstow, bar none. It costs a month's wages to walk through the door, so I need to eat beans on toast for the next fortnight. On the phone, Miranda said she knew the owner and the food is second to none. I thought, but didn't say, 'It bloody ought to be.' As I pull up in the harbour carpark, I hope Uncle Pete doesn't pop by the shop this afternoon, as he'll find it closed. There's no way I could eat, and get from Polzeath to Padstow and back, all in my lunch hour, so I'll work a little later to make it up. Not that we've been that busy latterly, but then it is November.

The restaurant is a whitewashed stylish Georgian townhouse five minutes' walk away. Once again, I'd wondered what to wear. It's not every day you have lunch with a famous writer, after all. I'd settled for my old black leather boots, a calf-length bo-ho green velvet dress with long sleeves and a high neck, and my favourite red 'Paddington Bear' duffle coat. My hair is in two plaits tied with green ribbon and just a hint of make-up. I went for 'I've made a bit of an effort, but want to be comfortable', and hope Miranda has gone for similar. A friendly waitress shows me into a spacious dining room to where Miranda waits at a lovely table next to a huge sash window overlooking the street. I'm pleased to see she's in a red polo neck jumper, with green jeans tucked into black leather boots similar to mine.

She stands as I walk over and gives me a kiss on both cheeks, her smile as sunny as the bright winter sunshine streaming through the window. 'Lovely to see you again, Sennen.' She holds me at arm's length, her blue eyes sparkling. 'And where did you get that dress? It's gorgeous.'

'Thanks, I've had it years, but it never seems to age.' I sit down. 'You look lovely too.'

We order drinks and look at the menu. Stunning choice, but I'm thinking of going for the one course rather than the two, because I'll have to be eating beans on toast for a month, not a fortnight, if I don't.

'It's my treat, so pick whatever you want to,' Miranda says with a smile.

Is she a mind reader? I open my mouth to protest but she won't hear of it and then the waitress comes back with our wine. 'This is so lovely of you,' I say, taking a sip.

'It's so lovely of you to come. I'll be honest, you're the first one of my cousin's girlfriends that I've wanted to meet. When we met the other night, I just knew we'd get on. I also know you will be wonderful for Tremaine. It's about time he was happy, poor lamb.'

This picks my heart up and floats it around in my chest. I need Velcro. 'Thank you, but it is early days, you know.' I add a smile so she doesn't think I'm putting her off.

'Oh, I know. I'm just hoping it will last between you.' Miranda tucks her shiny dark hair behind one ear and takes a sip of her wine. 'As I said, I want him happy.'

Curious to know more, I ask, 'Was it the other girlfriends that made him unhappy?'

The waitress arrives to take our order. We go for the two courses of pasta and fish and then, once the waitress has gone, she says, 'Not really. Well, I suppose the last one did, but the truth is, poor Tremaine has always been unhappy.'

My heart squeezes as I think of his moody expression banished by a sunlit smile and imagine what he was like as a boy growing up unloved and shipped out to Miranda's parents every holiday. 'Really? That's unbearable. I know he doesn't really get on with his dad and that he came to your place at holiday times.' She gives a sympathetic nod, so I continue. 'I also know he wanted to do something in the art line but his father told him he couldn't. Or at least if he did, he'd be kicked out and cut off with nothing.'

'Yes, all true, sadly. And I'm even more impressed that he told you all that. Tremaine *never* shares stuff. He must really be smitten!' She clasps her hands together in delight and beams at me across the table.

I laugh and shake my head, but I'm secretly pleased he divulged things to me that he's not shared with others. 'I must admit I was a little surprised given the way his moods can change like the wind. He's hard to figure out sometimes.'

Miranda nods, leans her crossed arms on the table and holds my gaze. 'He can be. Give me a "for instance".'

'Okay. For instance, a while back he was in my shop and I'd got some food on my top. He pointed it out and had a laugh at my expense. Not unkindly,' I add quickly. 'But then, when we were up at Nancarrow and he dropped some butter from his scone on his shirt, I laughed because it evened the playing field, but he didn't think it was funny in the slightest. He was quite sniffy about it. Once he'd changed the subject though, he was perfectly fine and things got easier between us, and he opened up about his past to an extent.'

Our food comes and we take time to appreciate the delicate pasta shells filled with crab and topped with caviar. It is amazing. Wait until I tell Jas. A far cry from the usual sandwich or pasty I have for lunch. Then Miranda says, 'Okay, before I comment on what you told me, is there any more?'

Not wanting to hold back, as something tells me I can trust her implicitly, but mindful that I might sound like I'm complaining, I continue, 'The very first time we met, he came across as snotty and up himself, deserving of the "entitled snob" description another of my friends gave him. But once I got to know him, I've found him to be sensitive, kind, caring and so sweet. He gets me, you know?' Miranda smiles her understanding and takes a sip of wine. 'Then sometimes, maybe in the next few seconds, he can switch back to grouch mode. When I asked if my friends could come to the party, he was not at all happy. But when he actually met them, he loved them. They even arranged a surfing day between them without even asking me!' I give an incredulous laugh.

Miranda finishes her food and pushes her plate away. 'I'm not surprised by any of that, I'm afraid.' She presses her lips together and puts her head on one side, her intelligent blue eyes regarding me keenly. 'I want to explain a little more about Tremaine and why he's like he is. That's why I asked you here – because I know how hard it is for him to share his past. Though I'm glad to find out that he's shared some with you already. Look, can I trust you to keep it between us? My gut tells me I can, but I need your word. He's a very private person and would hate it that I shared things about him without his permission.'

I'm impressed by her loyalty and reply, 'I promise whatever you tell me stays between us.' *And Jasmine of course. We tell each other everything.*

She butters a piece of bread and takes a bite. 'God, that's delicious, like the rest of the food here.' I agree and butter my own bread while she talks. 'Okay. And please don't think I make a habit of this, but I know how much my cousin likes you, and I wanted to ensure you had the whole picture. As you say, he can come across as a very annoying and puzzling character if you don't understand why. I didn't want you to dump him before you had a chance to know the real Tremaine. So, here it is. Tremaine's mother Katherine is my dad's younger sister, but they're like the proverbial chalk and cheese. My grandparents, like Tremaine's, were stinking rich, and Dad and Aunt Katherine had a privileged upbringing. Dad uses his money to help others, always has. He heads up three charities here and abroad, and he and Mum organise and run food banks and homeless shelters.'

'They have a very different attitude to money than Tremaine's parents then.'

'You could say that.' Miranda heaves a sigh. 'Aunt Katherine was always out for number one, despite never wanting for anything. When she met Julian Nancarrow, Dad said it was a match made in heaven. He said she never really wanted kids, but Julian wanted an heir. He had to carry on the family name.' She rolls her eyes. 'I do wonder if he's a Victorian throwback.'

Julian's perspective and actions are making perfect sense to me now. His father, Edward, obviously inherited the dubious legacy of his grandparents – Victoria's in-laws. If Julian had the outdated norms and expectations drummed into him, then he'd most likely do the same to his own son. I long to share what I know about Victoria with Miranda, but that would mean telling her about the parting glass, and I'm keeping that tucked safely away. Maybe I'll share it all one day, but I know instinctively that now is too soon.

I swallow a mouthful of bread and ask, 'So did Julian go to boarding school too?'

'Yes.' Miranda places a hand over her heart and exaggerates her upper-class accent. 'All the Nancarrow boys did, going back for a hundred years or more. It builds character, sets them up for manhood, don't you know? They need to learn how to lead, to provide, and to be masters of their own destinies, my dear girl.'

I give a wry smile. 'Poor Tremaine. He must have longed for some normality. He told me he loved being with you lot in the holidays.'

Her smile is warm. 'Yeah. We had fun. Tremaine, my older brother Jack and I were always off surfing and tree climbing. Not at the same time, obvs.'

I laugh. 'Don't talk to me about surfing. I'm not a huge fan of ocean swimming, but as I mentioned, I've agreed to go this Sunday with my friends and Tremaine. I'm nervous already! Luckily, I managed to get a wetsuit from Ann's Cottage in Polzeath. The assistant was so knowledgeable and actually put me at ease ... but it didn't last long!'

'You'll be fine once you're out there,' Miranda replies

and then does an exaggerated shudder. 'But you wouldn't get me in the water nowadays. I prefer a heated pool!'

Our mains arrive and we give the smoked haddock and black pudding in a vichyssoise sauce our full attention for a few minutes. 'Wow, this is amazingly good,' I say. 'Such unusual flavours but they work so well together.'

Miranda nods. 'God, yes. Paul works wonders with his menu. I try to come here once a month at least. Tricky with work at the moment though, as I'm advising on another series of *A Place to Call Home*, which is quite time-consuming.'

'Yay! Another series, can't wait.' Oh dear. What's wrong with me? I sound like a proper fan girl, but Miranda gives me a big smile.

'Glad you like it. I must admit I was very pleased with the outcome. I know so many writers who feel that TV or film has ripped the heart out of their original idea.'

'It was fab. Me and Josh...' Damn! I didn't want him slipping into our conversation. Now she'll want to know who he is.

Right on cue she says, 'Josh?'

'Yeah. He's my ex. I was going to say we never missed an episode, but I try not to talk about him. I'm still very angry about the way it ended.' I tell her everything, then add, 'That's why I keep saying it's early days with Tremaine and me. There's no way I want it to be a rebound thing as I really do like Tremaine. I just couldn't face getting rejected again – my heart won't take it.'

Miranda reaches a hand across the table and pats my arm. 'Poor darling. I don't blame you. And I'm sure

Tremaine feels the same. Ever since he was little, he's had to be perfect. He's always had to be the best at whatever he attempted, because if he came up short, he'd be ridiculed and humiliated by Uncle Julian. That's why he would have hated dropping the butter on his shirt. He'd have felt stupid and clumsy. And when you asked your friends to come to the party to help you feel more comfortable, he'd have felt inadequate – as if he wasn't good enough.'

I nod. 'Yes. That's the impression I got. Poor Tremaine.' A tide of sadness surges through me as I think of Tremaine as a little boy having to go through all that. I want to go down to London and give Julian Nancarrow a slap. Katherine too – cold-hearted cow.

'Olivia, his last girlfriend, did a bit of damage too. I think she's the only one he's been halfway serious about, to be honest. The others were mostly air-heads, models, wannabes, just gold-digging.' Miranda dabs her napkin at the corners of her mouth and pushes her plate away. 'Olivia's a gold-digger too, reminds me of Katherine in some ways, but at least she had the brains to go with her beauty.'

The sadness tide takes a turn and comes rushing back, netting jealousy and surprise in its wake. 'Olivia? He's never mentioned her.' But then I never mentioned Josh to Tremaine, did I? I push my plate away too and take a large mouthful of wine.

'He wouldn't, they're over now. Have been for about six months. And as I said, he's not one to share if he can help it. He met her at work, she's a lawyer too. They were going out for about a year and there was talk of her moving into

Nancarrow with him when it was done, as well as into his place in London. Then he heard rumours that she'd been putting it about with one of her clients. Eventually, Olivia admitted it, but said it was just a fling and she wanted only Tremaine. Despite her begging for another chance, he told her it was too late. There's no way he would have let her back. As you can imagine, because of what I've told you, Tremaine would have felt terribly humiliated and foolish. Anyone would, but for him it would have been ten times worse.'

Sitting back in my chair, I fold my arms and think about this. Tremaine and I have had similar experiences, and recently. What if we are both on the rebound? Not a good combination. Miranda puts her head on one side and asks if I'm okay, so I tell her my thoughts. 'And another thing. Why did an intelligent man surround himself with all those shallow gold-digger types? The people at the party too. With a few exceptions, they were all very pompous and about as genuine as a prehistoric iPhone.'

Miranda throws her head back and laughs. 'Great analogy. And I think the answer is because he wants to be liked. His parents did some serious damage and Tremaine's very needy, but he covers it up well with his snooty side. I suppose if he fills his house with people, no matter how unsavoury, he can tell himself he's popular. He might very well be, as he's an attractive personality, as you have found, but most of them there the other night were there because Tremaine can do something for them in some way. Maybe he can help them as a lawyer, or put them in touch with the right people, or put in a good word for them somewhere. Networking is crucial in Tremaine's world.'

'Hmm. A very different world to mine.'

Miranda sighs and her mouth curves into a gentle smile. 'Yes. But it needn't be. You told me that Tremaine wanted to be an artist and I'm sure that with the right encouragement he could drop the lawyer career, move to Nancarrow House permanently and pursue his dream. Happiness is the most important thing in anyone's life, and he needs to realise that.' Miranda looks at me closely. 'And, Sennen, I'm not just saying this, but I think you will be the person to make his dreams come true. Yes, okay, you might both be on the rebound, but whatever darkness the past has dealt you, your future path is waiting and it's bright. You can walk it together.'

Embarrassed to find sudden tears in my eyes I blink rapidly and say, 'Nice words. I can tell you're a writer.'

'It's true. I know you two are meant to be together.'

———

Outside the restaurant, as Miranda and I say goodbye, she gives me a big hug and makes me promise to keep in touch. 'You know I'm here for you if ever you need to ask me anything about my cousin, or simply to have a chat.'

'Thanks, Miranda. It's been a lovely afternoon and we'll do it again soon – my treat next time.'

'We'll deffo do it again. Bye, Sennen.' She squeezes my arm and then flings a wave over her shoulder as she goes off down the street.

Though Miranda didn't have much Velcro in her bag, I do feel like I might be a bit more grounded as I walk to my car. I know more about what makes Tremaine tick, which means I have a better understanding, and I know about Olivia too. I also know that I have a friend in Miranda. Someone I can call on if I need a listening ear and advice. Yes. All in all, things are definitely looking up.

Chapter Fifteen

My stomach is churning and swirling in time with the waves out on the ocean and the idea of eating the ham and pickle sandwiches, sausage rolls and cake I packed for the picnic is making it worse. Tremaine lifts the lids of the lunch boxes, and the smell of food wafts under my nose, courtesy of a fresh breeze.

'Who's for having a quick bite before we take the plunge?' he asks our little band of intrepid adventurers, as we gather at the foot of the dunes on Daymer Bay.

'I thought you weren't supposed to eat before swimming?' Robert says, folding his arms and looking at Jasmine for confirmation.

She lifts a finger and wiggles her eyebrows. 'Technically, we aren't swimming, are we? We're surfing. And in reality, we're most probably going to be sitting astride our boards waiting for a wave, most of the time we'll be out there.' She nods at the navy-blue swell of the ocean threatened from above by a huddle of bruised clouds.

'I could eat a horse,' Tremaine says with a grin at me.

'Well, I forgot to pack one of those, I'm afraid,' I answer, trying to come across as jovial, instead of terrified.

'Hmm. I think I'll wait until afterwards. I'm a bit nervous to be honest,' Rob says, running his hands through his short dark hair while looking out towards the horizon. He points. 'Looks like rain's coming in.'

Relief that I'm not alone in my apprehension, I comment, 'Yeah, it does. And isn't it a bit silly picking a day in November to have our first go at surfing? It will be bloody freezing in there, even though we're wearing wetsuits.'

Tremaine slips an arm around me and kisses my cheek. 'That's just a few collywobbles speaking. You'll love it once you get in there.'

'She will,' Jasmine confirms. 'I reckon the sun's trying to get through the cloud too. It'll all be grand.' She grabs Rob's hand and kisses him on the lips. 'Come on, let's get to it!'

Tremaine grabs my hand too and we set off at a run, surfboards tucked under our arms. He calls to me that it feels exhilarating. I just feel like we're going into battle. Jasmine's shrieks and Rob's yell as they charge through the freezing shallows don't help my nerves and as I splash in up to my knees, my breath is taken by the cold. I can't even breathe, never mind shriek.

'Nooo!' I manage, as Tremaine pulls me in up to my waist. 'I thought wetsuits were supposed to protect you against the c-cold!'

'They are, you'll warm up soon – promise.' Tremaine

pulls himself onto his board and begins to paddle forward with his arms. 'Okay, now you!' he shouts, over the roar of the waves.

Easier said than done, I think, when your hands are pink from the cold and can't grip the board properly, while the sand keeps shifting under your feet as you try to launch yourself onto a bit of fibreglass bobbing about in the surf. And why the hell would any sane person want to? On what must be my tenth attempt, I manage to fling myself inelegantly across the board and lie there, like a dead seal on an iceberg.

'Yay! You're on. Well done!' Tremaine says paddling alongside me. 'Okay. Just do what I do and follow me. We need to get out of these breakers and wait for a good wave to ride back to shore.'

I'm horrified. 'You don't expect me to try and stand up on my first attempt, do you? 'Cos you'll be sadly disappointed.'

'No. But you can sit astride and get the feel of it, or use it like you would a body board.' His eyes shine with enthusiasm and the full force of his broad sunlit smile puts a prickle of desire in my belly.

'I'll try my best,' I answer, with more conviction that I'm actually feeling, but I want to show him that I'm not completely hopeless. To my right I see Rob's on his board too and paddling steadfastly after Jasmine. Okay, you can do this, I tell myself. Fortunately, myself is paying attention, and the dead seal slowly comes back to life.

An hour later, we're wrapped in dry robes, sitting on the rocks with a mug of tea in one hand and a sandwich in the other. A positive charge is rushing through my veins and every inch of my skin is tingling, invigorated by Tremaine's nearness, added to by the cold ocean and the thrill of riding a few waves. Well, I have to admit I never actually got to my feet, but I rode the waves to shore, nevertheless.

'More tea?' Jasmine asks, lifting her flask.

'Yes, please. I'll need a gallon to warm me through,' Rob says, holding out his cup. 'If someone had told me I'd be surfing in November and then having a picnic on the beach with sea water dripping off my beard, I'd have told 'em they were mad.' He looks at us all, his blue eyes sparkling with merriment. 'But you know what? It's been bloody brilliant!'

'What about you, Sen?' Jasmine asks. With her messy red ringlets twisted up into a damp ponytail, green eyes sparkling and her face glowing from the cold, she looks like happiness personified and I'm thrilled she's turned a corner.

'What about me, what?' I ask, just to irritate her, because I know what she's asking. I smile as a frown creases her brow. We always wind one another up, it's the law. Has been since schooldays.

'Have you enjoyed it, you daft mare?'

Tremaine laughs at that and I pretend to be offended. 'Daft mare, indeed! How very dare you?' Jasmine narrows her eyes and cultivates a death stare, so I say, 'Yeah. I loved it. Maybe we can do it again … when the Atlantic isn't pretending to be the Arctic.'

'A Sunday roast cooked by my own fair hand and glass or two of wine will warm you up,' Tremaine says, dropping a kiss on my forehead.

'Can't wait,' I say and take a few sips of tea.

Jas gives me a sly wink when he's not looking, which means she knows what else would warm me up. I roll my eyes but must admit I have been spending an unhealthy amount of time imagining what it would be like to go further than a few kisses and caress with Tremaine. Heat flares in my cheeks when I think of how I almost got to find out, the night of the party when I was about to suggest I stay over. What would I say if he suggests the same later? Is it too soon? My libido says no, my sensible head says, probably. I leave them to argue it out and say to everyone, 'Well, I'm all for going back to Nancarrow House before my poor frostbitten fingers fall off.'

Tremaine laughs and drains his cup. 'Come on then, folks. Let's go.'

If Jasmine says, 'Oh my God!' one more time, I will gag her. Yes, Nancarrow House is impressive, but her constant repetition of that one phrase is doing my nut in.

'Oh my God! I know I saw it when we came to the party, but it was dark and I couldn't really see outside. Look at the view from the kitchen,' she implores, even though we are already doing just that. She hurries through into the living room. 'And it's even better in here!' We follow in her wake to find her at the French windows which open out onto the sweep of lawn and the ocean beyond.

Rob joins her at the window and slips his arm around her shoulders. 'It's certainly very impressive.' There's a slightly envious tone to his words and I can see why. He must be thinking he could never afford a house as grand as this, and Jasmine's over-the-top praise must be irking him a bit.

'Thank you,' says Tremaine. 'I'm growing to love this place more and more. When I set out for London on a Tuesday morning it's becoming harder to leave it behind … Cornwall too.'

'Why don't you stay then?' Jasmine asks. 'We have lawyers down here, you know.'

Tremaine smiles. 'Easier said than done.'

I can see Jasmine gearing up for a Spanish Inquisition and know that he won't want to tell her the real reason he can't leave corporate law in the capital, and his father's influence, so I say, 'Everything always is. How about we have a drink and warm up round the log burner?'

'Yes. And I need to check on the beef in the Aga. I put it on to slow roast before we went surfing.'

After a glass of red wine and some cashew nuts, I'm beginning to get some feeling back in my fingers and toes. Jasmine and I are sitting opposite each other, cosied up in two huge comfy armchairs, wrapped in yellow and red checked blankets. Rob and Tremaine are sitting on the sofa in front of the wood burner, talking about global warming and how Tremaine plans to make this house more sustainable. The wood burner is new and fits in with the latest regulations, but he plans to fit some solar panels to the roof at the back of the house and what remains of the old stable too. Once it's been refurbished and made into a garden room it will be the perfect place to watch the sea on inclement days.

'They seem to be getting on like a wood burner on fire,' Jasmine says with a nod across the room towards the two boys.

'Yes. I'm so glad. That way we can spend more time all together.'

'Yeah. Though it might be nice to spend some time in just twos, eh?' Jasmine tips me one of her cheeky winks. 'If you follow me.'

I give her a withering look. 'Of course. How could I not?' She sighs and I have the feeling she needs to have a chat. 'Fancy a grand tour of the upstairs?'

Jasmine jumps up like a puppy invited for a walk. 'You bet your sweet ass I do.'

I tell Tremaine where we're going, and we leave them to it.

———

'This house is absolutely incredible,' Jasmine says as we stand at the top of the wide staircase ready to go back down. 'That master bedroom feels like you're standing at the prow of a ship with the bay window overlooking the ocean. Can you imagine waking up to that every morning?'

'Yeah. It would be wonderful, proper set you up for the day.' I smile and turn to go downstairs, but her hand on my arm stops me.

'You could, you know.' Jasmine's serious expression and intense stare puzzle me.

'I could what?'

'Wake up every morning to that view. And to that hunk of a man downstairs too.'

'A bit previous, aren't you? I've not known him five minutes.'

'That's not important. What is important is the way he looks at you. The way he is with you.' Jasmine smiles and I'm surprised to see her get a bit teary. 'And the way you are with him too.'

'I think that wine's gone to your head, mate.'

'No. But Tremaine has gone to yours. I can tell.'

A rush of panic inside my chest pushes her words away. It's all getting a bit too serious too fast. 'I haven't noticed he looks at me in a particular way. Yes, I like him, but it's all very new.' I turn and go down the first three stairs.

'What are you afraid of, Sen?' Her quiet tone stops me again.

'You're not serious?' I turn and shoot her an incredulous look. 'Maybe the fact that I've recently been hurt, and we're both on the rebound, perhaps?' I lower my voice and go back up the stairs. I'm beginning to feel like a broken record. 'We've been through all this when I told you on the phone about what Miranda said.'

She shakes her head and takes my hand in hers. 'Maybe you just can't see what's in front of you. I've never seen you like this with anyone before. You light up when he's around. It's as if you're glowing from within.'

I laugh and take my hand back. 'That's 'cos I'm radioactive. You need to stop reading those romance novels.' Jasmine opens her mouth to say more, but I head her off at the pass, as my gran used to say. 'Never mind my love life. Yours seems to be doing pretty well, too. Rob's lovely and you can see he thinks the world of you.'

Her bright smile makes her look like she's glowing from within too. 'Yeah. The feeling is mutual…' Jasmine leans in to whisper. 'I stayed at his last night.'

Without thinking I say, 'Bloody hell, that's a bit quick, isn't it?'

Her face falls. 'When it's right, it's right. Anyway, I don't think a night of passion would do *you* any harm either. Might stop you being so grouchy and frightened of love.'

It's like a punch in the gut. Frightened of love? That's ridiculous. Isn't it? A response evades me as I open and close my mouth, goldfish-like. Before a mischievous light in Jasmine's eyes prompts me to say, 'That's not true. I'm just being cautious. It's called self-preservation.'

'It's about time you found some guts.' Jasmine sniffs and brushes past me. 'Come on. Show me the steps that lead down to the forgotten beach. Maybe the ghost of Victoria's there and will give you a good talking to.'

The grey clouds threatening the ocean earlier have brought reinforcements. A bully of a wind whistles in our ears as we stand at the top of the steps, competing with the high-pitched squeak of the danger sign as it's battered back and forth on its chain. The indigo ocean makes a great fist of its waves and pounds the shoreline as if showing the clouds its mighty strength, and I shove my hands into the pockets of my coat and turn my back to the wind. Jasmine puts her hood up, wraps her arms around her middle and peers past the sign at the steps. 'Looks like they're finished!' she calls above the wind.

'No. Tremaine says next week. They've just got to put the last section of handrail in!'

As she turns round to face me, the wind yanks her hood down and makes streamers of her hair. 'Bet you can't wait to get down to that cave!'

I'm about to say *once again* that I'm not sure looking for the parting glass is a good idea, when the thought of Gran and Victoria's determination to find happiness stops me. Finding the parting glass is of paramount importance to me, even though I keep trying to dismiss it. I can think of so many good reasons to forget all about it, but even more convincing ones tell me I mustn't. Maybe Victoria's spirit is here after all. Gran's too. I gaze up into the angry sky and say, 'Yeah. I'll do it when Tremaine's in London. It's something I have to do alone.' I look out over the raging ocean and a watch a couple seagulls flying backwards. Then

I take a huge breath of salt air and say, 'With Gran's help of course.'

There's a chilled-out ambience in the kitchen, the kind that only a wonderful meal, excellent wine and great conversation with good friends can bring. 'I can't eat another thing,' Jasmine groans, patting her tummy while gazing longingly at the remains of the tiramisu in the dish before us.

'That's what you said before you had your second helping of pudding, Jas,' I reply with a giggle.

'It's all his fault!' She jabs a finger thorough the air at Tremaine sitting opposite. 'If he wasn't such an extraordinary cook, it wouldn't have been so hard to say no.'

'You didn't say no,' Rob reminds her with a cheeky twist of his mouth.

She gives him a playful punch. 'Don't you bloody start!'

'There is always room for a third helping?' Tremaine raises his eyebrows and picks up the serving spoon from the side of the dish.

'No thank you. I would actually pop!' Jasmine pushes her dish away to reinforce her decision. 'How on earth did you get to be such a good cook? A perfect roast and then a tiramisu made from scratch.'

'My aunt taught me when I was at their house during the school holidays.' Tremaine stands and begins to clear the plates. I can tell from his demeanour and body language that he wants to nip that conversation in the bud, so I follow suit.

'Cheese and biscuits for you, Jas?' I quip, as I collect her dish and wine glass.

'Oh ha, ha.'

'I wouldn't mind a coffee, if that's okay?' Rob says, picking up the tiramisu and taking it over to the fridge. Jasmine walks over, slips her arms around him and whispers something. An ear-to-ear smile curves Rob's lips and he nods to Tremaine, who's measuring coffee into the machine. 'Hold mine, Trem. I think we might be heading off soon.'

My heart sinks as I'm sharing a taxi with them. It's only 7.45 and I'd hoped to spend a bit more time here. 'Oh, right. I'd best not have a coffee either, then.' My tone is flat, deflated.

'You don't have to go now,' Tremaine says with a hopeful smile. 'We'll get you a later taxi.'

From behind his back, Jas makes googly eyes and forms a heart shape with her fingers. 'Yeah, you should stay and er' – she does a lascivious wink – 'chat a bit more, Sen.'

Upon witnessing his girlfriend's antics, Rob coughs to hide a snort and calls a taxi.

After they've gone, Tremaine and I sit on the old leather sofa in front of the wood burner, our feet up on the matching pouffe, coffee in hand. We chat about the day as we toast our toes, mine in blue fluffy socks and his in garish orange ones. I tap my foot against his. 'Dayglo orange socks aren't normally you. You're more the city-slicker, man-about-town kind of dresser.'

'That's because most of my clothes are for work and London. I do have quite a crazy taste in socks, as it goes.' He laughs and strokes his foot along mine. 'And PJs too, truth be known.'

Intrigued, I lean into his shoulder and say, 'Ooh, spill all.'

Tremaine pulls a grave expression. 'If I tell you, I'll have to kill you.'

'Aw, go on. I promise I'll take it to the grave.'

'Hm. Okay, my favourite ones at the moment have the Millennium Falcon, Chewbacca and C3PO all over them.' He looks at me through narrowed eyes as if daring me to laugh.

Though surprised, as *Star Wars* pyjamas don't fit in with his corporate lawyer persona, I don't find it funny. I think it's a bit sad, to be honest, because I know he was never really allowed to be a kid when he was one. Maybe the orange socks and PJs are an outlet for his fun side. A side that was repressed for so long. He gives me a questioning look and I send him a warm smile. I tell myself not to over-analyse everything, and that he might just like *Star Wars* and brightly coloured socks when he's relaxing. But my heart tells me I was right the first time.

I slip my arm through his and lay my head on his chest, because I want to be close to him, to comfort the sad and lost little boy that still lives within the man. As the flames send dancing shadows up and down the walls, and I listen to the crackle of the logs in the fire and the thump of his heart through his soft arran sweater against my ear, I feel my senses calm, and a sense of belonging find a home within me. Being here in his arms feels natural, right. '*Star Wars* PJs eh?' I nudge him. 'Well, all I can say is that I'd love to see you in those bad boys.'

There's a brief silence, then he pulls me tight against him and says into my hair, 'Are you suggesting that you'd like a sleepover? Because I don't see how you can … as you haven't brought your own pyjamas.'

That jolted me out of my reverie and I pull away slightly. 'No. I didn't mean that, I—' I stop when I notice the mischief dancing in his eyes.

'Got you there.' Tremaine gently kisses my forehead and trails a finger down my cheek and across my bottom lip. 'But you know you'd be very welcome if you did want to stay.'

Do I? The light touch of his finger has ignited a fire within me, but a range of emotions sweep in and through my heart, some sticking, others dismissed like miscreant schoolchildren. The schoolchildren mainly consist of regrets, fears, what ifs and maybes. The stickers are hope, happiness and desire. 'I'm not exactly sure… I think I might want to, but I need to share a few things about my past first.'

Tremaine looks deep into my eyes. In the flickering light from the wood burner's flames they draw me in, intensify, until I feel I'm falling into them. Into him. 'Of course. And I have something to tell you too. But right now, I need to do this.'

Being me, I immediately worry about what he wants to tell me, but every nerve ending is on fire, sending desire rocketing through my whole being. And as his sensuous mouth finds mine, I find that I really couldn't give a damn about anything except his kiss, and the caress of his hands.

Chapter Sixteen

Monday morning slips into afternoon, but I barely notice. Customers have come and gone, along with various conversations about the weather, the fact it's December already, their ailments, and could they order in X, Y and Z for Christmas presents? I navigated all this on auto-pilot because my head was, and still is, packed full of Tremaine and the wonderful night I spent in his bed.

I finish packing a beach-scene dish into a box with pink scrunched-up tissue paper, and then flick the kettle on in the back kitchen. As the water boils, I get a bit steamed up too as I think again about Tremaine's naked body, glorious under candlelight, lying next to mine, his moans of desire as my fingers caressed his taut stomach muscles and lower. The heat and intensity of his kisses all over my skin, the flicker of his tongue over my most intimate places sending me into rapture. I smile as I sip my tea and I remember that I'd planned to just talk to him about Josh, and the fact that I was worried that Tremaine and I might be having a rebound relationship. But all thoughts of that went out of the window. I must discuss it with him though, very soon.

The shop bell tinkles and a blast of cold air as the door opens whisks me back to the shop on a chilly winter's afternoon. I sigh, putting thoughts of being in bed with Tremaine out of my mind and resigning myself to reality. I put my mug on the side and go back to the counter.

'Uncle Pete! Not seen you for a bit. I was only thinking about you the other day…' The rest of the words die on my lips as I notice his serious-as-the-grave expression. It looks incongruous on him, as if he's breaking it in for someone less cheerful. Uncle Pete never looks miserable. He's always got a smile and a joke ready, always upbeat.

Heaving a sigh that sounds like it's come from his boots he says, 'Not sure you'll want to see me again, after I tell you why I'm here.'

My heart jumps as a hundred hideous scenarios flash through my brain. I grip the edge of the counter. 'Has something happened to Mum? Dad?'

He raises his hands palm up and says quickly, 'No. No, it's nothing like that, thank God.' Then he pulls off his green woolly hat and rakes his fingers through his mop of grey and caramel hair in an attempt to straighten it. 'Can we put the closed sign up and go through to the kitchen?' I see a flash of green as his eyes flit from the counter to the floor, to the display to his left, and back. He can't look at me.

Shit, whatever this is, it's serious. I nod at the door. 'You do the sign. I'll put the kettle on.'

My fingers tremble as I lift the kettle. I drop it back

down with a thump when Uncle Pete comes in and says, 'Not for me. I just want to get this over with.'

I fold my arms and plop down on a stool because my knees are copying my fingers. 'For God's sake just tell me.'

He sits too and at last lifts his eyes to mine. His mouth works and his jaw clenches and then he blurts, 'I want to sell the shop.'

For a moment his words don't register. It can't be true. 'But, why? You love this place; I love this place! I...' An image of Phillipa shimmying over to me at Tremaine's party comes smashing into my consciousness. Cold, calculating, confident that I'd sell. Handing me her business card before stalking off, telling me to ring when I'd changed my mind. Not if. When.

'I know, I know. But you see, I've had a ridiculous offer for it. It's a life-changing amount.' Uncle Pete's eyes grow round and he flings his arms to the side for emphasis. 'Life-changing.'

My worst fears are realised. Phillipa is behind it. Must be. 'I didn't know you were having money problems.'

He sighs and rubs his chin. 'I'm not. But the amount we're talking about would let me do all the things that I'd only ever dreamed of before.' Uncle Pete gives a little smile. 'When I say me, I mean us. Me and my girlfriend Greta. We've been seeing each other for a while now, met at choir – I expect your mum's told you?' He doesn't wait for my answer, just ploughs on. 'Thing is, she makes me happy, Sennen. I never thought I'd be happy again after your aunty Marianne died.' His voice cracks with emotion. 'But I am. I truly am.' A tear traces a slow path down his craggy face.

Torn between hugging him and screaming in despair at the prospect of losing my beloved shop and everything that goes with that, I look at my shoes and say nothing while I gather my thoughts. 'What is it that you and Greta want to do?'

'Go round the world. Visit all the places I've always wanted to see. Australia, America, maybe Japan?'

I say to my shoes. 'And how much are we talking about?'

'£850,000. The buyer started at £500,000 but immediately upped it when I said I wasn't sure.'

My eyes shoot up to meet his. 'Wow. So Phillipa wasn't joking about money being no object. I bet you could have got a million if you'd have tried.'

Uncle Pete's eyebrows disappear under his hair. 'You know her?'

I quickly fill him in and ask, 'One thing. Have you forgotten I own a forty per cent share in this place?'

'Of course not, my love.' He goes to touch my hand but thinks better of it. 'I know you have to agree to the sale, and I will totally understand if you decide you can't. Promise there will be no hard feelings. I know how much you love the place, I do too … but…' He lifts his hands and lets them fall.

I stare over his shoulder at the photo of him on his boat and know I'm beaten. I want him to be happy, he deserves it. Happiness is the most important thing in the world, after all. Victoria said so, Gran said so… 'But the offer is too good to refuse and it will let you do all the things you talked about. It will allow you to be financially secure for the rest of your life and to be happy.'

Uncle Pete's eyes brim over and he grabs a tissue from a box on the side. Dabbing his eyes he manages, 'Yeah. Yeah, that's about the size of it. And you'll get your share, of course. Maybe you could get your own little shop. But take a few weeks to mull it over. You don't have to decide right now.' He blows his nose and looks at me expectantly.

The fact that I'd get a very substantial chunk of cash hadn't registered in my mind amid all the shock and sadness. Now that it did, I couldn't care less. I didn't want the sodding money; I wanted my shop. The main thing is, I could never live with myself if I ruined Uncle Pete's dream. I could take a week or two to decide like he suggested, but I know I would arrive at the same conclusion. I have to give him my blessing. I get down from my stool and give him a big hug. 'Okay, you got your trip around the world,' I say, as I feel my own tears start.

Uncle Pete wastes no time in setting the wheels in motion and by the end of the following week the sale is underway. What will be left of the stock at the end is included, apart from my pieces. I'm still going into the shop part-time until it's sold, though I can't bear going in every day knowing I'm going to lose it. Already it feels as though the soul is being sucked out of it, less like my second home and more like an empty shell of a place. I'll hopefully sell quite a bit of my stuff before the last day. Any remaining pieces will be stored safely at Uncle Pete's. I haven't told Tremaine or Jasmine about it all. Tremaine would blame himself for bringing Phillipa down here to the party. If she'd not come to that, she would never have seen the shop. Jasmine would just go off on one, and probably go round to Uncle Pete's shouting the odds.

Mum and Dad know, of course, but, like me, realise that trying to stop Pete's dream would be the wrong thing to do. Besides, as Mum pointed out, I will have a huge lump sum in the bank to cushion the blow. More money than I could ever dream of. As well as buying myself a small starter home, I could try and find another shop in the local area, as there's nothing suitable in Polzeath. But it doesn't feel right. The thought of setting up somewhere else, from scratch, doesn't fill me with joy. Because of the money I'll have soon, I have the time to think about what to do next. There's no rush. Perhaps I could do some teaching? I've always fancied that, maybe with the local children. It's vague ... but it's an idea.

Chapter Seventeen

Tremaine and I have spent nearly every night he's been home, together. It's magical. We're never stuck for anything to say and I don't think I've laughed so much in years. The moody, pompous Tremaine is hardly around, and I must admit spending time alone with the happy-go-lucky, playful Tremaine is greatly preferable. Sometimes he's shared more bad stuff from his childhood with me, and we've talked it through. He said it's helped to have someone to talk about things with, and that, apart from Miranda, he's never found anyone else he felt he could talk to about those things. I metaphorically lick a finger and draw it down the air. In your face, Olivia. It's tricky not letting it slip that Miranda has already told me much more of it though.

This afternoon we're spending more precious time walking the cliff path together before he goes off to London in the morning. I'm finding it hard keeping up with his long loping strides and yell at him to slow down. At a slope in the path, he turns and laughs at me trotting along behind.

'You look like a cheerful little rabbit, hopping along in that brown fluffy jacket with your hair in bunches!'

'Nice. And you look like the miserable big bad wolf in your thick grey hoodie and gloves.' He doesn't. He looks like a Greek god as usual, especially with the sun on his face, the wind running its fingers through his hair and his eyes stealing colour from the sky and Atlantic below him.

Tremaine laughs again and points to a big flat rock wedged into the springy moss-grass just off the path. 'Want to park your bum for a bit and enjoy the view?'

'As long as you promise not to bite me, Mr Wolf.' I give him a cheeky wink.

He slips his arm around me as we sit down and nuzzles my ear. 'Not even a little nip?'

I answer him with a kiss, and then to stop myself getting carried away because of his roaming hands, I say, 'Cool your jets, Mr Wolf. At least until we get back inside.'

He sighs and folds his arms. 'Okay. You never know who might see us, I suppose.'

'Exactly.' I slip my hand into his and we stare out at the clear blue horizon drawing a stark line against the azure winter sky. 'I love days like this, even though it's freezing. Can't stand the dull grey days that never seem to get light.'

'Me too. The only time I spent holidays with my parents was Christmas. I suppose even *they* couldn't justify packing me off to my aunt and uncle's at that time of year.' Tremaine shoves his hair back from his forehead, his face pensive. 'It always seemed to be grey and miserable, but then that might have been because of their company.'

He glances at me, a half-smile on his face, but I can see hurt behind his eyes. I want to take him in my arms, pour sunshine into his heart and light into his dark memories – make it all go away. Swallowing a lump in my throat I say, 'I'm sorry you had such a crap childhood, Tremaine.' Then I kiss the side of his mouth and lean my head on his shoulder.

'I bet your Christmas holidays were a different story,' he says, still gazing out to sea. 'Tell me about them, and about your brother. I'd have loved a sibling to share the misery with.' He laughs.

I tell him about my happy Christmases past, but I tone it down a bit. I don't want him to feel even worse. Then I say, 'As for Ruan, he is one of my best buddies. We always got on, confided in each other about everything, and moaned about Dad sometimes.'

'You don't get on with your dad?' Tremaine asks, perhaps a little hopeful that I too might have some family problems.

'We do, mostly. But he's very old-fashioned, really. He'd always hoped that Ruan would follow in his footsteps in the restaurant. It had never been in his mind that I could go into business with him – because I was the girl, presumably. Though we never talked about it. If he had wanted me to, he'd have been just as disappointed, as I have no interest in that area, but poor Ruan wasn't let off the hook. Mum always had to remind Dad that Ruan was his own man and had his own interests.'

'How did that go down?'

'Not great. Things became even more awkward when, at the age of nineteen, two years ago, Ruan came out as gay and announced he was moving to Plymouth with Gio, his boyfriend. I'd known for years, and Mum had her suspicions, so it wasn't really news. But though Dad's not exactly neanderthal material, it did take a while for him to properly accept the situation. If he actually has.'

'Right. Well, it's nice to know it's not just my family that has problems,' he says brightly.

I give him a playful dig in the ribs and decide, as we are sharing more, it feels the right time to tell him about how the whole Josh thing has affected me. 'Tremaine, there's been something on my mind for a while, and I want to tell you about the guy who dumped me, the one I mentioned in passing when we talked about past partners?'

'Josh?'

I'm pleased he'd remembered. 'Yeah. Thing is, I found out that he'd been two-timing me and it really ripped my guts out.' I tell him all about it and he listens with his arm tight around my shoulder.

Then he says, 'Hmm. Sounds very similar to what happened with me and Olivia.' Tremaine had told me her name, but that was all, when I'd mentioned Josh before. 'She's a lawyer like me, and we had quite a lot in common, including clients. Olivia decided to sleep with one of hers and mine, and when I found out, I couldn't hack it.' He sighs and says to the ocean, 'Because of my past, her cheating put a big dent in my self-esteem. It had been drilled into me that I had to excel at everything, be the best.

Well, if my girlfriend was off looking for sex with someone else, I must be lacking. That's how she made me feel, and I didn't like it. I'd had enough of it during my childhood. I hate to feel exposed. Vulnerable.'

'Well, I can assure you I have no complaints in that department.' I turn his face to mine and place a lingering kiss on his lips. 'But I get what you mean about feeling vulnerable and exposed. I felt the same with Josh. I also felt stupid for having my suspicions and burying them because I wanted to be happy. It's humiliating.'

We talk some more about how we felt and he tells me more about Olivia. Though I want to tell him I already knew some of it, I have to respect Miranda's confiding in me. We agree that we're worried about getting hurt again and promise that we'll be completely honest with each other about everything. If either of us is unhappy in the relationship, they must tell the other before it's too late. We also agree that the big no-no is cheating, as that's what had hurt us both the most. As we walk back along the path hand in hand, I feel closer to him than ever before. The warmth of his hand and strength of his fingers entwined with mine give me a sense of belonging and send my spirits soaring up into the high white clouds above. For the first time in a long time, I'm feeling truly hopeful about the future. Let's hope I find this parting glass soon, too. If I'm lucky, it will tell me I'm right.

Over brandy, later, Tremaine takes me in his arms and tells me how much he loves being with me, and that he's so pleased we'd been able to have such an open conversation today about how we felt. I tell him I felt the same, and that I feel better having got everything off my chest. To avoid the dangers of a rebound relationship, we agree to take it slowly and see where it goes, but there have to be no secrets, and complete honesty between us.

Tremaine pushes his unruly curls back from his forehead, looks deep into my eyes, and traces the shape of my mouth with his fingers. My heart rate breaks into a gallop and a delicious shiver travels the length of me. I remember something he'd said about his pyjamas the first night I'd stayed over, and with a mischievous giggle I say, 'If the offer of seeing you in those *Star Wars* PJs still stands, I'd like to take you up on it.'

'Oh, it absolutely does,' he says and kisses me, slowly, deeply. 'And I'd very much like to see you without yours.'

Even though we bared our souls to each other a few days ago, I didn't tell him about losing my business. It's been difficult over the last while, keeping the shop sale from Tremaine, as he's picked up on my sadness. I've waved it away so far, blaming winter and the lack of sunlight for my mood, but I suppose I'll have to tell him soon. Not yet though. Today is one of those precious, winter-crisp, blue-sky, sun-filled, sleepy-ocean kind of days. Today, I have more of a spring in my step as I get out of the car at

Nancarrow House. Tremaine's in London, and the steps to the forgotten beach are well and truly finished. Today is D-Day. The day I look for the parting glass!

I crunch along the gravel path around the back of the house and slip between the shadows of trees in the little copse. A few more paces bring me to the top of the steps, and the unbroken view of the ocean. Adrenaline ups my heart rate, and anticipation floods through me as I kick the discarded old danger sign to one side and close my fingers around the smooth and sturdy wooden handrail. Tremaine told me last night the workmen had finished only yesterday afternoon, and that he hadn't even had time to set foot on the steps himself. So, I am the first to use them since Victoria. Well, apart from the workmen of course. This feels fitting and daunting at the same time.

Placing my foot on the first solid oblong of stone, I take a breath and ask Gran to walk with me. Her answer is in the winter sunlight on my face and the whisper of the wind in my hair. She's with me. The steps are well made and shallow and soon I'm at the bottom, and on the forgotten beach! At last. I'd picked the time carefully to make sure the tide would be out and I am quite surprised how deep the beach is. Admittedly it's not wide, maybe about a hundred metres, but there's certainly enough room to kick a ball around or have that beach party Tremaine talked about that first day I met him. To the right of the steps, there's just the base of the cliff and a few little rock pools; to my left is the main beach sheltering in the curve of the cliff, and at the end I can see the little sea-cave.

Looking out to the blue horizon, the light breeze tugging the ends of my plaits, listening to the ocean whispering its ancient song, I feel a lightness of being. All the heartache over the shop and uncertainty about the future seem less important now as I stand before this majestic expanse of water. It's been here since long before I was born, and it will be here long after I am gone. It's constant. Eternal. Taking in some deep breaths, I remember the gist of Victoria's words the day she came here and found the glass. '…*and as always, a feeling of calm and peace descended on me. There was also a feeling of anticipation and excitement running through my veins and I laughed to myself as I stood at the edge of the water looking out into the blue. I decided to come alone, as I wondered if Callum would think it a little silly, going in search of magic.*'

A smile stretches my mouth. I feel exactly the same. I'm going in search of that magic right now! All of a sudden, a sense of giddiness and excitement has me kicking my trainers off and rushing to the shoreline. I roll my jeans up and splash in the shallows whooping and screeching like the puzzled gulls coming in to roost amongst the cliff crevices. It's so liberating being here, as if I'm on a deserted island, happily with no chance of being found. I stop, spread my arms wide and call to the wisps of high cloud racing across the blue heavens, 'Gran! Are you ready? 'Cos I'm up for this!' The ocean shushes and a peaceful calmness settles across my mind. She's ready. Leaving my trainers at the foot of the steps, I hurry to the little cave at the base of the cliff near the end of the beach. It's shallow and damp at the entrance, dry at the rear, just as Victoria described, with a seaweed tide-line and barnacle-encrusted entrance. As she did, I have to duck my head to go inside, and as I trace my fingers along the rough, spiky wall, I wonder if Gran had done the same, over sixty-four years ago. A few more strides bring me to the back of the cave and, giddy with excitement, I lean against the rough rock to steady myself. Straight ahead, I see the natural recess at eye-level, covered in sand, and I slide my mum's little gardening trowel out of my coat pocket.

My heart is racing as I whisper to Gran, 'Okay, Morwenna, here we go,' and gently insert the trowel until the tip meets with a solid object. I release a long breath and quickly scrape away the sand. I soon uncover an old metal box, more rust than metal actually, and I worry that once I've opened the lid, the whole thing will disintegrate into a brown powdery mess. My fingers tremble as the lid opens with a crack and a creak, but it remains in one piece. I swallow a marble-sized lump of emotion, because there, on a faded red-velvet bed, lies the parting glass. As I carefully remove it from the box, a series of images take quick formation in my mind. Gran and Jory, Victoria and, I presume, Callum, and others I don't know, their faces lit from within by joy and love. In shock, I lean against the cave wall until my head clears. My God. What just happened?

Hurrying back out into the light, I lift the glass to the sun and catch my breath at the beauty of it. The stem is short and twisted, the bowl deep and triangular, around the top of which have been expertly engraved dancing figures interspersed with sea shells. The figures are wearing, at a guess, eighteenth-century clothes and as I twirl it slowly around, the figures look like they're moving. Carefully putting it back into the box, I wonder about the images that came to me in the cave. Could they be the spirits of people from the past who had lifted this glass to their lips on New Year's Eve? Or is it just my imagination working overtime? The former is too weird to contemplate.

There's a big flat rock nearby, perfect for sitting on and contemplating my extraordinary find. I stride over and sit down while studying the glass. It is incredibly beautiful with breathtaking craftsmanship and would have been a coveted treasure back in the eighteenth century. Running my finger along the twist in the stem I notice something sticking up from under the velvet base of the box. Further investigation reveals a slip of paper, and I roll the velvet back to retrieve it. Excitement flutters in my chest when I realise it's a note, and my heart jumps as I recognise the handwriting:

To whom it may concern,

This glass gave me the truth I'd hidden from my heart. It gave me the courage to go for the impossible dream and welcome the love of my life into my arms. We shared the briefest, yet most joyful time together, and I don't regret a single moment. Not one. May the glass bring you the same good fortune, and that you too will be lucky enough to find the same joy. Brief or long lasting, love and happiness are the greatest gifts of all.

Morwenna.

A sob breaks free and I hug the letter to my chest as emotion overwhelms me. Gran walked with me today, and now she's allayed all the fears and apprehension I had about the glass being evil or cursed. If she could still be thankful, and grateful for the love she found, despite the cruel way Jory was taken from her, then I can surely give it a chance too. I need to forget all the nonsense with Josh, keep an open mind, let Tremaine in and trust my feelings. Life is for living and I could do worse than to follow in Morwenna's footsteps. I fold the note and put it back under the glass, replace the lid, wipe away tears and take a deep breath. Gazing out across the turquoise and navy expanse, I exhale. Clasping the box safely to my chest, I make my way back up the steps.

Chapter Eighteen

M um is a bit shocked when I turn up at my parents' house unannounced, with puffy eyes and a sniffly nose. I'm a bit shocked too, because I hadn't planned on jumping in the car at Nancarrow and driving over here at all. It was as if Mum had a magnet or a beacon, directing my subconscious mind. Dad's working, as I knew he would be, which is what I wanted, as I don't want him in on the surprise. He wouldn't get it and might even make a joke about it. If he did, I wouldn't be responsible for my actions. 'You look upset, Sen. Everything okay?' Mum asks, as she leads the way through to the conservatory.

'It is now, but I was a bit upset earlier. Don't worry, I cried happy tears.' I give her a smile and a hug and sit at the table, placing my rucksack next to me on the chair.

'Cup of tea? Something stronger?' Mum puts her hand on my shoulder and unexpected tears push behind my eyes. God. I really am a mess this afternoon.

'A cup of tea would be good, but I've got something to

show you first.'

'Sounds interesting,' she says sitting opposite, but her knitted brow and turned-down mouth don't match her words.

A tickle of excitement grows in my belly as I undo the zip on the rucksack. 'Remember Gran's parting glass?' I watch her face carefully, relieved to see real interest replace worry. 'Well, today –' I pull out the box with a flourish and push it across the table towards her '– I only went and bloody found it!'

'Really!' Mum's face is wreathed in smiles. 'Wow! Let me have a look.' She carefully opens the lid, gasps, then words shoot out of her like rapid machine-gunfire. 'Oh, it's just as gorgeous as I imagined. Aren't you clever? What did Tremaine say? Will you wish on it this New Year's Eve? Oh my God, it's so beautiful.'

I laugh and sit back in my chair. 'I haven't shown Tremaine. I haven't even told him about it, or Gran yet. I'll do that soon. I wanted to make sure it was there before I came at him with such fantastical tales.' Mum stares round-eyed at the glass, her lips curving into a smile. 'Take it out and hold it to the light,' I say. 'If you turn it round slowly, it looks like the figures are dancing.'

Mum hovers her trembling fingers over the glass but withdraws. 'God, I daren't. What if I drop it and it shatters into a thousand pieces?'

'It won't! Just be careful.'

She does as I suggest, and her mouth drops open in delight as the figures begin their sparkling dance under the beam of the wall light. 'Oh, it is so lovely.'

'It is.' I notice her eyes glistening and I wonder if Gran's letter might be too much for her. I was a mess after reading it, but … something tells me she'd like to see it. 'Put the glass down, Mum. I was overjoyed to find it today, but what brought me to tears was a little note.' I swallow hard and nod at the box. 'It's there, under the velvet.'

Within seconds of unfolding the flimsy note paper, Mum's cheerful expression slides from her face, pushed from within by an avalanche of emotion. 'Oh, Sennen… Oh, Sen, that's so beautiful.' She flaps a hand in front of her eyes, but the tears keep coming. She takes a moment and lays the note on the table. 'It's true what my mum says. So true. Love and happiness are the most important things in the world.'

A lump forms in my throat and I pat her hand. 'They are.' Then I tell her all about Victoria, her notebook and all the worries and misgivings I've had about the parting glass. She is silent as I explain my fears of being hurt again, and that I was scared of letting Tremaine in, in case everything ended in tragedy, like it did for Victoria and Gran. 'But at last, I have come to realise, with the help of two very wise women, that it truly is better to have loved and lost, than to have never loved at all.'

Mum nods and says, her voice thick with emotion, 'And this time you might not lose it. Think positive.'

I send her a bright smile and blow my nose. 'I think it might be a little early to talk of *actual* love…' Mum opens her mouth to say something, which if I know her will be a searching question, so I deflect it with 'Anyway, how about that cuppa now?'

While Mum makes the tea, I hold the glass up to the light and give it a twirl. When would be the best time to spill all of Gran and Victoria's beans to Tremaine? What if, like Dad, he's a bit sceptical about these kinds of things? I smile to myself as I ponder that. What kind of thing might that be, Sennen? This glass is unique – one of a kind. I sigh and put it back in its box. The whole magical 'out there' theme might be too much for him. It was too much for me to start with, especially after the images I saw today in the cave of those long passed. Luckily, I have an open mind. Tremaine strikes me as a down-to-earth, no-nonsense, logic-based kind of man. But I won't know one way or the other until I tell him, will I? I decide against telling Mum about the images. It could just have been a mix of suggestions from my heightened senses, emotion and imagination.

———————

Mum and I pass a lovely hour talking about Gran, Victoria, the parting glass, my brother Ruan's upcoming visit and the fact it's only two weeks to Christmas. With the upset of losing the shop and everything, I haven't even given Christmas more than a passing glance as I've whizzed through the month of December. But I need to start paying attention to it, I suppose. A half-baked idea is cooking in my mind and I'm not sure if it will be to everyone's taste. I'm not even sure it will be to mine, but it's almost ready to come out of the oven, nevertheless.

'You look miles away, love. Everything okay?' Mum asks and pushes a plate of biscuits towards me.

'Yeah.' I crunch into a custard cream. 'Um … but I have an idea. You know that Ruan and Gio are down here next week?' She nods expectantly, but then I have second thoughts. Shouldn't I broach it with Tremaine first? 'Oh, don't worry. Not sure it will work.'

'Eh? What won't?' A crease forms between her eyebrows.

Oh God. Why did I start this? It's been an afternoon of surprises, finding the glass, racing over here, now an ill-thought-out idea waits to be tipped squirming out onto the table between us. Mum must wonder what the hell is wrong with me. A question waits on my tongue like a predator, and I keep it there. I need to just get it out, but if I release it now, it might feel like it's pouncing on her, and Mum won't be able to escape its jaws. She's already looking a bit wary. Then she folds her arms and holds me in her steady gaze. That makes me feel bad. But then Mums are experts at that, aren't they? Emotional archery – an arrow through the heart before we've even finished our tea.

I heave a sigh and say, 'I was wondering if you wanted to meet Tremaine. You and Dad, I mean, and Ruan and Gio.' Mum's eyebrows shoot into her hairline in surprise, and I can't tell if that's good or bad. Heat blooms in my cheeks. 'You know. Like a meal here, or at Nancarrow? Thought it might be nice for you all to get to know him.'

'Right. Well, that would be lovely!' Her beaming smile is a salve for the open emotional wound I've self-inflicted.

'It would? But are you sure? I hardly gave you much choice. You might just be saying that to make me feel better.'

'That's daft. Why wouldn't we want to meet Tremaine? I was only saying to your dad the other day how well you seem to be getting on, and that I wondered when we'd get to meet him.' Mum's eyes twinkle with excitement and a few tense knots unravel in my gut.

Then they tense again as I wonder what Tremaine will think. What if he doesn't want to meet them? If he says no, I'll have to make something up to tell my parents. It will be like making excuses for Josh all over again. Why the hell didn't I wait and ask Tremaine first? I'm such a bloody knob-head! I drain my cup and contemplate keeping this to myself, but as I look at Mum's puzzled expression, the truth elbows its way out. 'I'm just worried that I should have asked Tremaine first. I mean, we haven't been together that long and he might think it's all a bit much. A family meal, you know?' I hold her gaze. 'He hasn't had much of a family life. Well, any family life, to be honest. He might feel it's all too much pressure. And…' I throw my hands up. 'Oh, I don't know, Mum. I maybe shouldn't have jumped the gun, that's all.'

Mum sighs, pushes her hair from her forehead and flicks her eyes, shimmering moss-green with the remnants of tears, to the table and back to me. Then rolling up the sleeves of her purple V-neck jumper, she puts on her a no-nonsense expression. 'Look. This is the way I see it. You want us all to have a nice meal and get to know each other, which is perfectly natural, because you obviously think the world of him. Love him, maybe.' She holds a hand up when I start to protest. 'And I'm guessing you're worried he'll say no and then you'll have to make up a big fib for him like you used to for that jerk Josh.'

My mouth drops open. 'You knew they were all excuses? That he didn't want to see you?'

'Of course.' Mum shrugs. 'But what could we say? You had to walk your own path, but I can only say thank goodness you binned him at last, as the youngsters say.' She winks and gives a little chuckle.

The lump in my throat from earlier is back and getting bigger. 'I'm so sorry, Mum. I feel like a rubbish daughter for letting him dictate our lives. For lying to you.'

'Don't be. You were manipulated, hurt, and now you imagine Tremaine is going to be the same. Josh has a lot to answer for.' She spreads her hands. 'Okay, Tremaine might think it a bit soon, especially as you say he's had a crap experience with his family. But just tell us the truth, okay?'

I nod and eat another biscuit to shift the lump. Then I say, 'I'll ask him tonight when I've told him about the parting glass. No time like the present, eh?'

I love the new petrol-blue velvet top I treated myself to after I left Mum. It's been quite a day for spontaneity. As I drove through Polzeath the top spoke to me from the window of Ocean Blue, a boutique that I adore, and I just had to have it. The colour reminded me of the sparkling shallows at the forgotten beach, and it picks out the seaside blues from the grey in my eyes. I apply mascara in my bedroom mirror and, deciding to leave my hair without its plait tonight, I brush it through while thinking about how to approach the meal idea with Tremaine. Though this is making a dainty little butterfly flit around my stomach, the thought of telling Tremaine about what I found on his private beach releases a huge dinosaur crashing about in there. Best to get the dinosaur out first, then the butterfly will be easy.

Tremaine's in the kitchen wearing a white shirt open at the neck with jeans. Over these he's got a black chef's apron with 'Head Chef' printed on it. The food smells delicious, and as usual Tremaine looks good enough to eat. His hair's damp from the shower and his eyes twinkle at me in the candlelight. Having finished work for the week he's relaxed and happy, which makes him even more attractive, and after giving him a long lingering kiss hello, I'm wondering if the butterfly and dinosaur would be banished by an interlude in the master bedroom.

'You smell gorgeous.' He kisses my neck and then holds me at arm's length. 'And is that a new top?'

'It is. How clever of you to notice.'

'I notice everything about you, my dear.' He grins and then hurries off to check something in the oven.

'What are we having?'

'Moussaka! Not had it for ages and I just fancied it ... looks ready to me.' Tremaine takes it out of the oven and nods to the fridge. 'Pour us a glass, will you?'

Hmm. Looks like I'll have to put the master bedroom on hold. Probably for the best, with all this information bubbling around in my head like a potion in a cauldron. 'Okay, I'm looking forward to it.'

As usual the food is delicious. Tremaine is a brilliant cook, and despite planning to drop the biggie first, that thought builds a stage for the meal scenario. I swallow a forkful of moussaka and clear my throat. 'My brother Ruan and his boyfriend Gio are down next week for a visit.'

'Oh, nice.' He dabs his lips with a bit of kitchen roll. 'It would be great to meet him.' He takes a forkful of food and says from the corner of his mouth, 'I know you think the world of him, so I'm sure we'll get on. Maybe he and Gio can come here for dinner?'

My breath leaves my body with a whoosh. I can hardly contain my happiness. After all that worry and a butterfly or two, Tremaine was the one to suggest it! 'That would be amazing!' Go on, Sennen, go for the clincher. I cross my fingers under the table. 'And maybe my parents could come too?'

His eyebrows do the wiggle dance they sometimes do when he's surprised or wrong-footed, which makes the dinosaur stamp its feet and bellow at me. Seconds later his forehead turns Botox-smooth and he smiles. 'That would be lovely. The more the merrier.'

'Really?' I search his face for hidden disgruntlement, but there's none. 'Are you sure you want to meet them all at once? Because you don't have to say yes just for me. I will totally understand if—'

'Hey!' He holds up his hands. 'You should know me by now. If I didn't want to meet them, I'd tell you.' Tremaine takes a sip of wine. 'I was a little surprised at first, as it's not the kind of thing I'm used to with my own dear mama and papa, but it will all be cool.'

He takes our plates, and whistling a merry tune goes off to get our desserts. Wow. My heart is floating on a tranquil sea of happiness and the dinosaur is disappearing across the ancient plains, its bellowing a distant whisper on the wind. How perfect is this man? He's gorgeous, kind, sensitive, cooks like a Michelin chef, is a fantastic lover, and now he wants to meet my family. Then a wicked little voice pipes up. *But he doesn't know about the bloody parting glass yet, does he?* Damn it! The dinosaur turns, gives me a wink, and trundles back, the ground shaking underfoot. I have to tell him now. My nerves won't take any more. I grab the wine bottle as he brings a chocolate pudding and crème fraiche over to the table and pour myself a huge glass.

'More wine?' I tilt the bottle over his glass and notice my hand is trembling.

'Just a splash, thanks.' Tremaine looks askance at the swimming-pool measure in my glass but says nothing. 'Chocolate pudding?' I nod and give a brief smile while trying to wrangle my words into the right order. He pushes a dish towards me and the pot of crème fraiche. 'What do you think I should cook for your folks' dinner party?'

My words are nowhere near in the right order, but after a huge swig of wine they escape anyway. 'Tremaine, remember the day we met and I told you I wanted to see the house where my gran used to work in the 1950s?' He nods and opens his mouth to say something, but I don't give him the chance. 'Well, that was only half-true. There's a lot more.'

He listens, mostly in silence with only a few eyebrow wiggle dances, while I tell him everything. Then he frowns. 'Bloody hell, Sennen. So all this time you only wanted me for my forgotten beach, hey?'

Oh God. My heart's pounding and I feel my cheeks flame. 'No. No, it wasn't like that at all. I...' My words dry up as he laughs and points at me.

'Got ya!' He sighs and takes a sip of wine. 'But I do wonder why you didn't tell me until now about it all.'

I find myself smiling, mainly because I'm relieved he's not upset. 'That's easy. I didn't tell you because I thought you'd think it was all a crazy idea and it might not have been in the cave at all. Then I'd feel even more stupid. I had to wait for the steps to be finished to find out.'

Tremaine nods. 'Okay. Makes sense.'

'There's some more too.' I take Victoria's notebook out of my bag and explain how she fits into the story while he reads it. Eventually he sets the notebook to one side and releases a long sigh. Tremaine clasps his hands behind his head and leans back from the table, his pudding abandoned. 'Poor Great-Granny.' I can see he's moved by what he's read. 'My God, that's a hell of a tale, Sennen.'

'Yeah. You could say that.' The dinosaur is quiet now, but it hasn't gone. 'Do you believe it? You know, that the glass is somehow magical?'

He shoves his hands though his hair and twists his mouth to the side as he considers my question. 'I believe that Victoria and Morwenna believed it. Whether the glass has magical powers is something else altogether.'

Okay. At least he's not ridiculed the whole thing. 'Would you like to see it?'

'Of course.' Curiosity is twinkling in his eyes and one side of his mouth turns up.

I hurry to the hallway, grab my rucksack and take out the box. Once I place it on the table under the flickering candlelight, it looks even more mysterious and ancient. I watch his face as I open the lid. '*Et voila.*'

'Wow!' Tremaine lifts it gently and, without being told, slowly turns it around and around, the soft candlelight providing the perfect showcase for the dancers. 'That is so beautiful,' he whispers, his eyes following the step and flow.

'Breathtaking,' I agree. I'm not looking at the glass but at him. All the little details of his face, the set of his jaw, those incredible eyes, his aquiline nose and full sensuous lips. As usual whenever I'm near him, there's the warmth of desire running through me, but it's morphing into something else lately. Something deeper. Something I only imagined I'd felt with Josh…

He watches it for a while longer then sets it carefully on the table between us, a faraway look in his eye. 'So much to take in.' Then he stares at his pudding dish as if he's only just remembered it's there, digs his spoon into the sponge and demolishes it in a few seconds. Pointing his spoon at me he says, 'Great Uncle bloody Jory had some balls, didn't he? Back then, going against the Nancarrow way would have been unthinkable.' Tremaine takes a big glug of wine. 'He was a damn sight braver than wimpy old me.'

Oh no. Moody-ocean Tremaine is on the way back and I haven't seen him for quite a few weeks. 'You can't compare yourself to Jory. You had different experiences. Your parents weren't in your life … you say you never felt loved. It's true what Miranda said, they did so much damage. And then Olivia—'

'Damage?' Tremaine's calm blue eyes become a storm at sea as he glowers across the table. 'You've been talking to Miranda, behind my back?'

Shit! Me and my big mouth! I knew I would slip up, eventually. I briefly consider trying to wriggle round the truth but can't see how. 'Hey,' I begin, reaching my hand across to his, but he pulls away as if I've electrocuted him. 'It wasn't like that. We went to lunch, as you know, but we weren't really talking behind your back.'

'Was I there?' He draws his mouth into a tight pout and folds his arms.

What the hell? 'Well, no. I—'

'So, behind my back, then.'

I'm getting the full-on lawyer sneery questioning and I don't like it. 'Tremaine, listen. Miranda wanted to tell me about your past and Olivia because she knew you could be a little tricky to get to know at times. She said she wanted me to understand your background because then I'd be more likely to…'

'Damaged, she said, and you agreed? You make me sound like a reject. Something half-formed, broken. Well, well. It's nice to be pitied.'

His expression is fighting with anger, sadness and indignation all at the same time and he's having trouble holding back tears. All I want to do is take him in my arms and kiss away the pain, but instinct stops me. I know he wouldn't welcome it. 'It wasn't like that. Believe me.'

'You should have talked to me if you wanted to know. Bloody hell, Sennen. I bared my soul to you. Shared everything.' Tremaine slaps his hand on the table, and the cutlery rattles together on his plate. 'And now I find you already knew?'

My heart sinks. 'Not all of it…' I say in a small voice. He has every right to be pissed off. 'Please believe that Miranda had the very best intentions. She loves you; you know that.'

Tremaine heaves a sigh and gives me a sad little smile. 'Yes, I do. I just wish you hadn't kept things from me. That kind of thing doesn't help the confidence of a "damaged" individual.' His tone searches half-heartedly for humour and falls short.

'I'm sorry. I promise there will be no more secrets.' I reach for his hand again and this time he doesn't pull away. 'I wouldn't hurt you for the world. God knows you've been hurt enough.' I squeeze his hand, and he returns it. 'That's why you honestly shouldn't compare yourself to Jory. He had Victoria. It's clear from the notebook how much she cared for her sons and—'

'Yes, but Jory didn't know that, did he? He was only little when she fell down the steps, and you can bet your life her in-laws made sure he never did get to know how much she loved him.'

I realise I have stupidly made things so much worse,

with the whole Miranda slip-up and now with Jory. I take a spoonful of pudding but I've lost my appetite. 'Who knows?' I push my dish away. 'But the main thing is Jory and Gran were happy, as were Victoria and Callum.' He's looking moodier again by the second. There's a black cloud darkening those turquoise blues and he's staring at a spot somewhere over my left shoulder, his jaw clenching and unclenching, and I can almost tell what he's thinking. 'Yes, I know they weren't happy for long, and that *did* bother me for a while. I thought the glass was cursed and decided I didn't want to find it. But soon, Victoria convinced me, and so did Gran.' I pin on an encouraging smile, fish out Gran's note and show it to him.

Tremaine finishes reading and it's his turn to stretch his hand across the table. I take it and we stare into each other's eyes. His face is a blur as emotion takes over and he hands me a tissue. When I've dabbed away a few tears, I see his eyes are copying mine. He wipes them on his sleeve and sighs. 'So much love, and so much loss. Was it too much to ask that they lived happily ever after?'

I shrug. 'It would have been nice, wouldn't it? But it wasn't to be for them.' Spontaneity strikes one last time, because from somewhere comes: 'But it might work out for others.'

Tremaine stands up and pulls me up into his arms. He kisses my cheek and nuzzles my neck. 'Who knows,' he whispers. 'But at least we know what we'll be doing on New Year's Eve.'

My heart is so full I can hardly stand as he kisses me again. Then the dinosaur gives one last bellow and leaves.

Chapter Nineteen

Jasmine's beret is navy, her boots are lilac, her trousers are green, her jumper is orange and her puffer jacket is red. She looks like a six-year-old has created her with a pack of Crayolas, and her face, right now, matches her jacket. I'm guessing from her expression that's more to do with anger than embarrassment. She stops on the beach, tightens the scrunchie on her ponytail and fixes her emerald eyes on my face. 'Are you fucking kidding me?' she asks. I'm about to answer in the negative, but realising it's a rhetorical question, shrug and wrest a hank of hair from my mouth put there by an offshore breeze. She sticks her neck out and continues, 'And you just let it happen with no more than a whimper?' Jasmine lifts both arms and lets them fall to her sides with a slap. She now looks like a disgruntled penguin, finding out for the first time that it can't fly.

'Yes. What else was I supposed to do?' I copy her wing-flap. 'Tell Uncle Pete that I'll drag him through the courts? Deny him his dream in the autumn of his life?'

Jasmine opens her mouth to say something, thinks better of it, pulls her beret further over her ears and resumes walking. I fall into step beside her and look out over the shouty ocean. Today, maybe emulating Jasmine's mood, it's tossing its waves about until a white foamy chop punctuates every undulating roll. The sky is pretending it's July, but the sun's showing it up by running out of battery. I pull my old yellow and red striped scarf tightly about my neck, match Jasmine's punishing pace and wonder how long she'll take to realise I had no choice about selling the shop.

Turns out it's a matter of seconds, as she comes to another abrupt halt and fishes a used tissue out of her pocket. 'Bloody wind's making my nose run,' she grumbles. She blows it and turns to me. 'I suppose it *would* have been a bit shitty fighting your own uncle in a legal battle. Especially as he let you have a big chunk of his business and taught you everything you know about potting.'

'It would.' I tip her a smile and start walking again. There's a hot chocolate and a mince pie with my name on it at the café on the beach.

'But you bloody love that place,' Jasmine says as she hurries to catch me up.

'I do.'

'What does Tremaine say? Your parents?'

I tell her that Tremaine doesn't know, and my parents agree there was only one decent course of action I could take. Predictably she goes nuts about keeping Tremaine in the dark and so I explain why.

'Jeez, Sen. You can't keep things from him like this, though. You know he has trust issues and he'll think you didn't trust him enough to confide in him. How do you know he'd blame himself because of that bitch Phillipa? He might even be able to help.'

I'm beginning to grow a bit weary of all this criticism now. But mainly it's because she's right. I shouldn't have kept it from Tremaine. I promised no more secrets and here I am with another whopper under wraps. Pride won't let me admit it though, and there's a snap to my tone when I say, 'To be honest, Jas, I wasn't even going to mention it to you. I only told you when you noticed the shop was shut twice this week and badgered me until I told you why I was only going in now and then. I knew you'd go on and on and on and…' I stop and notice her expression's borrowed from a wounded animal and relent. 'Look' – I put my hand on her shoulder – 'it will all be okay. I'll get a lump sum and then take my time considering my next move.' I shrug and squeeze my eyes shut against an ocean of tears. 'Besides. It's already sold. I signed on the dotted line this morning.'

I stride on, hoping the wind will dry my eyes. Jasmine's trotting beside me suggesting different things I could do with my future and making sympathetic noises as the wind fails to do its job. But I have to focus on something other than images of me in the shop, arranging displays, making pots, chatting to customers, feeling the thrill when a customer tells me how much they love one of my pieces, or how much it's moved them. Focus. A hot chocolate and mince pie. That'll do the trick.

In the café, Jasmine starts a conversation about runny noses, which brings me out of my mood. It's hard to be fed up with her for long.

'It's because we're in a warm café after being out in the cold, I suppose,' I say, wiping my own nose, and take a sip of the delicious hot chocolate complete with marshmallows.

'Yes, but *why* does being in the warm after you've been in the cold make it run?' she says earnestly, sniffing and blowing her nose for the umpteenth time. 'The wind was making it run on the beach, now it's the warm? Evolution went wrong somewhere.' Jasmine shakes her head and shovels a huge spoonful of mince pie and cream.

I sigh and decide to drop the whole reason for meeting up with my friend into the mix. 'Anyway, the mystery of running noses and the failure of evolution aside, I have interesting news. I found the parting glass!'

Jasmine's shriek has every customer's head turning so fast, I fear they will all have whiplash. Eyes rounder than a bush baby's and with a blob of cream on her chin she says, 'Oh my God! Why didn't you say before?'

I wiggle my spoon at her. 'Erm, because you went off on one about the shop, so I never got the chance, perhaps?'

'Fair point. Okay, tell me all about it! Does Tremaine know you found it?' I tell her everything, and about Tremaine's reaction. 'Oh, bless his heart. He was genuinely moved about his great-granny Vicky?'

The cream on her chin wags in time with her words and

I burst out laughing and hand her a napkin. 'Wipe your chin. And I'm not sure Victoria would appreciate being called Vicky.' She does as I ask, inspects the napkin and rolls her eyes. 'Yes, he was moved. And he told me yesterday that he's going to have a word with his father next week when he drops off their Christmas presents to see if he can find out any more about her, his granddad Edward and Great Uncle Jory.'

'Good. I'd love to know what they were told about their mother's death.'

I nod. 'Me too. But we might never know. I've let him keep the notebook to show his father. It belongs to the family, after all.'

We fall silent while we give our full attention to our mince pies, and then I stir my marshmallows into my hot chocolate while Jasmine opts for picking each one out with a spoon. I toy with the idea of telling her I'm going to try the parting glass magic this New Year's Eve with Tremaine. She'd make a huge deal of it and it's something I want to do quietly with him. Our secret, I suppose. I take a slurp of my drink and ask, 'How's it going with Rob?'

An expression of pure delight transforms her face, and a banana smile curves her lips. 'Really well. I'm thinking of asking him over to Mum and Dad's for dinner before Christmas, so they can meet the man I can't stop banging on about.'

'Ha! Would you believe my parents and Ruan and Gio are going over to Nancarrow House next week to do exactly the same?'

She laughs. 'What? To meet Rob?'

'Oh, you're hilarious.'

'I know.' Jasmine pulls a silly face. 'And a family dinner party, that's great. Who would have thought mean and moody Tremaine City Lawyer Pants would want to do that when you first met him?'

'Not me.' I fold my arms and think of how much Tremaine's changed since the early days. 'He's hardly moody at all now.'

'Must be your influence.'

'Hope so. And Nancarrow House too, I think. You can see him visibly relax when he's home from London and first walks in the door.'

She raises an eyebrow. 'I'd visibly relax too if that fabulous house was mine.'

'Yes. It is beautiful.'

'You'll be living there once you're married.'

I nearly spit my hot chocolate on the table. 'You what?'

'You heard.' Jasmine makes the shape of a heart with her fingers and smiles at me through it.

'You're away with the fairies.'

'It's true. You'll marry him and go and live there.'

I shake my head. Any such notion is far, far away in the future, if it's there at all. Yes, I am very fond of Tremaine, but it's all early days. 'Na. We're both taking it slowly, seeing where this thing's going … if anywhere.' An image of Tremaine nuzzling my neck and whispering that we'll be testing the parting glass on New Year's Eve comes to mind and I hide a smile.

'Says she who's just arranged a family dinner for him.' Both eyebrows are raised this time.

Maybe she has a point. 'Hm. Perhaps I shouldn't have done that... It is a bit soon really.'

'Oh, for goodness' sake. You did it because you wanted to – because you felt it was right. Stop setting up stupid guidelines for yourself that you don't really want to abide by.'

'What stupid guidelines?'

Jasmine folds her arms and does the death stare. 'Let me see now. How's this for an interpretation? Because I was hurt once by shit-for-brains Josh, I mustn't let myself go. I have to play it cool. I must make sure I always hide my feelings behind an emotional electric fence.'

That rankles because it's only half-true. 'That's not how it is. It might have been at the beginning, but I've eased off a bit. I do think your idea of us even thinking about marriage is ludicrous, though.'

'Ludicrous or not, it *will* happen.' Jasmine turns off the death stare and swirls the last bit of hot chocolate around her cup. 'Nancy Cornish said so, and she's never wrong.' She drains her cup and grins.

My heart jumps. 'Nancy Cornish the psychic?'

I get a withering look. 'No. Nancy Cornish the brain surgeon.'

'When did she say this?'

'I ran into her at the post office the other day and we got chatting. She was wondering what kind of Christmas gift to get for her mum, and I gave her one of your cards. She got the vibe from that.'

A jumble of thoughts surface and do a quick circuit of my brain. Nancy Cornish is a psychic, and I'm not sure I believe in all that stuff. Okay, when she predicted Jasmine and Rob would get together, I believed it. It was a bit of fun, and it didn't really concern me. But this does. She predicts I'll marry Tremaine. *And how do you feel about that, Sennen?* Having no definitive answer I say, 'Yeah, well, I'll believe it when I see it.'

Jasmine says nothing, just does a little knowing, serene smile and looks out of the window at the ocean.

Ruan looks at me from under his unfeasibly long lashes and runs some gel through his floppy chestnut fringe. 'I think you're hoping to get lucky tonight wearing that, sweetie.'

I glance down at my new low-cut, clingy red dress and tug the neckline up to cover my boobs a bit more. 'Hm. It looks a bit tarty, doesn't it?'

'No, it does not!' Ruan stops applying some subtle eyeliner, turns from the mirror to face me and puts his hands on his snake hips. 'And stop covering up your assets. I think you look absolutely gorgeous, and this Tremaine fella should think himself lucky.'

'Do you really think so?' I flick my heavy plait over my shoulder and fiddle with the scrunchie securing the end. 'Maybe I should have my hair loose?'

'Maybe you should chop the sodding thing off. I've been saying so for years. It would drive me mad having to wash and dry that mop every other day.' Ruan picks up my mascara and looks at it thoughtfully.

'Don't you dare put that on. Your eyelashes are already the length of the Nile.' I've always been jealous of his lashes since I was a kid. Mine are average length and insist on sticking straight out until I wrestle them into an upswing with my eyelash curlers.

'Ha! As if. I don't wear it very often, and I certainly won't put it on tonight. Can you imagine the old man's face? He'll have kittens when he sees my eyeliner as it is.'

'Oh, I don't know. He might be coming round a bit. I heard him saying how proud of you he was to Bob the builder the other day when I was round at theirs. Bob and Dad were chatting at the gate and I was upstairs in the bathroom, the window was ajar – heard every word.'

Ruan's dark green eyes glow with pride and not a little astonishment. 'Really? Bloody hell, it would be nice if he could say that to my face.'

I give him an 'as if' glance. 'I'd take that for now if I were you. You know our dad isn't one for sharing his feelings in public.'

'Hm. Well, it's about time he did. It would make our relationship better, that's for damn sure.'

I keep quiet. There's no point in debating Dad's shortcomings. He's definitely warming towards Ruan and Gio's relationship, and maybe he'll surprise us one day. I turn my thoughts back to my heavy, cumbersome plait and wiggle it at my brother. 'Do you really think I should cut it?'

Ruan sits down on my bed, crosses his legs and sweeps my hair with a look of disdain. 'No, Sen. I think I should.'

My heart gives an anxious squeeze. 'What, now?'

He nods and pulls his scissor wallet out of his bag. 'Why not? Gio is going to be another half an hour Christmas shopping, and I've been dying to make you look even more gorgeous for about a hundred years.' He grins and snips at the air with the scissors.

'But I'm all ready to go out.'

'Then put your dressing gown on and a towel over your shoulders. It will all be fine.' Ruan pulls a serious face. 'Trust me. I'm a hairdresser.'

It looks like an old piece of rope from a fishing trawler, but it isn't. It's my hair. Across my lap is eighteen inches of dry, badly conditioned hair that feels like coconut matting between my fingers. How come it didn't feel like this when it was still attached to the rest of my hair? It's as if the scissors have cut its lifeblood and killed its vitality and shine. Maybe Ruan is actually Jack, and here lieth the beanstalk, hewn, rootless, dead. Once more I lift my eyes to the mirror that he's propped up on the kitchen table and can't believe the transformation. Still past my shoulders, the 'wet beach' colour seems to have dried golden in the sun, and having shed the weight, natural curls bounce when I move my head this way and that.

'Stop fidgeting a minute, will you?' Ruan grumbles. 'I need to finish thinning the back.'

'Sorry. It's just so light and bouncy! I really love it, Ruan. Thanks.'

'You're very welcome. I've been telling you for years that it needed a good chop, but would you listen?'

I laugh and scroll through the pictures on my phone while he finishes off. 'I know I sent you a photo or two of Tremaine ages ago, but they were a bit blurry. Here are some recent ones. Mind you, you'll be seeing him in the flesh in an hour.' I hold the phone up over my right shoulder so he can have a look.

The scissors go silent and then, 'Oh my God! He is one. A god, I mean.' Ruan laughs. 'Don't tell Gio I said so, but bloody hell, Sennen. How do you keep your hands off him?'

This makes me laugh. 'I don't, normally.' Then I see my face grow pink in the mirror and a bashful smile twists my lips.

'Good girl!' Ruan puts his scissors on the table and dusts his hands free of hair. Through the mirror his eyes lock onto mine. 'Seriously, does he make you happy? That's the main thing. He could be as ugly as a box of frogs, but happiness is such a precious gift.'

I smile. He must have been channelling Victoria and Morwenna. Though I've told him most things about Tremaine, Ruan's not been privy to any of the parting glass news. Not because he would ridicule it, but we haven't really had time since he arrived in town this morning and telling him over the phone wouldn't have felt right. 'He does make me happy, but he has a lot of baggage, as you know.'

'His dad sounds a right old bastard.'

'His mum's not great either.'

'Hm. Are you strong enough to carry the baggage, Sen?

Do you even want to?' Ruan tips his head on one side and zhuzhs my hair up.

'I am, and I do,' I answer, without hesitation, which surprises me a little. 'And before Gio comes back, I have a bit of a story to tell you that started with our gran.'

Chapter Twenty

Anticipation and excitement run hand in hand from my tummy to my chest and back again, their tiny light footprints tickling my insides as they go. The evening ahead is unknown territory, but I'm ready for it. I feel like a new woman in my dress and new hairstyle. It lifts my face somehow. Ruan says it just adds to what's already there. And what's there at the moment, according to him, is an inner light put there by love. I roll my eyes and harrumph at him, but Gio jumps in on his side and says, 'It's true. I've never seen you look so radiant.' Then he winks and adds, 'Positively indecent.'

I launch into a protest, but Gio holds up a finger to silence me, checks his appearance one more time and asks Ruan to sort out his already perfect close-cropped blue-black hair. They argue about what needs to be done to it with much gesticulation from Gio, showing his Italian heritage. Gio has an Italian dad and Mediterranean looks. He has sparkling dark eyes, olive skin and a very well developed yet understated sense of style, which he has passed on to my brother. Both are wearing dark trousers and matching cashmere jumpers. Deep red for Gio and olive-green for Ruan.

When I tell them both to shut up, they give me cheeky grins and I return a withering glare and do another twirl in front of the cheval mirror in my bedroom. Behind me, Ruan and Gio continue to bicker about his hair and end up play fighting on my bed. They are obviously so much in love, and I'm so glad my little brother has found the man of his dreams at last. It wasn't easy for him growing up in the closet, but he felt, living in a small Cornish town with many of his peers being casually homophobic, that he couldn't come out of it until he was almost ready to leave the nest.

While Gio pays a quick trip to the bathroom before we leave for Nancarrow House, Ruan sidles up and puts his arm around me. 'It's so great to spend time with you, Sen. Wish it could be more often, but it's mad at work.' He gives a sheepish grin. 'And you know me – the control freak. I hate leaving Frankie in charge. Yes, she's very competent, but I do worry about the business when both Gio and I are away.'

'I miss you too. Maybe I'll come over to see you in the new year for a few days?'

'Yeah. Bring lover boy too.'

'I don't know, we'll see.'

Ruan's expression grows serious. 'I hope you and him make it. I know me and Gio were enjoying winding you up before, but it's true. There's magic in your eyes – must be a combination of Tremaine and the spirit of those who used the parting glass before. The ones you saw in the cave.'

Immediately I regret telling Ruan that bit of the story. It sounded totally weird when I said it out loud. 'Yeah, well, I think that was more a product of my imagination, to be honest.'

He shrugs. 'Whatever it was, I'm sure that glass will bring you happiness, not grief.' Gio comes into the kitchen and Ruan drops a kiss on my forehead. 'Right. Let's go and meet this Tremaine person.'

We all arrive on the drive at the same time. Mum waves at us through the drizzle on the windscreen as she cuts the engine, and Gio swings our car up next to theirs. Dad jumps out and gives me a hug. He's wearing his best suit and tie, which seems a bit over the top, but at least he's making the effort. Mum's in a smart grey shift dress and red cropped woollen jacket with black buttons.

I take down the hood from my raincoat and say, 'You look gorgeous, the pair of you.' I'm suddenly conscious of them staring at my hair in disbelief.

Mum holds me at arm's length. 'My goodness, look at your hair!' She turns to Dad. 'Look at her hair, Mark!'

'I'm looking! Really suits you, Sen.'

I grin. 'Thought it was time.'

Dad and Ruan do a brief, awkward hug and pat each other's backs, then Dad shakes hands with Gio and Mum gives him and Ruan a warm embrace. We stand in front of the entrance in a loose circle making inane small talk, until Tremaine's voice from behind me says, 'There you all are. Come inside out of this mizzle and get warm!'

He's looking effortlessly incredible as usual, in a light green shirt and dark jeans. The sparkle of excitement in his eyes and wide smile light his face as he looks at everyone, and then his jaw drops a few inches as he notices my hair. I touch it self-consciously and say, 'Thought it was time for a change.' It only just occurs to me that he might not like it shorter.

'Wow! Is all I can say. You were a beauty before, but…' Tremaine pretends to faint and grabs the door jamb to support himself. 'But now I'm unable to speak, presented as I am with such unrivalled perfection.'

This breaks the ice and he links arms with me and ushers everyone inside. I introduce him to everyone, and as we divest ourselves of our coats in the hallway and walk to the kitchen, he whispers in my ear, 'My God, you look absolutely stunning with the new hair and dress. Maybe I'll see you without it later, if I'm lucky?'

I raise an eyebrow and whisper back, 'Perhaps. As long as you're on your best behaviour with my folks.'

Tremaine leads the way through the kitchen to the living room and everyone oohs and ahhs at the view, despite it being mostly obscured by a grey sheet of rain right now. Gio is effusive in his praise of the house and says, 'Bellissimo!' while he gesticulates at everything, his hands flapping like a he's conducting an orchestra. While Tremaine is holding court about the restoration, Ruan nudges me and whispers, 'He's even better than his photos. Lucky cow.'

I giggle and reply, 'Gio has hardly been bashed with the ugly stick. Now shush, before he hears you.'

Gio frowns at our whispering and looks like he's about to ask a question. Before he can, Ruan raises his hand to Tremaine like he's a kid in class. 'Sorry to interrupt,' he says, with a twinkle in his eye. '...but what are we having for dinner? It smells divine!'

'Nice swerve,' I say, under my breath.

'Traditional roast beef, Yorkshire pud and all the trimmings. It is Sunday after all,' Tremaine answers, with a big smile.

'Oh lovely,' Mum says, her words carefully enunciated as she uses the voice she reserves for formal occasions. 'We love roast beef, don't we, Mark?' Her smile is too stretchy and doesn't reach her eyes properly. There's a nervous air about her and I can tell she clearly feels a bit out of her depth. I'd forgotten the effect this house and Tremaine can have on people. Hopefully she'll realise there's no need to stand on ceremony once she gets to know him and relaxes a little.

'Can't go wrong with a good bit of beef.' Dad nods, shuffles his feet and straightens his tie. Blimey, is he nervous too? Surely not.

'Talking of which,' Tremaine looks at his watch, 'I need to check on it. Now. Would you like drinks in here or the kitchen?' There're no answers, just some shrugging and questioning glances at partners. Tremaine looks at me. 'What do you think, darling?'

My stomach flips. Not sure he's ever called me darling in public like this before. Silly, but it makes me feel like I belong here. Belong with him. 'Oh, the kitchen, I think. It's cosier, and we can chat to you while you cook.'

'Might we give the poor boy a hand too?' Dad asks, finding some of his usual bluster. He walks over to Tremaine and puts his hand on his arm. 'Did my daughter tell you I'm a chef?'

Half an hour later the atmosphere is as warm as the mulled wine we're sipping. Well, Mum and Gio as designated drivers have only had one, and are now on the fruit punch, but they are clearly enjoying themselves. We've had a tour of the house and the conversation is in full flow about Nancarrow in the past, what it's like to be a London lawyer, hairdressing, and now Dad is chatting to Tremaine about cooking. Dad's been helping (interfering) with the meal as much as he can, but Tremaine's taking it all in his stride, and they seem to be getting on like the proverbial dwelling under an arson attack.

As we'd looked in the master bedroom on the tour, Mum had noticed my dressing gown on the back of the door and raised an eyebrow. Now, as Gio and Ruan are looking at the prints on the wall in the hallway, and Dad's making gravy with Tremaine, she leans across the table and says in hushed tones, 'So you have your dressing gown in the master bedroom, and I'm guessing that's your spare toothbrush in the bathroom?'

I'm twenty-five, for goodness' sake, so why do I feel like a teenager being caught doing something sneaky? The blood rushes to my face and I bite my cheek to stop a snarky comment coming out. 'Yes, Mum. I keep a few things here. Do you have a problem with that?' My voice is sickly sweet and I turn one corner of my mouth up.

She gives me a cheeky wink. 'Nope. I think it's about time you moved the rest of your stuff in. He's a gorgeous and lovely man and I'm so pleased you're happy together.'

Pleasantly surprised at this, my cheeks grow hotter as I realise that Tremaine's overheard. He points at himself, then me, makes a heart shape with his fingers, flutters his eyelashes and does a soppy grin. 'Behave, Tremaine,' I say, narrowing my eyes at him. Mum snaps her head round, and just as quickly, he turns back to his cooking.

Her eyes grow rounder than the shape of her open mouth and she whispers, 'Oh, my goodness, did he hear me?' My blush has jumped across the table to her cheeks and she flaps her hand against them.

'Yup.'

'I feel awful now,' she mouths, and takes a glug of wine.

'That will teach you to interfere,' I say, with a giggle and soon she can't help but laugh too.

———

'That was one bloody good meal, Tremaine, and I've had a few,' Dad says, pushing his plate away after polishing off three helpings. 'Cooked a few too.'

'Thanks, Mark. I've always loved cooking; I find it's relaxing after such a hectic work schedule all week.'

'You should give us a few tips,' Ruan says, nudging

Gio's arm. 'We're awful for getting takeaways, aren't we, hon?'

'Yeah,' Gio admits with a sheepish grin. 'But we have a hectic work schedule too and open late two nights. It's not the same stress as your job though.'

'Hmm. You could say that again,' Dad comments, with snort. 'Being a corporate lawyer and a hairdresser don't really compare, do they?'

Ruan frowns and heaves a sigh. 'No. Gio *did* just say that.'

He's obviously disgruntled, and rightly so. I hope Dad's not going to go off on one.

'Did you learn about cooking from your mum, or dad?' Dad asks, draining his glass.

Relief that he's leaving the hairdressing thing alone is anchored by my heart sinking. Mum knows about Tremaine's parents but she's either not told Dad, or he wasn't listening, as usual, when she did. I wonder if I should change the subject but Tremaine seems unfazed.

'No, Mark. I didn't spend an awful lot of time with them growing up. I was at boarding school from the age of seven and spent the holidays with my uncle and aunt.' He takes a sip of wine and smiles. 'Even if I had been at home more, I wouldn't have learned anything from them. They always had a cook.'

Dad pours another big measure into his glass and my stomach ties itself into a double knot. I have a bad feeling about this. Dad's enjoying himself, but he can go unintentionally too far with his blunt comments when he's had a drink. 'A cook! Very *Upstairs, Downstairs!*' He laughs and Tremaine joins in.

'Yes, you could say that. My parents are ridiculously wealthy and sometimes do behave like they are part of the aristocracy.'

'Must have been a bit harsh on you growing up, then?' Ruan asks with a sympathetic smile.

Tremaine looks thoughtful and toys with the stem of his glass. 'It was. The only praise and encouragement I ever got was from my uncle's family. And the teachers at school. It's not the same as coming from parents though, is it?'

It's Ruan's turn to snort. 'No. No it certainly isn't. Being starved of praise can really damage you.'

I can almost see the hackles on Dad's neck standing up. The lines on his forehead resemble a furrowed field and he says, 'You trying to say that me and your mum didn't praise you, then?'

Dad's irritated tone has Ruan spreading his hands and pulling his neck back. 'I think you'll find I said nothing of the sort.'

He drains his glass and places it carefully back down. Ruan might seem calm, but the tell-tale clenching of his jaw sets my stomach churning. I don't think this is over. About to change the subject, I open my mouth but he gets there first.

'I was just saying that praise is very important to a child's self-esteem.' Though his voice is controlled, Ruan's eyes have turned to green sea-glass. 'Teenage years are important too, in fact even more so. Especially if that child is a bit different from his peers in some ways.'

Dad bangs his glass down. 'Like you, you mean? You being gay?'

Ruan shrugs, never taking his eyes from Dad's.

'So you *are* saying that you didn't get enough praise from me and your mum?' Dad crosses his arms.

'Mum was fine … but…'

The 'but' hangs in the air like a bomb ready to go off. I frantically think of the best way to defuse it, but thankfully Tremaine beats me to it.

'It's difficult to know how much praise a child needs, I suppose,' he says hurriedly. 'Having no children, I can't speak from experience, but I think it would depend on all kinds of things. Confidence is a big one. I had little, because I never felt good enough, due to my parents' distance. I blamed myself, concluding there must be something wrong with me, if my parents never wanted me around. As I grew older, I realised it was them that had the problem. I am good enough. But being a parent must be hard too, I suppose.'

I'm so proud of my boyfriend. He's come so far in such a short time, sharing his feelings and trying to understand those of others. The stand-offish snob is long gone, thank goodness. Yes, we're from different worlds, but now I can see them merging a little. Perhaps our differences can be overcome by our strength of feeling for each other. Unfortunately, however, I can see by Dad's stormy expression he's not ready to let Ruan's comment go, and having polished off half the glass he's just poured, I dread to hear what he'll say next.

'No. I expect parenting is not as easy as you imagine

when you're a kid,' I say, mainly to try and calm the situation. I notice Mum looking like a rabbit caught in the headlights, with Dad as the oncoming car. I need her help. I smile at her and ask, 'Did you find it hard, Mum?'

'Yes, at first. Nobody gives you a handbook!' Mum's false high-pitched laughter shatters the tension and we all chuckle and smile. Apart from Dad. 'We all learned together as we went,' Mum says, looking beseechingly at Ruan. 'Parents make mistakes, but hopefully not too many.'

Ruan reaches his hand across the table and she takes it. 'Don't worry, you didn't, Mum. As Tremaine said, he knows he's good enough. And if people don't appreciate that, then it says more about them than it does about you.'

Dad's storm finally breaks and he growls at Ruan, 'Why don't you just come out and say—'

Tremaine stands, cutting Dad off with the sound of his chair scraping back across the kitchen tiles. 'Who's for pudding? It's apple pie and custard!'

Dad's mutterings are drowned out by a rumble of agreement, and Ruan excuses himself to visit the loo. Phew! Gio, Mum and I catch each other's eyes and we smile our relief. Dad plays with his spoon but says nothing. He and Ruan have clearly got unfinished business, but at least it won't be dealt with here. Hopefully this lovely evening can be salvaged, now. Dad goes off to 'help' Tremaine with the pudding, and we fall into an easy conversation about Christmas crackers and how bad they are for the environment.

Ruan appears in the doorway, wearing a puzzled expression. 'Er, there's someone here to see you, Tremaine.'

Tremaine turns from the oven with the pie. 'Really? I'm not expecting anyone...'

'Darling! You made my favourite!' comes a woman's voice from behind my brother. He stands aside and in strides a tall, curvaceous, curly-haired brunette, wearing a short, sparkly red dress, killer heels and a smile to match. She tosses her mane and flicks her amber eyes over our little party gathered at the table. Her gaze stays on my face the longest, and her lip curls in disdain. Then she hurries over to Tremaine and plants a kiss on his cheek. 'Why didn't you tell me last night that we'd be having guests today, sweetheart?'

Last night? Sweetheart? What the fuck! I grab the edges of the table to make sure it's solid and I'm not in some freakish nightmare. My heart is doing a marathon in my chest and the Sunday roast is showing signs of wanting to make a reappearance. I glare at Tremaine who's putting down the pie with trembling hands and shoots me an apologetic glance.

He clears his throat, and into the pin-drop silence says to the woman in soothing tones, 'I thought you were on your way to London. Let's get you settled somewhere quiet until you're feeling better.' Tremaine slips his hand under her elbow and tries to guide her out of the kitchen, but she's having none of it.

'Better? There's nothing wrong with me, darling, as you found out last night!' She tips him a lascivious wink and rakes her fingers through her shiny curls. 'And aren't you going to introduce us?' Her words are running into each other and she's getting more agitated by the minute. Her fingers go back to her hair, then she gives a twitchy smile, then she tosses her hair, then the smile again. It's as though she's a robot, short-circuiting.

Tremaine sighs and takes her elbow again. 'This is Olivia, an old friend who popped down to see me last night unexpectedly and—'

Olivia shakes his hand off. 'Old friend! Ha! I'm his girlfriend.' She directs the last comment only to me, and as I struggle to hide my shock and disappointment, a flicker of triumph appears in her eyes.

'Ex. Now, come on. Please don't embarrass yourself,' Tremaine says in a low voice as he tries once more to guide Olivia from the room.

'Don't be ridiculous.' Olivia pushes him aside and sits down at the end of the table. 'Be a darling and get me some apple pie and a glass of bubbles.' She tosses her hair and says to us all wide-eyed, 'Now. Do tell me who you all are.'

Everyone looks at me, and then back to Tremaine, then back at me like nervous meerkats watching a tennis match, but nobody speaks. Tremaine shakes his head at Olivia, his eyes fiery with anger and his lips a thin line in his pale face. He bends to whisper in her ear, but she quickly turns her head so his lips find hers instead. He steps back and grabs her arm again, but that's me done. I can stand no more. I need to get out of here before I scream, cry, rage or all three.

Jumping up so fast that my chair falls over backwards with a clatter, I say to my family. 'I'm going. Gio, will you drive me home, please?'

Gio's already standing; Ruan too. Mum comes over and hugs me, while Dad sits staring with utter contempt at

Olivia and Tremaine. 'Mark. Come on,' Mum says, and takes his arm.

Tremaine abandons trying to remove Olivia and hurries over to me. 'Please don't go, Sennen.' He goes to put his arms around me but I step backwards. 'Let me explain everything and—'

'No. I can't be here right now.' My voice sounds little, distant, wounded. I hurry out into the hallway followed by Gio and Ruan. I hear Dad's strident voice saying something I can't catch and Tremaine answering, but I don't care what Dad says to him now. All I want to do is get under my duvet and find oblivion – banish Olivia's supermodel image from my head. Images of her here last night with my Tremaine. In the bed we've shared so many nights. No, No, NO! Tears spill from my eyes as I blindly snatch my coat and run to the car.

Chapter Twenty-One

Delicate fingers of winter sunshine stroke the edges of my bedroom curtains, as if trying to coax them open. They won't win. I'm staying in my bed wallowing in self-pity, misery and woe for the rest of the day. Maybe for the rest of the week. My head feels like there's an elephant in there trying to escape through my eyes, due to the ridiculous decision I made to drink three glasses of wine when I got home last night. Tossing and turning until the early hours didn't help either, going over every painful moment of Olivia's entrance.

Little snippets of the conversation I'd had with my brother and his partner flutter into my mind as I try to go back to sleep, despite it being nearly 10.15 a.m. I cringe as I remember telling them to go back to the hotel because they were 'doing my fucking head in'. But to be fair they *were* making light of it all. It's okay for Ruan and Gio to say it could all be easily explained away if I'd give Tremaine a chance, but they aren't me, are they? They don't have to live with the brutal humiliation of having a family dinner party crashed by someone who looked like she'd just stepped out of *Vogue*. Someone who says she's his girlfriend. Someone who stayed the night at Nancarrow House. I ignored Mum's calls too, but I did fire off a message saying I was okay and would call her today. Can't face that, either.

Hot tears push their way under my closed lids as I think of how great I felt with my new red dress and hairstyle, and then I saw Olivia. How could I ever hope to compete with her? Tremaine had said I was perfection when he saw me at the front door. He lied. And now I feel foolish. Foolish and ugly. My phone rings out and vibrates an urgent little dance on the nightstand as if in protest at my thoughts. I reach out a hand and drag the phone under the duvet. It's Tremaine. Again. Tough. Ten missed calls so far and thirteen messages telling me it wasn't how it looked, that she isn't his girlfriend, that nothing happened the night before last. I can't ring back. I can't allow him into my head. My heart.

Josh's betrayal had faded over the last few months, now it's back in vibrant colour to torment me and slash at my fragile ego with a sharp knife. I can't go through this again. Not again … please not again. Not with Tremaine. Questions that puzzled me all night come back again for a repeat performance. If it's all innocent between him and Olivia, why didn't he tell me that she had stayed over the night before? My phone starts up again, silencing more pointless conundrums demanding answers, and I'm ready to reject the call, until I see it's not Tremaine, but Jasmine.

Great. She will have found out from either Mum or Ruan. I think about rejecting, but then answer it. She'll only come round if I don't. Though there's an outside chance she doesn't know what's happened and wants to chat about something else.

'Hey, Jas, what's up?'

'I might ask you the same. What the hell's going on with you and Tremaine?'

The outside chance just packed up and left. I let out a weary sigh. 'I don't want to discuss it right now.'

'Yes, that's what Tremaine said. He's been trying to get in touch so many times. But you know that from your missed calls. He rang me as a last resort. Poor guy's in bits.'

I sit bolt upright in bed. 'He's in bits? *He's* in bloody bits? What about me?' I'm incensed. How can my best friend have sympathy for him over me?

'Hey, don't shoot the messenger! I don't know what's happened at all. He just said there's been a huge misunderstanding and he didn't want to go into details, because you should be the first to hear it. But he was terrified – his words, not mine – that it could mean the end of your relationship.'

'Damn right it could!'

'Oh no. Please don't say that. You two are made for each other.'

'Yeah? Well, maybe he's made for someone else.'

There's a sharp intake of breath. 'What? He's cheated on you!'

'Yes. I think so … I'm not sure.'

'But who with?'

'Which part of the sentence "I don't want to discuss it right now" didn't you understand?' Jasmine's wounded silence kicks me in the gut harder than words could ever do. It's not her fault, is it? I sigh. 'His ex, Olivia, who looks like a goddamn supermodel by the way. It's all a mess and I feel like my heart's been ripped out and trampled on by a Shire horse, yet again.' I bite back a sob. 'Suffice to say your psychic Nancy Cornish friend is a fake.' A humourless bark of laughter escapes as I think about the woman's prediction that we'd marry.

'Jeez.' There's a long pause and I can imagine Jasmine striding round the house biting her nails, desperate to make me feel better with her next words. 'Look. You've just admitted you don't know if he's cheated on you. Why not give him a chance to explain at least? Face-to-face, not over the phone, so you can tell if he's lying.'

I consider this for a few seconds but my gut says, 'No. I can't see him today. I'm an emotional wreck and I've not slept or eaten. I'll have a bath and a fry-up and a nap, then I'll be as right as rain.'

'Acid rain, perhaps.'

'Yeah, well, at least I'll be able to think more clearly.'

'Why don't I come over?'

'Er, I don't think—'

'I won't stay long. Just bring you some of my mum's famous chocolate cake – your favourite. She made some yesterday. And I can give you something else that you obviously need more than anything right now.'

'What's that?'

'A big hug.'

Jasmine rambles on at breakneck speed about how a trouble shared is a trouble halved and ten trillion more clichéd phrases, and I switch off until there's silence. I know argument is futile so close my eyes and say, 'Okay. See you soon.'

A hot shower, clean clothes and a plate of scrambled eggs on toast have left me feeling slightly more human and I'm contemplating ringing Mum when the doorbell goes. Hell, Jasmine's hardly given me time to draw breath. Still, the sooner she's here, the sooner she will leave me in peace.

Jasmine's on the doorstep with a large container of cake and a pink face. Her eyes dart about like a couple of green fireflies and land anywhere but on mine. I frown. What's she embarrassed about? No. Not embarrassed, shifty. 'Hello, Sen.' She gives me a quick peck on the cheek and pushes me backwards with the cake container.

'Oi, steady on, you nearly shoved me over then,' I say, standing to one side. Ignoring that, she giggles nervously and pulls me towards the kitchen. 'Hang on, I need to close the front door…' The remainder of my sentence sticks in my throat because it's blocked by a ball of anger.

Tremaine slips in, white-faced, and closes the door behind him. He looks like he's had a similar night to mine; his normally lively blue eyes are dull and red-rimmed, and his hair is as wild as the wind outside. Clocking my fury, he holds his hands up as if I'm about to shoot him and says, 'Please, Sennen. Don't be angry. It's the only way I could think of to—'

'What the hell!' I glare at him and then at Jasmine. 'How could you betray me like this, Jas?'

At last Jasmine alights her fireflies on my face. 'I know you're angry now, but this needs to be sorted.' I'm about to launch into a stream of expletives, but she shoves the cake at me and hurries to the door, chucking over her shoulder as she opens it, 'I'll leave you to it. But you know where I am!'

Incredulous, I stare at the door shutting behind her, and then I point wordlessly at it, and back at Tremaine. 'Get. Out.' Though my voice is quiet, it's freezing cold.

'Please let me talk,' Tremaine implores, clasping his hands together in front of him as if in prayer. Then he starts pacing to and fro in my hallway like a caged tiger, raking his hands through his curls until it sticks out at the sides like Einstein's. 'I can only imagine how you must be feeling after last night. As if it wasn't bad enough that bloody Olivia turns up unannounced, she has to do it in front of your family!' He stops pacing and reaches out a hand to me, but my death stare makes him think better of it. 'Please believe me, Olivia is my ex. Nothing happened. She wanted it to, but there's only one woman for me, and that's you.'

The tremble in his voice makes me look from the front door to his face. Standing tears make his eyes into two rockpools, and he swipes them away with the back of his hand. His voice shares the tremble with his lips and fingers as he reaches out to me again. Compassion threatens my resolve, but, determined not to just cave at this first tug at my heartstrings, I step away from him and walk towards the living room. 'You have ten minutes.'

We sit on opposite chairs. I don't want him near me on the sofa in case he tries to hold my hand. I can't bear his touch right now. I don't know where he's been. Tremaine clears his throat and holds my gaze. That's a good start; at least I'll be able to detect any trace of a lie. I've not known him for long, but I do know he can't tell fibs without a certain amount of blinking and lip twitching. A few weeks ago, for a laugh, he'd tried to make me believe he'd climbed Everest on his gap year. Didn't work.

Tremaine leans forward, hands clasped, elbows on knees and maintains eye contact. 'Okay. Olivia came to Nancarrow the night before last around nine. She was completely out of it on cocaine and booze.'

Wow. I wasn't expecting that. 'Cocaine? Is that usual for her?'

'No. She used to like a drink, a bit too much, but coke's a recent thing. She said she got into it after we split up. Apparently, she couldn't cope without it after she heard on the grapevine that I'd found someone else.' He shrugs. 'A bit rich considering she was the one who cheated on me and caused the split in the first place.'

'Hang on. How did she get to yours if she was off her head?'

'Taxi. She'd got a train down from London. Anyway, she said she was sorry she'd cheated and that she'd do anything if I'd give her another chance.' Tremaine's eyes shift from mine and he heaves a weary sigh. Then he looks back at me. 'To be honest she's been texting me for a few months begging my forgiveness, but I didn't tell you as we were just starting out, and I didn't want her making waves.'

'Just like you didn't tell me she'd stayed over, hey?'

'Yes. Exactly. Can you imagine how you'd have reacted? If Josh had done the same to you, would you have told me? Besides, your brother had just arrived and I didn't want to ruin the mood for you.'

Maybe he had a point, but I'm not telling him that. 'So why couldn't you have called another taxi and packed her off again?'

'Oh, Sen. I couldn't. Olivia was a complete mess. Crying, begging, throwing up… I felt sorry for her, which was more than she bloody deserved.' He spreads his hands and sighs. 'So, I ran a bath, made her some food and ,once she was more or less sober, put her in the spare room. She went out like a light.'

'Funny that she said, "There's nothing wrong with me, darling, as you found out last night" then, isn't it?' The memory of it sends a barb through my chest.

'Olivia said that to wind you up. Just like she pretended not to know who everyone was. I'd told her you were all coming for dinner, and then she'd demanded to know what you looked like. Asked to see photos of you on my phone, so she knew exactly who *you* were. I showed her, hoping she'd realise she was on a fool's errand, but no.'

I remembered her sneer of derision when she looked me up and down. Up to now, his story is ringing true, and I've been watching his face closely. So far, there've been no blinks or twitches. He's about to say something else, but I hold up a finger and tell him I need a moment to process what I've heard so far. There's a long deep silence, across which we stare like opposing forces in No Man's Land.

I lean back in my chair, fold my arms and try to appear nonchalant and in control while my heart is galloping about in my chest as if it's a corralled mustang. 'Can you look me in the eye and swear that nothing happened between you and Olivia on that night?'

'I can.' He gives me an unwavering stare. 'Nothing happened between me and Olivia on that night, I swear on all I hold dear. I'll admit, she *did* come into my bedroom naked in the early hours and slipped under the covers, but I gave her prompt marching orders.'

My stomach churns as I imagine Olivia's perfect body sliding into the bed I've shared so many times with Tremaine. Wrapping her arms around his sleeping form, kissing his back...

'Oh please! You expect me to believe that you turned down Miss sodding Universe?'

Tremaine frowns. 'Eh?'

A tumult of emotion races through my every part of me and I jump to my feet. 'She's bleeding stunning! What man in their right mind would turn her down?'

He shakes his head and holds my gaze. 'Yes, she's stunning. But she can't hold a candle to you, in my opinion. As I said earlier, you're the only woman for me, and yes, I did turn her down. There was no need to tell you she'd come into my room, but I want you to know everything.'

My heart slows and the churning in my gut eases, as the

honesty in his eyes shoots across No Man's Land like a bullet. He wants me. Only me. I swallow what feels like a golf ball, sit back down and take a deep breath. I can't put up the white flag yet, I still have questions. 'How come she turned up yesterday then, if you told her there was no way back for you?'

'Despite me putting her on a train for London in Bodmin yesterday morning, she got off at the next station and spent the day in the pub, drinking and snorting coke, before getting another taxi back when she knew you'd all be at my house for dinner.' He gives a wry smile. 'Olivia is nothing if not determined.'

'She'd been on the coke again ... that's why she was behaving like a robot malfunctioning,' I say, almost to myself.

'Yup.'

We do some more staring at each other. Well, it's more like gazing now, because a wave of affection is washing away a lot of the anger from my shores. 'What happened after I left last night?'

'Your dad asked me what the hell was going on. I told him the truth in front of Olivia and said she would be leaving immediately.' Tremaine sighs. 'Then, once your parents had gone, she went off on one like before. Screaming, yelling, tugging at her hair. But this time I didn't give in. I called a taxi and put her in it, told the driver to take her to a hotel I know near Bodmin Station, and told her to be on the morning train to London. I also told her that if she came back, she'd be outside in the rain as the bolt was going across my doors.'

My shoulders come down from up round my ears and I relax back into the sofa cushions. 'So that's it. All of it?' I ask in a soft voice.

'Yeah. She didn't come back, thank God. Hopefully she'll be back in London now and hopefully she'll bloody stay there…' He gives me a long and loving look. 'Please say you believe me, Sen. I can't bear all this upset between us.'

The golf ball is back in my throat, so I can only nod. Every fibre of my being is calling out for his arms, his lips. But he has to be the one to make the first move across No Man's Land. I'm too worried about emotional snipers. I'm scared that I've messed everything up by not answering his calls and jumping to the wrong conclusions. But then given the circumstances, it did look dodgy. Even now, a little part of me is imagining Olivia bursting through my front door screaming and yelling that he's lying. But the most part of me knows she won't, and he isn't.

'I do believe you, Tremaine. And I can't cope with all this either.' I give him a little smile and swallow hard. 'Maybe I should have listened to you earlier, but in my defence, I couldn't, because the betrayal of Josh came flooding back and mixed with how stunning Olivia looked, and the humiliation of it all happening in front of my family, plus the pain and despair when I thought I'd lost you … well, it just made me run for cover.'

He nods. Then he jumps up, hurries over to sits by my side and takes my hand in his. 'I understand, absolutely. Josh has left his mark. And you know I found it hard to love and trust people because of my past, and after Olivia cheated. But meeting you changed me, moving to Nancarrow changed me. I feel like Cornwall is my home, it's where I belong. I have learned to love again.' Tremaine's eyes draw me into their depths and he moves closer. 'Actually, I have learned to love for the first time. Sennen, I love you, my darling.'

I put my hand over my mouth to stifle a sob, but my eyes insist on overflowing. Because I don't want to end up a snotty bawling mess at such a tender moment, I hurriedly brush the tears from my cheeks. Months of keeping him at arm's length and trying to keep my feelings under control are out the window, and it's bloody liberating! He loves me? He LOVES me! Flinging my arms around his neck I press my lips to his, and as we melt into each other, I wish this kiss would never end. When it does, I say, 'I missed you … and I'm glad you feel that way about me, because I feel the same about you.'

'You love me?'

Suddenly shy, I just nod and look at our intertwined fingers.

'Tell me,' he says, kissing my damp cheeks. 'I want to hear you say it out loud.'

Shyness forgotten, I look up into his eyes and say, 'I love you, Tremaine. So much.'

A while later, after making love for the second time, we lie awake talking about the future, and our hopes and dreams. Tremaine is considering moving here permanently and either continuing being a lawyer or branching out into something new. He doesn't know what yet. One of his New Year's resolutions will be to learn how to make pots. I promise to teach him and we laugh about re-enacting the scene from the film *Ghost*. Guilt takes the edge of our contentment though, as I still haven't told him about losing the shop. Because he's been totally honest about everything, and our relationship has taken a big leap forward, I decide I can't keep it to myself any longer.

Propping myself up on one elbow I face him and say, 'Tremaine, I have a bit of a confession to make about my shop. You see—'

'You sold it to Phillipa.'

My falling jaw nearly snaps its hinges. 'How do you know?'

'Jasmine.'

Why am I not surprised…

'Jasmine? That little madam does like a good old meddle in my life, doesn't she?'

'But regarding both today and the shop, it's a good job she did.'

Puzzled, I snuggle closer to him and say, 'Today, I understand. But why is it a good job she told you about the shop?'

Tremaine settles back against the pillows and does a dramatic sigh. 'Looks like the present I got you for Christmas will have to be an early one.'

'What? Why?' I ask his back as he pulls his boxers on and hurries out of the bedroom.

A few moments later he's back with an envelope in his

hand and a huge grin on his face. Slipping under the duvet he drops a kiss on my nose and says, 'As I said, I wanted this to be a surprise, but it seems fitting you should have it now. Jasmine told me all about the shop sale, your Uncle Pete, and the fact that you didn't want me to know you'd sold it, because you didn't want me blaming myself for bringing the delightful Phillipa down here.'

Mute, I nod. The envelope looks official, and as he waves it under my nose, I have a tingly feeling running the length of my spine and a bubble or two of anticipation popping in my chest. 'That's true, yes. But what's in this enve—'

He holds a finger up. 'I did feel a tad responsible, but that wasn't the real reason I did what I did. I did the thing that's in this envelope because I wanted to make you happy, and I knew I had the ability to make that happen.' Tremaine kisses me softly on the lips and places the envelope in my hand. 'Merry Christmas, darling.'

My fingers won't function properly, they're shaking too much. What the hell is in this damned envelope? Eventually I pull out the thick embossed sheet of paper upon which many words are written. But the only ones that leap out at me are: 'deed', 'Sea Spray Gifts', 'owner', and 'Sennen Kellow'. My brain cuts through all the legal jargon and tells me that I am the sole owner of my shop. Me. I have my shop back. But that's impossible. I look up from the document. 'I … I don't understand. How can I be the owner?'

'You aren't, until you sign on the dotted line right there.' He runs a finger along the bottom of the sheet. 'But as to how? Well, I decided to buy it back for you.' He holds his hands up at my immediate protest. 'Not for the exorbitant price that was paid, but at normal market value.'

My heart thumps a tattoo against my ribs. Have I fallen down a rabbit hole? This whole thing is so surreal. How on earth did he manage that? 'Phillipa made a huge loss? Why would she do such a crazy thing?'

'No. Not Phillipa, her boyfriend. He's the one she gifted it to, and let's just say I know a few things about him that he might not want bandied about town.'

My stomach churns. 'You blackmailed him?'

'Didn't have to. Before he dabbled in art, he was in the same game as me, but he tended to rip people off when he could. A real nasty piece of work, so don't spare any sympathy for him. I found out about his involvement in one of the dodgy deals and I questioned him about it. Thing is, it would take a bit of work to prove it, but I would if necessary. Anyway, I just told him that you'd made a mistake giving up the business and you'd like it back. He knew when he was beaten.'

'But you still had to pay for it. I can't let you do that. I have the money from the sale – I'll reimburse you.'

'No, you won't. I have pots of money, and it makes me happy to use some of it to give you a lovely Christmas present. Save that money for something else.'

Bewildered, I look into his eyes, full of love for me, and then run my fingers over the document again 'Such a wonderful thing to do … I really don't know what to say.'

'Are you happy with the gift?

'Happy? I'm bloody over the moon. It's unbelievable!

Totally unbelievable,' I mutter, mystified. 'Thank you. Thank you so much.' I wipe away a new procession of teardrops from my cheeks.

Tremaine laughs and pulls me into his arms. 'You're welcome. Okay, stop with the snivelling and kiss me.'

Chapter Twenty-Two

The Old Black Bull is full to the rafters. With only elbow room at the bar, Tremaine and Rob inch forward, chatting as they wait, while Jasmine and I have a bloody good catch-up. We've not seen each other since the week before Christmas, and tonight is New Year's Eve.

'Just think, your gran and Jory were here in this exact place, exactly sixty-seven years ago. Isn't that wonderful?' Jasmine says, squeezing my arm. She adjusts the plunging neckline of her sparkly purple top to cover her boobs more and nods at the linen bag between us, lying by my side on the long padded bench. With an expression borrowed from an over-excited pixie, she says, 'Let me have another peek.'

'No. It's wrapped up in a soft cloth, I'm not getting it out in the middle of a busy pub. Don't want to tempt fate.'

'What do you mean?'

I roll my eyes at her. 'Well, what if someone barges past as you're looking at it, nudges your hand, and it shatters into a thousand pieces? No, thank you. You can look another time.'

Crestfallen she grumbles, 'Okay. Where are you going to do it? In here, or outside in the beer garden?'

'Not decided yet. It's more crowded than we expected, so probably in the garden.'

I get a warm smile. 'You don't really need the cup of kindness, or parting glass, whatever it's called, to tell you the truth within your heart anyway, do you?' She nudges me in the arm and the strap of my emerald velvet dress falls down 'Not now you've found the love of your life, your Prince Charming, the owner of the most gorgeous house in the world, and the man who gifts you shops for Christmas.'

I laugh and pull my strap back up. 'Shops? I think you'll find it is just the one. But yes, I am very lucky to have found Tremaine. Even though we come from very different backgrounds, we are discovering more common ground each day. Gran felt the same about Jory, but she wanted to make sure one hundred per cent that he was the one she wanted to walk alongside for life. I want to do the same. And don't tell Rob about it, will you? I still want it to stay between us until after tonight at least.'

'As if. He's not what you call particularly open-minded when it comes to that sort of thing. Very down to earth is our Rob.'

We watch our respective partners at last push their way to the front of the bar and get served, their almost identical bottle-green arran sweaters and blue jeans giving them a Cornish fisherman vibe. 'They seem to be getting on really well,' Jasmine says. 'Maybe we should go out for a meal together or something in the new year. We've not done anything as a four since the surfing day.'

'No. But then we did have a little problem named Olivia to iron out in the run-up to Christmas.'

'She needed bloody ironing out, the mad bitch.'

'Hmm. Tremaine reckons she's just going through a really bad time. He's worried that if she doesn't get help for her addiction, she might end up losing her job. Nobody wants a lawyer representing them who's completely "out of it", do they?'

Jasmine raises an eyebrow at me. 'You sound like you feel sorry for her.'

'I do, in a way. She made a huge mistake cheating on him and didn't realise he was the one for her until it was too late. Tremaine's with me now, and there's no way she can get him back. If I was her, I'd be distraught too.'

'Yeah, but you wouldn't have cheated on him in the first place, would you?' she counters.

'True.'

'Sennen Kellow, you're too kind for your own good sometimes. I reckon she's bad news with a capital BN.'

I'm saved from further comment by the two men coming back with our drinks. 'Rob's been telling me about the new shop he's opening in Bude in the spring,' Tremaine says, handing me a glass of Merlot. 'You're going to be pretty busy helping to get it up and running, eh, Jasmine?'

Jasmine puts on an affected tone and pretends to examine her nails. 'I will, dear one. But Rob needs his most trusted and innovative manager onboard to make sure it hits the ground running, don't you know?'

We laugh and Rob replies, 'Joking apart, you are indeed a bloody good manager and I wouldn't want anyone else beside me in the new Bude place.'

Jasmine's cheeks could grill a steak and her ear-to-ear smile demonstrates the pride and happiness Rob's comment has caused. 'Aw, that's nice, love.'

Rob scrubs his hand over his short dark hair and his cheeks catch a bit of heat from hers as he says, 'I wouldn't want anyone else beside me in life either.'

Immediately tears spring in Jasmine's eyes and this time it's me who catches them. I'm so pleased she's found happiness at last. Tremaine and I look on, gooey-eyed, as they give each other a loving kiss and hug. However, this loving kiss and hug go on for far too long and are bordering on the indecent, so I give her a nudge. 'Oi, get a room.'

They break apart with a self-conscious laugh on Rob's part, and a wicked giggle on Jasmine's. 'Don't worry, we will later.'

Ten minutes to midnight finds Tremaine and me out in the deserted beer garden – well, it would be, wouldn't it, at this time of year with an icy breeze coming off the Atlantic. Why I decided to go for a dressy-up-type dress which barely covers my thighs I don't know. Well, I do. It's New Year's Eve and I wanted to look glamorous. It's not just any old New Year's Eve after all. It's parting glass time. At least we are wrapped in heavy coats, scarves, gloves and fur-lined knee-length boots – me, not him. He has trainers on his feet, both of which he's stamping as he repeatedly flings his arms to the side and then hugs them around himself again, as if he's doing the weird ritual courtship dance of the lesser spotted crazy bird.

'What exactly are you trying to achieve?' I ask, giving him the side-eyes.

'Well, duh. Getting warm, obviously.'

'And is it working?'

He puffs a dandelion-head breath of air into the night sky. 'Not so you'd notice.'

I slip my arms around him and rest my head on his shoulder. 'This better?'

'Much.'

Then over the rooftops behind him, I notice the hands on the church clock and my tummy does a few flips. 'It's almost time. Come on, let's get ready!'

Carefully, I take the glass from the linen bag, unwrap it and set it down gently on a wooden bench next to a full glass of red wine. A spike of adrenalin shoots through me and I'm lost for words. We both stare at it and my hand finds his. 'Are you doing the honours or shall I?' he asks.

My heart thumps in my chest. 'I think it should be me.'

'I think it should be you too. It was your mission, after all.'

I tip half the wine into the cup of kindness and lift it to the moonlit heavens. The stars wink along the rim, as with trembling hands I turn it gently in their light. The engraved figures begin their ancient dance, and the sound of music and laughter from the pub seems to fade, until it's just me and Tremaine in this moment. A moment that we've always waited for, but never knew. There's no past or future, only now. Only us. The chill wind kisses my cheek and Morwenna and Victoria feel close by, guiding my hand. As the church bells ring in the new year, I stop turning the glass and take a sip. Immediately, heat fires through my whole body, every vein and sinew alive with an exhilarating energy, and in my heart, there's the unshakeable truth. My heart's desire is Tremaine. Tremaine. Tremaine, today, tomorrow and always.

Then the images I saw in the cave return in an explosion of light and music, people dancing and laughing, their hearts full of love. Music and laughter start up again in the pub too and fireworks shoot an arc through the black-velvet sky like a night rainbow. Tremaine takes my hand and kisses it, his eyes glistening, full of fireworks and emotion. Over his shoulder, I see Gran smiling, her face alight with love. She blows me a kiss, then she's gone. I can't speak. I pass Tremaine the glass, and he takes a sip as 'Auld Lang Syne' starts up. I think I can hear Jasmine's voice high and loud above the rest. Tremaine puts the glass on the table and pulls me close.

'Did anything happen?' he whispers in my ear.

Part of me wants to keep everything to myself, because I feel that in the telling, the experience might be diminished. Words can't do it justice. But I'll try my best. 'I'm not sure I have the words to describe it,' I whisper. 'Suffice to say I felt the presence of Victoria and Gran, and my heart told me that you are the one … now, tomorrow, and always.' A sob breaks free and I let happy tears flow unchecked down my face.

Holding me at arm's length he says, 'That's incredible. And while I can't pretend to have experienced anything like that, I did feel a contentment once the glass touched my lips. You are my now, my tomorrow and my future, Sennen. I adore you and want to be the one you walk alongside for life.'

I fall into his arms, laughter and tears mingling as we share our first kiss of the year, and the rest of our lives.

Chapter Twenty-Three

How can we be at the end of January already? I'm in the shop, sorting out a new window display, remembering how Gran used to say the older you got, the faster time seemed to fly past. Once she said she'd get a fly swatter and stop it in its tracks; failing that, she'd chuck a spider's web over it to make it slow down a bit. Gran had a weird imagination to say the least. Time does seem to be flying right now though, and I'm only twenty-five. Well, twenty-six on Valentine's Day. Tremaine told me last night he has a lovely surprise planned for me. I can't wait. Though in a way I could do with a bit of normality to anchor my feet to the ground for more than five seconds. The last few weeks have been a bit of a whirlwind.

First there was the shop, shortly followed by the parting glass experience, then last week Tremaine asked me to move in with him. I could hardly believe it, until he pointed out that I'm there more than I am at my flat anyway, so it made sense. Smiling to myself, I rerun the scene in my head at his reaction after I said yes. He leapt on the kitchen table and started to sing 'Take My Breath Away' at the top of his voice. It's crazy how much I love that guy. I've been moving my things over bit by bit. There's not much left at the flat now, apart from big things like my bed, kitchen table and sofa, and we decided that they could go to charity, as though they're still serviceable, they've seen better days.

Jasmine was predictably over the moon when I told her Nancarrow House was now my new home and lost no time in telling me that she told me so. Or rather, that Nancy Cornish told me so. I pointed out that actually, the psychic had said we'd marry and then live there. Jasmine said that was incorrect. Nancy hadn't stipulated which way round it would happen. I decided to leave it there, as Jasmine was trying her death stare on for size.

I pick up a large dish I made last week, depicting a clifftop scene. A swathe of green sits as a base for hosts of yellow daffodils nodding in a gentle breeze against a sleepy blue ocean. My fingers trace the petals of the daffodils. Delicate brushstrokes skilfully and thoughtfully applied, bringing the flowers into bloom. Tremaine's brushstrokes. He's a natural. I was amazed when I discovered just how talented he was, which made my dislike of his father even keener, despite never having met the man. How could he have crushed the young Tremaine's dreams to be an artist all those years ago, and rubbished his work?

As I make myself a coffee to go with the chocolate éclair I bought from the bakery across the road earlier, I think again about the day we'd spent in the workshop re-enacting *Ghost*. Well, not really; we got into even more of a mess than

Demi and Patrick did and a bit of clay landed in my eye and I had to wash my face. Reality is never the same as fiction, I've found. Tremaine has a way to go when it comes to potting, but he's got the raw talent. As far as his painting is concerned though, he is incredible. And to think he hasn't lifted a brush for over ten years. Half the éclair disappears in one bite, and as I chew it, an idea I've had brewing for some time now buzzes around in my mind. Tonight, over dinner. That's when I'll spring it on Tremaine. Hope he likes it. The shop bell tinkles, and I check my mouth in the kitchen mirror for any escaped cream before I go back into the shop.

'Ruan! What the hell are you doing here?'

'That's a nice greeting for your brother, I have to say.'

I laugh and give him a big hug. His cheek is icy, so I pinch it and pull his checked yellow and black scarf tighter round his neck. 'You're frozen. And you know what I mean. It's unusual seeing you here on a weekday afternoon when you're normally working in Plymouth.'

'Don't worry, I've left the love of my life in charge.'

'Oh, I hope Gio doesn't find out.'

'You're so hilarious.' He grins, walks into the kitchen and flicks the kettle on.

I follow him in. 'Anyway, why are you here?'

'I've just had a long walk on the beach, hence the frozen face, to think about the meaning of life and stuff.'

I perch on a stool and hand him a packet of hobnobs. 'O-kay. So, you've come from Plymouth on a weekday, when your shop is open, to walk on the beach and contemplate the meaning of life?'

Ruan pours water onto teabag, slips onto the opposite stool and crunches into a biscuit. 'Kind of. I was actually contemplating the conversation I had earlier with Dad and concluding that at last we can move forward in a positive way.'

'You came to see Dad?'

'Yeah. He called me last week and said the altercation we had at Tremaine's before Christmas had been playing on his mind ever since, and could I come over sometime and have a chat about it?' Ruan blows across the surface of his tea and takes a sip. 'I said I'd come as soon as I could. I mean, when have you known Dad to ever want to talk about bloody anything?' He chuckles. 'Well, apart from cooking fish and the restaurant clientele.'

'Never. Thinking about it, the few times I've seen him since they were round for dinner, he has been a bit subdued. Like he had stuff on his mind, you know?'

'Yeah. Well, he had, and now he hasn't, because he shared it all.' Ruan jabs a biscuit at me. 'Turns out that Tremaine is behind it, in part. Dad said he had a chat to him in the conservatory when you and Tremaine popped over for lunch at the beginning of January. You and Mum were in the kitchen making lunch, apparently.' Ruan stops and stares off into space as if contemplating the meaning of life again.

'And?' I raise my eyebrows.

'Hm? Oh, yeah. And Tremaine said he wished he'd had a better relationship with his father. Told him he'd gone along with his father's wishes, even when he knew his life would be the worse for it. Partly because he'd not had a lot of choice, but if he were honest, deep down it was because he wanted to please his father, even though he'd been made to feel never good enough. Tremaine said his self-esteem had been rock bottom for years because of the way his parents had treated him, and now he was older, he wished he'd been braver in standing up for himself. Apparently, this got Dad thinking about me and him, and what I'd said at the dinner party. Tremaine said he should talk to me before it was too late. Dad agreed.'

'Blimey! Tremaine never said anything.'

'Maybe he didn't want you to know before Dad had talked to me.'

'Perhaps. So, what happened?'

'We had a couple of beers and I told him how he'd made me feel about being gay. That he'd never come right out and said he was disappointed, but his whole attitude towards me had changed and he'd become distant. I felt like I wasn't his son anymore.' Ruan blinks a few times and looks into his tea.

My heart squeezes. I hate to think of my lovely brother suffering like that. I reach for his hand. 'Well done for being so honest, Ru. I know Dad's not easy to talk to about serious things.'

'No. He's not great at empathy either. But I was relieved because he just blurted how he felt. I reckon he'd been planning what to say for a while.' He takes another biscuit from the packet, looks at it and puts it down. 'Best not. Still trying to get rid of the Christmas excess nearly a month on.'

I can relate to that, but take one anyway; I need sustenance. 'Go on, tell me what he said.'

'Basically, Dad said it was true, he was disappointed that I didn't want to carry on in his footsteps. He'd had great hopes for us going into partnership together in the restaurant. Thing was, he'd had it all mapped out since I was a kid.' Ruan shakes his head in bewilderment. 'He wanted a re-run of him and Granddad. Okay, he admitted Granddad was a fisherman, not a cook, but he'd taught him all there was to know about fish, and the two of them were inseparable. Dad wanted that close relationship with me, but when I showed no interest in being a chef, and chose hairdressing, he couldn't get a grip on it.'

My heart goes out to Ruan, and less so to Dad too, for his blinkered vision. 'Hm. Silly sod had built his own dream without consulting you in the matter … as if you didn't have a choice.'

Ruan nods. 'Yeah. I pushed him over the gay issue too, and he took a while to consider it. Then he admitted it was a shock when I came out of the closet, as that wasn't part of his ridiculous plan either. Grandchildren were. A big part, it seems – you know, to carry on the family name? But then he held his hands up and told me that everything he'd hoped for was selfish, and all about him.' Ruan takes a moment and wipes a few tears away. 'Dad said he was so sorry for the distance he'd put between us, and could I forgive him and move on?'

'Bloody hell, that's so un-Dad-like. Must have been so hard for him to admit. What did you say?'

'I said he was a selfish old bastard, and there's no way I'd forgive him, so he could fuck off out of my life for ever.'

I nearly fall off my stool. 'Shut up! You didn't!' I examine his deadpan expression for signs of cracks. There are none.

At last, there's the big daft Ruan grin. 'Course I didn't, you soft mare!' He laughs. 'I said I forgave him and we did a manly hug, complete with awkward back slaps and embarrassed smiles.'

A relieved giggle breaks out. 'Oh, that's good. Do you think you'll be okay now?'

'I think we will, if we work at it.' Ruan absently takes a biscuit and crunches into it. 'The heavy lifting's been done now, so let's hope it will get easier between us in future.'

I slip off my stool and give him a big non-man hug. 'I'm so pleased, Ru.'

'Me too.'

'Tremaine should take a leaf out of his own book and go see his father,' I say, leaning against the countertop and downing the last few dregs of coffee. 'In fact, I'll mention it to him tonight.' Then I remember the other thing I was going to mention tonight and decide maybe this one can wait until another time.

Dinner is down to me this evening, and I'm a bit nervous, given that Tremaine is such a master chef. I've only made a few sandwiches and salads for him so far, so tonight is the first time he'll get to taste my culinary efforts. He's due home from London at seven, and then that's him back for a week. I can't wait, as he's been away for three days. Though recently he's been slowly cutting back on his case load and spending more and more time here at home. Home. Tremaine's and mine. It's still incredible to think I live here in this amazing place. I remember the first time I laid eyes on it and knew immediately the house was sad – sensed the neglect and loneliness. I thought its huge bay windows on the ground floor were half shuttered, like eyelids lowered in grief, and my heart ached for it. I wondered about its future. Would anyone live there again, make the house into a home? Little did I know that the 'anyone' would be me.

The aroma of chicken casserole and dumplings in the oven gives the kitchen a welcoming feel, and a glance at the clock tells me it's time to set the table and pour the wine. I take a sip, sit at the table and find myself smiling. I find myself smiling an awful lot these days, and there's a lightness of being in my soul that floats me round the place too. I can't believe my luck to have found such a wonderful man, who loves me just as much as I love him. Though there's a nagging voice that likes to pop up at these times too. It mentions that in the past Morwenna and Victoria would have been floating around as well, but then they fell to earth with a bump. Victoria literally. I tell the voice to do one, and go to check on the casserole.

'Hi, honey, I'm home!' Tremaine calls a little while later, as he comes through the kitchen door, bringing with him on his coat the breath of sea air and winter. He picks me up and swirls me round before pulling me into his arms.

Dropping a kiss on my cheek he says, 'I've missed you SO much! Mmm. Something smells dee-lish-ous!'

'Missed you too! And it's me you can smell.'

Tremaine winks and snuggles my neck. 'Yes, it is, but it's also something you've got cooking in the oven.'

'Chicken casserole, herby dumplings and roast potatoes. Just the thing for a cold January night.' I smile.

'Wow! Sounds great. I'm starved. I'll quickly get changed and then we can eat.'

By the time he's back, the casserole and potatoes are in the middle of the table and I'm pouring him a glass of pinot. 'How was your day?'

'Grim.' He pulls a face. 'But then every day is grim when you hate your job.'

This is news. 'I know you don't really like it much, but hate? Really?'

'Yeah. It's been worse since I got this place and met you. All the lies I used to tell myself about it not being so bad, or it would get better, fall on deaf ears now. I'm fed up with lying.'

Poor love. That's awful, yet it does help me regarding my big idea. 'Right. Well, I might have the solution to that, but let's eat first.'

Tremaine raises an eyebrow and lights the candle in the middle of the table, the flame catching a twinkle in the blue of his eyes, like a sunburst on the ocean. He gives a half smile. 'Solutions. I like those.'

We help ourselves to casserole and I say, 'And guess who came into the shop this afternoon?'

'The Queen?'

'No.'

'Ed Sheeran?'

'No.'

'I give up.' He shrugs and takes a big mouthful of food. 'Ruan.'

'God, this is superb,' he says, fanning his mouth with his hand. 'Hot, but superb.' He takes a gulp of wine.

'Well, you did put half the plateful in your gob at once.' I laugh, pleased that my first dinner is appreciated.

'True.' He takes a smaller mouthful and speaks out the corner of his mouth. 'Sorry, Ruan, you say? Shouldn't he have been at work?'

I tell him the whole story and add, 'It was really nice of you to have a chat with Dad like that. Ruan and he wouldn't have met up today if you hadn't. Thanks, darling.'

Tremaine dabs at his mouth with a napkin. 'My pleasure. I could see things needed fixing when they were here at the ill-fated dinner party. One of them just needed a little push.' I nod, and we eat in silence for a few minutes, but I can tell by his vacant expression he is far away and pondering. 'You know what?' He scoops up the last bit of potato and pushes his plate to one side. 'I think I'm going to take a leaf out of my own book. I'm going to go up to London next week to talk to Father.'

My heart leaps. 'Oh good! Because I was going to suggest you do that, but didn't know how to broach it.'

'Great minds, eh?'

'Yeah. And I'm so pleased you enjoyed the casserole. I was a bit nervous as you're so good in the kitchen.'

'Why, thank you.' He tosses his tawny curls and wiggles his brows. 'How about in the bedroom?'

'Even better,' I say with a slow smile. Then I remember the big idea I was supposed to mention and decide this is a good a time as any. 'You know you said you hated your job, and that you have been talking about maybe trying something else?'

He pours us both more wine and relaxes back in his chair. 'Yeah?'

'I've had an idea about that. After I saw how talented an artist you are, I thought maybe you could paint some of my ceramics, but also create some artwork of your own, and I could sell it in the shop? I know it won't bring in anywhere near the kind of money you're used to, but it would be something you love to do. Something you always wanted to do before you were prevented from following your dream.'

He leans forward, rests his arms on the table and looks deep into my eyes. 'Now that, Sennen, is one of the best ideas I've heard for some time. I don't need a huge income anymore, as I have more than enough in the bank after working ten years or so in the corporate world. There's the pot of gold that dearest Daddy put in my trust fund too when I toed his very demanding line. I've not really done much with it, apart from buy and refurbish this place, so it's just sitting there. Don't need it really.'

I laugh. 'Except when you draw out a few hundred thousand to pay for a Christmas present for your girlfriend.'

'Best money I ever spent.' Tremaine reaches across the table and takes my hand. 'Do you really think I'm talented enough to paint your stuff, and make a real go of creating my own work?'

The self-assured city lawyer before me morphs into the vulnerable teenager he used to be, seeking praise and validation, and the hope in his eyes twists my gut. 'You are, my love. One hundred per cent.'

He squeezes my hand and sighs. 'You don't know how happy that makes me feel. I've been thinking along similar lines, but there's always been the self-doubt put there by you know who. The sneering, the pointing of derisory fingers reaching from the past to trip me up in the future.' Tremaine takes a big gulp of wine and sets the glass down with a thump. His eyes are full of candlelight but there's a deeper fire of passion burning within them. 'I'm going to tell that old goat a few home truths. I'd like to build a few bridges like Ruan and your dad have begun to, but if not, I'll burn them.'

Knowing a reconciliation would be the best for his mental health in the long run, I say, 'Hopefully that won't be necessary. As you said, you don't need his money now, so if he doesn't approve of you leaving the law, so what? He has no power over you anymore, Tremaine.'

I get a slow contemplative nod. 'Yes. And a man without power is open to reason, with any luck. I also want to ask him what he knows about Victoria and Edward, her son – my granddad. I was going to ask them when I dropped off the Christmas presents but turns out they'd popped over to visit friends in France.' A wry smile finds his lips and I know he's hiding the hurt. Yet again. 'Anyway, I'll take the notebook and let him read it.'

'A good idea. I'd love to know more,' The last bit of my plan, and one I've always wanted to put into action, is next. 'And talking of money, I've been thinking I might set up a little art school, part time? Using some of the money I had from the sale of the shop I could buy materials and maybe rent a workshop? It would be for local children, in the school hols, free tuition of course. Kids here need encouragement and opportunity, not fewer facilities. Cornwall is one of the poorest counties in England, and I'd love to feel I was making a difference to children's futures in a small way.'

Tremaine's broad smile could light up Blackpool Tower. 'That's a wonderful idea, Sennen! Perhaps I could help too once I've had a bit more practice?'

'Yeah, that would be brilliant!' I go round and sit on his lap. 'What an exciting year we have ahead. There's been so much change in my life lately, but good change.' I dip my head and kiss him.

'Oh, Sennen. At last, my dreams are about to come true. At last, my life is going to have some meaning, and it's all because of you.'

I trace the contour of his jawline and look into those beautiful eyes. My heart is too full to reply, so I let my lips do the talking.

Chapter Twenty-Four

My birthday and Valentine's Day dawn bright, cold and full of excitement. Tremaine has been very mysterious about what he's got planned for me and told me not to organise anything for the day. When I said I usually pop over to see my parents on my birthday, he'd said not to go, but not to worry, it was all in hand. Last week, he worked his final day as a lawyer, and he got back from seeing his father very late last night, so I'm keen to hear what his father made of it all. I only saw him briefly when he came to bed, as he was exhausted, but said the meeting had been good and he was glad it had happened.

As I'm opening a card from Jasmine, a raunchy one with a near naked man on the front, a near naked Tremaine comes into the kitchen, rubbing his eyes and yawning, his hair resembling a birds' nest. He stretches languidly and I run my gaze over his well-defined abs, and the contours of his bare chest. I'm about to follow my gaze with my fingers, but he ties the belt of his robe so I just say, 'Morning, sleepy head, fancy a full English?'

'I do. But I'll be the one making it because it's your birthday and Valentine's Day!' Tremaine takes me in his arms. 'Happy birthday, sweetheart. I love you.'

'Thank you, and I love you too.'

We kiss, and through the thin cloth of his pyjama bottoms, I can feel how happy he is to see me this morning. 'Fancy a birthday roll in the hay before breakfast?' he murmurs into my hair.

'Yes, please,' I whisper, and lead him upstairs.

Back downstairs we eat a leisurely breakfast at the kitchen table, and then Tremaine says with a wicked glint in his eye, 'I bet you're wondering what's going to happen today and what your present might be?'

He's right. I'm dying to know, but I reply, 'Maybe. But you're present enough.'

'Liar.' He laughs and pulls a card from underneath the fruit bowl and pushes it across the table towards me.

On the front is a lovely seascape and inside he's written:

To the one I love, today, tomorrow and always. Happy birthday, Sennen xxx

My heart swells with joy. 'That's beautiful, thank you.'

'Do you like the picture on the front?'

'It's stunning. Where did you get it?'

'I painted it and had it made into a card.'

'That's brilliant! You could maybe sell those too?'

'Yep. That's what I was thinking.' Tremaine stands up and moves to the doorway. 'I was also thinking we need to take a walk around the garden this fine, bright morning, and also to the forgotten beach for a paddle.'

'Sounds good to me,' I say, convinced by his mischievous grin that he has more than that up his sleeve.

'And I'll tell you all about what happened between me and Father too.'

Dressed warmly in jumpers, jeans and padded jackets, we walk around the garden in the pale winter sunshine. Despite the offshore breeze, in sheltered spots the sun tells us it's not far off spring, and she strokes our faces with a little warmth, encouraging our hearts to believe her. Some green shoots by the copse back her up too, and near the cliff edge in the longer grass, a carpet of snowdrops allow a few yellow daffodils to join their party.

'Won't be long until it's spring,' I say to Tremaine, crouching to stroke the delicate petals of the daffodils.

'I was thinking the same. I love this time of year. Everything is fresh and new, full of hope.'

I stand up and slip my arm through his. 'Like us.'

'Exactly like us,' he replies, and then points to the markings out of the swimming pool, now overgrown and abandoned. 'Shall we bother with a pool? I keep putting off making a decision.'

My mind's eye presents an image of children splashing around with inflatables in a sun-drenched pool, and Tremaine and me laughing as we watch. Judging it might be a bit soon to share it, I say, 'No need to decide now. Though it might be nice in the future.'

'When we've got a couple of ankle biters, you mean?'

My jaw drops. Is he a mind reader? 'I...'

He stops me with a kiss. 'You look a bit shocked.' He laughs. 'Don't let me railroad you. Let's go down to the beach, eh?'

His words have placed a bubble of contentment in my chest, because now I know that one day, with any luck, we will be parents. We make our way down the steps, firmly gripping the handrail as they are wet from the rain the night before. I always think of Victoria when I use them, how could I not? Would her life have been saved, if there had been a sturdy handrail there in the past? How different things would have been then.

Once on the beach, Tremaine taps me on the shoulder and says, 'Tag, you're it!' and sets off at a run along the beach.

I pull off my trainers and socks and set off in pursuit. I know he's hiding behind some boulders near the little cave, because I can see his hair waving above them in the breeze. It's hardly a beach for hide-and seek, being relatively small, with few places to hide. Nevertheless, memories of this childhood game put a tickle of excitement in my belly and trying not to let my laughter free and give the game away, I run lightly up to the boulders and climb over the back. From my vantage point I can see him crouched into a tight ball and he keeps peeping round the boulder down the beach towards the steps, then pulling his head back in again, like some crazed turtle. Splaying my toes wide on the wet, barnacle-encrusted boulders, I edge forward, tap him on the back and yell, 'Tag, you're it!'

Tremaine gives a start and turns round, his face a mixture of surprise and mirth. 'How the hell did you get up there?'

'I'm magic!'

'You are. But I'm gonna get you!' He gives a roar and launches himself at me, but I'm too quick and head for the sparkling azure slash of the ocean. Today the waves are topped with meringue peaks and cold as ice as they wash over my feet. I look behind me and laugh as Tremaine kicks off his shoes as he runs, and because I have my jeans rolled to the knee and he hasn't – he's wearing straight legs with no give in them – I imagine he'll stop as soon as the waves get to his toes, but I'm mistaken as he charges straight in and tags me, wet jeans and all.

'Stop!' I yell, as he picks me up and does a few tight turns in the water. He stumbles a bit because of the buffeting waves, and I think he'll end up dunking us both.

'Only if you promise to let me win. If you won't, you're going in the Atlantic!'

Tremaine's laughter is verging on the maniacal and he's wearing an expression stolen from a child hyper on sugar. Right now, I think he's capable of anything. 'Okay, okay!' I giggle. 'You win!'

He puts me down and we run out of the water hand in hand. On a boulder by the steps, we sit to get our breath back and watch the scene. Because the shape of the beach is a horseshoe, it's framed on two sides by the cliffs and we're sheltered for the most part against the wind. In the last few minutes, it's changed direction and is now coming off the land, so in the intermittent sunshine, it's quite pleasant. We watch a line of seven seagulls coast in from the right, calling to each other in raucous voices. From the left, two jackdaws swoop into the picture fast and low, landing on the boulders near the cave, and peck at something in a rockpool. Maybe an unsuspecting shrimp or two have appeared, just in time for brunch.

For a while, we sit in companionable silence, watching the clouds roll in and out of view, playing their own game of tag with the sun and shadows. A stillness envelops me as I acknowledge the peace without, and within. Time becomes static as I inhale deep breaths of the fresh salt air and exhale with it any remainder of worry or stress. And as I do, my soul rejoices in being alive. Being here. Tremaine's fingers snake through mine, warm, strong, dependable, and I rest my head on his shoulder.

'Ready to hear about my meeting with Father?'

'If you're ready to tell me, sweetheart.'

'Okay. I met him at one of his London houses. Mother was in Paris at some fashion show or other, so we could talk uninterrupted. However, he did let me know that he'd had to move some very important appointments to make time for me. Father knows exactly how to make a person feel welcome.' Tremaine rolls his eyes and sighs. 'Anyway, I jumped straight in and told him I'd left practising law, and all about my regrets of not following my dream because of his threat to cut me off from my inheritance. I said I aimed to put that right as soon as possible, and he could stick his bloody inheritance as far as I was concerned. I also told him about you, including that you're the granddaughter of the woman whom Great Uncle Jory fell for, and that we are living together.'

'Wow. Bet that shocked him!'

'Yeah, you could say that.' He's quiet for a moment, seemingly lost in thought as he watches a group of seagulls chase off the jackdaws. I don't interrupt, even though I'm so proud of him for standing up to his father like that and I'm bursting with questions. Tremaine needs to tell me in his own words and his own time. Then he says to the horizon, 'Predictably at first, he started gesticulating, pontificating, pacing the room, banging on about me throwing away a perfectly good career for an uncertain future, and had the audacity to ask if you were behind the changes. I said that yes, you were in a way, and I thanked God I'd found you, because you were the only person who'd shown me real love in a very long time. If ever.' Tremaine squeezes my hand and takes a moment.

My heart is with him and I want to take him in my arms and kiss away his pain, but I don't want to halt his train of thought. I kiss his cheek and squeeze his hand instead.

'He asked what I meant by that, so I told him in no uncertain terms how he made me feel over the years. The threatening to cut me off without a penny thing again, how they both made me feel, packing me off to boarding school, never wanting to spend time with me, the fact that my aunt, uncle and cousins showed me more love, affection and encouragement than my own parents ever did. That I never felt worthy of them. Never felt good enough. Always a failure. I also said that just recently, with your help, I realised that none of it was my fault. Instead, it was theirs alone. They had caused so much damage, and they should be ashamed.' Tremaine looks at me and his eyes fill with tears.

I find mine have followed suit, and I throw my arms around him and hold him as if I never want to let him go, and I don't. I won't. 'Oh, my poor baby. I'm so proud of you getting all that off your chest. It must have been incredibly hard to say it, but I'm glad you did. How did he take it?'

Tremaine wipes away his tears with the back of his hand and sighs. 'Surprisingly well. I expected more shouting and remonstration, but no. Father sat in his chair by the fire and stared into space, expressionless, as if someone had removed his senses. Then his gaze slowly came back into focus and he looked at me and shook his head. Father told me he had worried for some time that he'd been too harsh on me in the past, especially over the inheritance thing, but he did it only because he wanted to do the best for me. He said he was raised exactly the same way by his parents. At a distance. Boarding school fostered a strong sense of independence and strength of character. His father taught him to never settle for second best – failure wasn't an option. It might have been for some lesser men, but not for a Nancarrow.'

I know I'm trying to keep quiet, but this is too much. 'Hell, he sounds like he belongs in the nineteenth century!'

Tremaine chuckles. 'That's exactly what I said to him! I

also said that I knew he'd been to boarding school and that he was following in Grandad Edward's footsteps, he'd told me enough times over the years. Then I asked him if he'd actually been a happy child. Father answered "not particularly", but he'd understood that it would be all worth it in the end when he was as successful as Granddad Edward. I told him that wasn't good enough, because how could he raise me the same, knowing what an unhappy child he'd been himself? Aren't we supposed to learn from the past so that we don't repeat the same mistakes in the future?'

'Wow! What did he say to that?'

'Nothing. Said he'd not had much idea of how to be a parent. He just did what he thought was right. He admitted that Mother wasn't maternal. She was very fond of me, but Mother had always done her own thing. Parties, fashion shows, cocktails with friends, travelling. Things she enjoyed.' Tremaine shook his head, incredulous. 'I said to him that my mother also did exactly as Father told her to, so really boarding school and the raising at a distance was his idea, not hers.'

He looks over the ocean again and I can see him struggling for composure. I say, 'Let's stop now, if you like. Tell me another time.'

'No, there's not much more to say and I'd rather get it all out in one go if you don't mind?'

'Of course not. I just can't bear you hurting so much.'

'It gets better, don't worry.' Tremaine gives me a gentle smile. 'In the end he threw his hands in the air in defeat and said that he had no idea I'd felt so wretched, and that he would try to heal the rift between us. He admitted he had made mistakes, but maybe we could repair them together. I'd have to help point him in the right direction, as he wasn't very good at relationships. Then I got a warm hand-clasp and a back slap. No hug of course. That would be far too intimate.'

'Well, it's a good start and you're in a much better place than you were before you went.' I give him a hug. 'I'm so proud of you, Tremaine.'

Tremaine gives me a broad smile and his cheeks pinken. 'Do you know what? I'm proud of me too.' He puts his arm around me and gives me a squeeze.

'Good!' I chuckle and lean into him. Then I remember something. 'Oh, did you give him Victoria's notebook?'

'Yeah! He read it and was quite moved. Well, sort of – this is Father we're talking about. He got glassy-eyed for about a second, and said, "Well, well, well." Apparently, Father was told by my granddad Edward never to rely on anyone because they always let you down, just like his mother Victoria had. His grandparents told Edward his mother had run off with the gardener – or planned to – and left him and Jory with them. She didn't of course because she'd slipped and broke her neck.'

'But Victoria says in her notes that Edward and Jory were told to wait at the top of the steps with their belongings. Edward was seven, so didn't he remember any of that?'

'He did. But it was all very vague, as it would be, given the trauma of it all. Callum came up the steps distraught and took them back to the house. He was told later by his grandparents that she hadn't planned to come back for them at all. He didn't know what to believe, but as time went on, he accepted what they told him.'

Anger on Victoria's behalf simmers on my back burner. Her poor boys brainwashed like that. 'I expected as much! No wonder Edward found it hard to trust, and to love, probably. He passed it down the line to your dad and your dad passed it to you. Maybe your father is as much a victim of all that as you?'

Tremaine nods. 'Yes, perhaps. But as I said to him, if he was such an unhappy soul, why did he inflict the same on me? Times have changed. I was born in the 1990s, not the 1950s. We are so much more aware of various aspects of mental health and parenting. People have counselling and are more open about their feelings nowadays. Father should have learned something, surely?'

I have no answers for that. 'Who knows, my darling. But one thing is for sure. You have set the wheels in motion for a better relationship between you. We can only hope that Julian Nancarrow realises what a wonderful man his son is.'

All the pain etched into his face is suddenly obliterated by his sunshine-on-a-moody-ocean smile. He stands up and shoves his hands into the pockets of his puffer jacket, and just stares at me grinning like a loon. 'Anyhow. Enough of all that. It's time for your surprise.'

An excited butterfly does the rounds in my chest, and I get off the boulder and brush my jeans clean of sand. 'Come on then. Don't leave me in suspense.'

'I'd prefer it if you sat back down.' He gives a nervous laugh and his face turns pink again. 'Thing is, after Father had read the notebook and we'd finished talking about Victoria, he suddenly remembered he'd got some of her things that Granddad Edward had in an old box. It was all he'd had left of her, and despite all the hateful comments about his mother, he'd kept them safe all his life.' Tremaine swallows hard and shuffles his feet in the sand. The wind is trying to blindfold him with his hair, so he pushes it out of his eyes and drops to one knee. From his pocket he pulls a small, faded blue velvet box and opens it. 'This was Victoria's.'

I gasp. Inside, winking in the pale winter sunshine, sits a beautiful vintage sapphire ring corralled by a circle of diamonds. 'Oh my God,' I manage. Though I don't know how, because my heart's in my mouth.

Tremaine shifts his gaze from the ring to my face, and he asks in a tremulous voice, 'Sennen Kellow, will you do me the honour of being my wife?'

For a few seconds, the scene seems to freeze in time. I think I hear Victoria and Gran on the breeze whispering their blessing, then the waves crash to shore, breaking the spell and I hear myself say, 'Yes. Oh my God, yes!'

'You will? Phew!' Tremaine takes my trembling hand and places the ring on my finger. 'It fits perfectly!' he yells, pulling me up and leading me in a mad crazy dance around the beach. Then we stop and our lips meet in the most tender and loving kiss.

'I can't believe what just happened,' I breathe, watching the ring on my finger glint and sparkle in the sunshine.

'Neither can I. But I'm overwhelmed with joy that it has.' Tremaine kisses me again and then laughs. 'And I'm thrilled you said yes, because family and friends are going to be arriving in a few hours to celebrate!'

My jaw drops. 'What? How? Where?' I say to Tremaine's back as he takes off like a hare for the steps. I yell, 'Tremaine! Tremaine, come back here and explain yourself!' But all I get in answer is his laughter on the wind.

Chapter Twenty-Five

I'm still pinching myself when, three hours later, there's a crowd on the forgotten beach milling between three barbecues and various cold buffet and drinks tables, all serviced by professional caterers. There's Mum and Dad, Ruan and Gio, Jasmine and Rob, Miranda and her husband Harry, some of Tremaine's less pompous friends from work, some of my friends who run neighbouring shops in town, and Bob the builder and his wife Grace.

Earlier, when I'd caught up with Tremaine after he'd run away up the steps laughing like a hyena, I'd got him to explain how on earth he'd organised it all. To be honest I had to admit to myself that I was a bit disgruntled. Did he just assume I would say yes? He must have, because, being Tremaine, he would have felt a complete failure if I'd said no, and then he'd have had to explain to everyone who turned up to the party.

I smile to myself when I think of his 'ingenious plot' as he called it. Turns out that he'd already decided to ask me to marry him on my birthday – that it was Valentine's Day made it seem doubly romantic. When he'd told me a while ago that there would be a surprise for me on the day, he'd already got another ring. But when Julian had shown him Victoria's ring, he decided he'd take the first one back as the sapphire ring was perfect, and he knew it would hold so much more meaning for me. The celebration on the beach had been organised for a few weeks, and if I'd said no to his proposal, it would have turned into just the birthday bash, not a joint celebration for an engagement too.

At the moment I can hardly contain my excitement, because so far, everyone thinks it *is* just a birthday bash. Tremaine told me to keep our engagement a secret and hide the ring until he announced it. He's like a big kid at Christmas, but I like that. He would have had precious few happy Christmases when he was growing up. Going forward I will do everything in my power to make sure he has the happiest life possible. I love him so much, that when we're apart, it feels like I'm only half of the whole. How is that possible in such a short time? I don't know, but I'm certainly not complaining. Josh's betrayal is just a distant memory these days. What I felt for him couldn't have been true love, because it doesn't even come close to what I feel for Tremaine.

Jasmine waves and comes towards me with a plate piled high with barbecue food, just as Tremaine jumps on a boulder and claps his hands a few times. She stops and frowns at him and raises a questioning eyebrow at me, but I just smile. She's going to go off like a firework when she hears what he has to say.

'Can I have your attention one moment, ladies and gents?' The low murmur of conversation stops and everyone looks at Tremaine expectantly. Mum, who's standing a few feet away, glances at me, and I suddenly feel bad for not telling her first, but there's not been time. I just point discreetly to the third finger of my left hand and give her a little smile. She gets it immediately, and her jaw drops. Then she puts a trembling hand to her mouth and her eyes fill as she looks back at Tremaine. 'Thank you so much for coming today to celebrate Sennen's birthday, but we have a double celebration.' His smile is beatific as he holds his hand out to me.

I run across the sand, the sparkly blue dress I hurriedly changed into not the greatest attire for a blowy mid-February day. Pulling my jacket tighter around me, I step barefoot onto the flat boulder beside him, and slip the ring in my pocket onto the tip of my finger. I give him the nod. 'Ready,' I whisper.

'It's a double celebration ... because a few hours ago I asked this beautiful, kind, clever and most lovely woman to be my wife.' He looks at everyone and does a throaty laugh. 'And she said yes!'

I take my hand out of my pocket and he pushes the ring all the way onto my finger. Then he holds my hand up so people can see, and after a second of stunned silence, everyone cheers.

Mum hurries over to us and I jump down from the boulder to give her a hug. Tears are pouring down her cheeks and for a few moments she can't get her words out. 'Oh, Sen! Sen! How wonderful!' she says into my hair.

'It is, Mum. I'm sorry I couldn't tell you, but it only happened a few hours ago.'

She steps back and fishes a tissue from her pocket and blows her nose. 'Don't worry about that. I'm so happy for you both. Tremaine is perfect for you.'

I'm about to reply, but I'm nearly knocked off my feet by the force of a firework crashing into me – otherwise known as Jasmine. 'Sennen! OMG! Sennen!' is all I can get out of her while she jumps up and down hanging onto my hands as if she's on a pump-trolley on a railway track. 'I knew it! I knew this would happen! Nancy Cornish is never wrong!' Her red corkscrew curls are blowing wildly about her face and she's wearing her over-excited pixie expression.

I laugh and hug her. 'Yes, okay. Calm down.'

'Calm down? Calm down, she says! How can I calm down? This is the best news ever!' Rob, standing nearby, is grabbed and dragged over to me. 'Isn't it brilliant, Rob?' she says shaking his arm as if she's checking it's fixed in the socket properly.

'It is! Totally wonderful,' Rob says and gives me a big hug.

'Look at the ring.' She grabs my finger and thrusts it under her boyfriend's nose. 'It's the colour of the ocean.' She points to the waves, presumably just in case he doesn't know what the word 'ocean' means.

'And guess whose ring it used to be?' I say.

Her pixie expression is replaced by a series of frowns and twists of the mouth as she contemplates this. 'You got me. I don't think it was Morwenna's, 'cos no offence, it must be worth a bloody fortune, and she wasn't rich.'

'No, not Gran's. It was Victoria's.'

'Shut up! OMG, that is flipping amazing!'

Jasmine wants to know all the ins and outs of the story, but I can see Dad hovering, waiting to speak to me, so I say, 'I'll tell you later, okay?' Rob reads my mind and leads her off to the drinks table.

Dad steps forward and I can see by his face that he's only just holding it together. In place of words, he pulls me into a bear hug, and we just stand like that for a few moments. I can't speak. When he releases me, we both have matching tears and he clears his throat. 'Look at me.' He sniffs and swipes at his cheeks. 'Over the moon for you, Sen. Over the bloody moon.'

'Thanks, Dad. I'm over the moon for me too.'

'He's a good bloke, that Tremaine feller. Posh, but salt of the earth with it.' Then he goes in search of Mum, who's busy telling Grace how she knew we would get together as she felt it in her water.

By this time Tremaine's joined me, and after Ruan and Gio have given us a hug and said how pleased they are at the news, everyone else comes up to individually congratulate us. It's been such a wonderful afternoon. I still can't believe it and want to keep celebrating for ever. But in just a few hours, as it's February and nearly five-fifteen, the sun decides to pack up the day until tomorrow. The caterers have packed up too, and there's just two left, disassembling a table. Tremaine suggests we all return to the house to get warm and have a cuppa, which is readily accepted by our little party.

Across the midnight sky, the moon sails above the ocean like an escaped party balloon. I watch it for a few moments, transfixed by the beauty of the scene, before closing the bedroom curtains and climbing into bed with my fiancé. My fiancé! I will never tire of saying those words, even though I haven't yet, except in my head. As I snuggle down next to him, he pulls me into his arms and asks, 'Was it a good birthday then, my love?'

'The best.' I run my hand over his chest and kiss him. 'You'll have to think of something to beat it next year. Because as you know, I'm a very demanding woman.'

Tremaine traces his fingers across my stomach. 'And are you too tired for some of my demands right now?'

'Never,' I murmur, and move my hand lower.

Four weeks later I'm still walking on air and spring is in full bloom. Like Tremaine, I adore this time of year, it's full of hope and promise. We've already put some of our plans in motion and we've found a workshop to rent for the school holidays. Next, we are going to do a leaflet drop to some local community centres and the nearest primary school to advertise our classes, and Tremaine is working on his paintings from home. Each day he seems to grow happier, blooming like the daffodils in the garden. It's wonderful to see. The weight of his past and his old job is diminishing day by day, and at last he can be his true self.

I'm in the shop this afternoon sorting through some orders and checking we have enough of the old favourites ready for the tourist season which will be upon us very soon. On the countertop is a postcard from Antigua, depicting a hammock strung between two palm trees on the beach. It came this morning. Uncle Pete and Greta are having a whale of a time on their travels and they want to wish Tremaine and me every happiness. Mum must have told him about our engagement, as they email each other every month. I'm so happy for him. Who would have thought when he came in here last year and told me he wanted to sell up that everything would work out for the best in the end? Certainly not me.

I'm just about to go and put the kettle on when my phone rings. It's Miranda. We met for coffee last week and I'm beginning to think we will be really good friends. She wasn't cross that I'd accidentally betrayed her confidence to Tremaine and she was over the moon that everything had worked out. I'm so glad Tremaine had her to spend time with when he was a kid. Although we haven't set a date for our wedding, we've tentatively pencilled in spring next year, and Miranda has a friend who makes the most stunning wedding dresses. Maybe this is what she wants to talk about.

'Hi Miranda, how's tricks?' A sob on the line twists my gut and I grab the side of the counter. Something is wrong. Very wrong, I can feel it. 'Miranda? Miranda, what is it?'

'It's … it's Tremaine,' she says, her voice thick with tears.

'Tremaine? What's happened!' My heart is thumping so

hard I can hear it in my ears. I slide down the wall to sit on the floor. My legs refuse to support me.

Miranda heaves a sigh. 'That crazy bitch Olivia called me to say there'd been an accident. She went to see him at Nancarrow and he was walking on the beach. She was out of it as usual on God knows what, and there was an altercation between them on the steps. Somehow…' Miranda exhales. I don't want to hear what comes next, but I can't not hear it. 'Somehow he fell and hit his head. She called an ambulance … he's in hospital—'

'NOOO! No, this can't be happening!!' My stomach rolls again and I rush to the kitchen sink dry retching.

Miranda's still talking in my ear. 'He's in a bad way, but where there's life, there's possibility. Don't give up hope.'

Don't give up hope? People say that when they know things are hopeless, don't they? I can't believe it. My brain is flailing, trying to process what's happened, but not really comprehending the conclusion. It must be some kind of a mistake. He might have got a broken arm or something. Somebody somewhere at the hospital has got it wrong. A nurse or a doctor who's worked a ten-hour shift has given Miranda the wrong information. My lovely man can't be 'in a bad way'. He's strong, full of life … we're getting married, living happily ever after. We drank from the parting glass. Everything is going to be fine. Everything. A tempest of a storm builds in my chest, and despite putting a hand over my mouth a huge sob bursts out through my fingers.

'Oh, Sennen, my poor darling. Shall I come and get you, take you to him?'

Miranda's voice sounds like it's coming from a long way

off, as if I'm waking from a bad dream and the TV is still on, playing to itself. Maybe that's it. Maybe I've dreamed it all.

'Sennen? Sennen, are you listening? Shall I come and collect you – take you to the hospital?'

Her voice is clearer now. Less like background noise. Sharp, and clear ... and horribly real. Still, my brain rebels. I can hardly process her words. I clutch the edge of the sink; my world is spinning and I want to scream. Miranda's asking over and over if I'm okay. Eventually, I submit to the truth. I take a moment and slow my breathing enough to say, 'Yes. Yes, come and get me. And come quickly!'

Chapter Twenty-Six

The incessant beep, beep, beep of the heart monitor makes me want to punch the sterile white wall next my chair. I want to punch everything. I want to scream and rage and yell. I want to find Olivia and rip her limb from limb. How dare she do this? How dare she fucking walk into our lives and tear it apart like this? My Tremaine. My beautiful man is lying ashen-faced in the hospital bed in front of me. He's still and silent. Eyes closed, unruly curls covered by a bandage, tubes in his nose and mouth like synthetic vines. Machines are keeping him alive, measuring his existence in beeps and ticks. Hums and sighs.

Miranda shifts position in the chair beside me. 'Do you want more coffee? I know it tastes disgusting, but it's wet and warm.'

'No, thanks. And don't feel the need to come every day, you have writing to do. Mum is coming this evening and Jasmine will be coming soon.' I squeeze her hand. 'You've been wonderful over these past few days. Thank you.'

'I've wanted to be here with you, Sennen. I can't concentrate on anything when I'm home anyway.' Miranda tucks her dark bob behind her ears and touches Tremaine's hand. 'I still can't believe it's all happened. It's like being in some surreal dream.'

I nod. 'A nightmare, more like.' I stare at my fiancé and think again about what the consultant told us yesterday. The operation to reduce the swelling on his brain went as well as could be expected, and now he's in an induced coma to give it a chance to heal. When I asked the consultant if Tremaine would make a full recovery, he said time would tell. There could be some damage. But until the swelling has gone down, and he's had a scan, they won't know. I wish he'd lied. Wish he'd said of course he'd make a full recovery and he'd be as good as new in a few days. Because the truth is gut-wrenching. Terrifying. What if he doesn't recover? What if he's brain-damaged? What if he can't function? And the most horrifying 'what if' is always there hiding in the darkest corners of my mind, just waiting … what if we have to make the decision to switch off the machines?

I jump up and run to the window and press my forehead against the cool glass, wishing I could push through it, fly away somewhere to a parallel universe where none of this is happening. Since the accident, I've been trying to block 'what if' thoughts like this from my head, but they keep coming. Keep slipping through the flimsy barriers and gouging great chunks from my heart. I give a start when I feel Miranda's hand on my shoulder.

Her tone is hushed, gentle. 'Hey, come on. He'll be absolutely f—'

'Fine? Please don't say that, Miranda. You don't know, and neither does anyone else.'

'Yes, but we have to believe he will be well.'

'Think positive, yeah, right.' Why am I being horrible to her? She's been nothing but kind. I turn to face her. 'I'm sorry, Miranda. Ignore me. You aren't to blame.'

She gives me a quick hug to show she understands. 'No. Olivia is.' She wanders back to the hard blue chairs and sits down. 'I can't believe she thinks that everything will be okay for her, just because she called the ambulance and went to the police to admit she was under the influence of drugs and booze.'

An image of Olivia's perfect face floats in my mind's eye, and I want to punch it as rage, never very far away, boils in my veins. 'She's on another bloody planet! I mean, you said that she told you she went to Nancarrow to beg Tremaine to dump me and take her back, after finding out he was engaged. Said he'd made a mistake. What kind of a person is so sodding arrogant to think he'd agree?'

Miranda nods. 'Olivia is certainly arrogant. Entitled. But she told me she loved him so much she would try anything to get him back.' She looks at Tremaine and her eyes brim over. 'Wish it had been her who fell down the fucking steps.'

I agree and ask a question that's been nagging away for a while at the back of my mind. 'Do you think she pushed him? You know, after he told her there was no way he'd do as she asked, and tried to get her to leave?'

She seems unsurprised by this question. 'Who knows? But I doubt it, as she's totally obsessed with him. I can't see her deliberately hurting him.' Miranda sighs and looks back to me. 'No. I think that what she said is true. Tremaine told her to leave, took her elbow and tried to guide her up the steps back to the house. She stumbled and fell against him. He was at the opposite side to the handrail, lost his footing and slipped.'

As she's talking, I can picture the scene vividly. Olivia was probably wearing her bloody Louboutins or something, which would have made it even more likely that she'd stumble. Coupled with the fact she was off her head on booze and drugs yet again, poor Tremaine would have been trying to help her gently up the steps, as well as escort her to the house. Wish he'd have dragged her up them by the hair. Frogmarched her along with a swift kick in the pants at the top. I glance at Miranda. 'I wonder if she'll be charged?'

Miranda throws her hands up. 'If she is, it won't stick. She's a lawyer, don't forget, and she'll have lots of fancy expensive lawyer friends to choose from to get her off, if it goes to court.'

We sit in silence and stare at Tremaine, both lost in our own thoughts. A little while later the door opens, and in comes a nurse. 'Hello, there's two more visitors for Tremaine, but I'm afraid there's only two permitted at a time.' She looks at me. 'Maybe you could wait in the cafeteria?'

Miranda and I share a puzzled frown. We aren't expecting visitors. Well, apart from Jasmine, but she's not due for another hour or so. I'm about to ask the nurse who it is, when a tall man with grey hair and Tremaine's eyes squeezes past the nurse, pulling a slight, elfin-featured woman with dark curly hair in after him.

'Uncle Julian,' Miranda says, getting to her feet, 'and Aunty Katherine.'

I jump up and try not to look surprised. Miranda contacted Tremaine's parents after the accident happened, but they were in Australia visiting old friends. They were all on an outback jaunt, miles from civilisation, so it had been over twenty-four hours before she'd managed to speak to them. They said they'd get back as soon as they could. Because of what I know about them, I imagined it would be a while, but to get here so fast, they must have jumped on a plane immediately.

Julian nods. 'Miranda.' I get a quick scan and then he hurries over to his son's bed. Katherine follows, her composed expression crumbles and she sits on my vacated chair and rests her head on Tremaine's arm. Her shoulders start to shake and her sobs reverberate around the room. Julian puts a hand on her back and a single tear slips down his cheek.

I whisper to Miranda that I'll be waiting in the cafeteria, and she says she'll follow on after she's explained Tremaine's condition to her aunt and uncle.

───────────────

I'm on my second hot chocolate, and just ended a call to Jas telling her not to come, when the door opens, and in come Tremaine's parents. Miranda follows them and directs them to my table, then points at her watch and mimes that she'll see me later, then she's gone. Oh God. She can't leave me alone with them. I don't know what to say to them. I've had enough trauma to deal with lately, without being thrown to the Nancarrow wolves. Hastily dabbing at my mouth for chocolate stains, I stand and extend my hand. Julian shakes it warmly, and to my surprise, Katherine gives me a brief hug. Must be jet-lagged. Then I tell myself off. *Give her a chance. Tremaine is her son. She's obviously worried sick.*

'It's lovely to meet you, Sennen,' Julian says, sitting down. 'We've heard so much about you.'

Katherine follows suit. 'Yes, Tremaine is so happy to be getting married...' Her voice fades. 'Or was...' She dabs a tissue at the corners of her eyes.

Julian pats her hand. 'Now, let's have none of that. Our boy will be right as rain again soon, eh, Sennen?'

I want to ask how he knows this, and how he's the cheek to call him 'our boy', when all through his childhood 'his boy' was treated as an inconvenience by him, but of course I don't. 'That's the plan.' I manage a watery smile and realise tears are waiting in the wings. To distract them I ask, 'Can I get you a coffee, hot chocolate or anything?'

Julian stands. 'I'll get them. My backside is numb from sitting on endless flights. I need to stretch my legs.'

Katherine and I smile at each other, and then silence builds a slow but steady wall between us. 'Hell of a flight for you,' I say, just to halt its progress.

'Yes. And we had to travel four hundred miles in a jeep to start with. Our friends live in Sydney but we decided on taking a crazy trip to...' Katherine's voice is drowned out by a sob and she covers he mouth to prevent more escaping.

'Oh, Sennen. I can't get the image of my poor boy out of my head. I can't bear it. I don't know what I'll do if … if…'

Despite my recent thoughts about the way both she and Julian treated Tremaine in the past, I can't help but let my heart go out to her. She's rubbing her eyes with a balled-up tissue, obviously unconcerned about what remains of her eye make-up. Her fingers tremble as she absently starts to shred it. The woman is genuinely distraught. I put my hand over hers. 'Don't say it. Don't even think it.'

A half-smile finds her mouth and right then, she looks more like her son than her husband does. 'No. No, you're right. I need to be strong. Like you. You must be going out of your mind too.'

'The last few days have been tough, to say the least.'

Katherine pulls a clean tissue from her bag and gives her nose a delicate blow. 'I know you might not understand, not having children of your own. But until I saw him lying like a dead thing in the hospital bed, I didn't know quite how much I loved him. From being little, he's always been independent, strong, went his own way. Julian and I always encouraged it. Julian impressed upon me that it didn't do to mollycoddle a child.'

I bite my lip to prevent myself from coming out with *There was no bloody danger of that with you two cold fish.*

'Then, when he was older, I realised we had drifted apart, because we did our own thing. I've never been much of what you might call maternal … but Julian told me how our son was feeling about all that, and their heart-to-heart recently.' Katherine's eyes fill and spill over again. 'Oh, Sennen. I promise you and him that if he survives this, I will do my utmost to make amends. I will ask his forgiveness and do my best to be a better mother.'

At that moment, Julian comes over and puts a tray of coffee down on the table. 'That goes for me as well. We both want to be better parents and hopefully parents-in-law too.'

There's so much I could say, so many things I want to blame them for. So many questions I want to ask them and some harsh home truths I want to tell them. But right now, looking into their pinched faces full of emotion and regret, all I can say is 'Of course he'll survive. And because you're willing to work at your relationship, I know that things will work out okay between you. I can see how much you care for Tremaine, and in the end, love is all we need, isn't it?'

———

Later, as I close the bedroom curtains against another balloon moon and slip under the covers of a bed that's too big for me, I wonder if my comments to Tremaine's parents were just a load of rubbish. Is love really all we need? Thumping my pillow, I settle down and before I switch off the light, I stare at the parting glass, which has pride of place on the bookshelf. Right now, I want to smash it. Was I right after all? Is the damned thing cursed – not a cup of kindness at all, but a cup of cruelty? Why the hell did I insist on digging it out of the past? I should have left well enough alone.

I close my eyes and think about Victoria and Callum, and Gran and Jory, both incredibly happy on New Year's Eve, when the glass showed them the truth and joy within their hearts. Then a short time later, devastated, broken, desolate, alone. Will that be me? Will we suffer the same fate? I switch out the light, and as I'm drifting into oblivion, I hear Gran's voice reading out the words of her letter –

This glass gave me the truth I'd hidden from my heart. It gave me the courage to go for the impossible dream and welcome the love of my life into my arms. We shared the briefest, yet most joyful time together, and I don't regret a single moment. Not one. May the glass bring you the same good fortune, and that you too will be lucky enough to find the same joy. Brief or long lasting, love and happiness are the greatest gifts of all.

I mutter, 'Great gifts they certainly are. But will the memory of the time we've had together be enough to get me through the rest of my life, if I lose him?' Right now, I don't think so.

———

It's been almost two weeks since Tremaine's parents came to the hospital. They have been there every day like me, and we have got to know each other much better. I have one of Mum's old friends to help out in the shop, so I am able to be with Tremaine for at least half a day, every day. His parents are here for the other half and we overlap somewhere in the middle. I steered clear of asking probing questions about their 'parenting', of course, but during the endless hours of our vigil at Tremaine's bedside, we have talked more about our lives, our interests and our future plans. Well, as far as we can... Much of that depends on Tremaine's recovery. As far as that's concerned, nothing's changed. Last week they stopped the sedative drip and said he would start to wake up when he was ready. So far, he hasn't.

As I walk onto the ward this morning, I do as I always do. I make a wish and ask Gran and Victoria for any blessing they might send our way. My wish is always the same. *I wish my darling well again.* I tell myself he will be. The doctors say he's doing well and the swelling has reduced, but until he wakes, we won't know for sure. Outside the door to his room, I close my eyes and wrinkle my nose at the bouquet of disinfectant, hospital dinners and people's anxiety permeating the sterile air. How I wish he was home at Nancarrow, walking on the forgotten beach, the wind making streamers of his hair, the sun burnishing his skin, the sea salt on his lips...

I take a deep breath before I enter. I'm hoping to see a flicker of life in his face. A twitch of an eyebrow, a flutter of his long dark eyelashes, against his pale skin, anything to let me know Tremaine's in there, desperately trying to come back to me. Any sign will do. Anything at all but the prone, waxwork figure masquerading as my Tremaine that greets me every day. Silent, distant, lifeless. Swallowing my nerves, I push open the door and step inside. Despair casts a leaden net over my heart and drags it down. Against the crisp white sheets, he looks even paler today, if that's possible. I wouldn't be surprised if he disappeared. A ghost of the man I love.

In the mirror above the sink, I see a woman with tired blonde curls tumbling around a mask of grief. Faded blue eyes edged by a pair of crow's feet stare out from under a deeply furrowed brow and bright-red lipstick failing in its attempt at cheery is slicked across a mouth turned down at the corners like a crazed clown's. Old beyond her years. What happened to me? I swallow down a lump in my throat. *The accident is what happened to me.* Then I glance at Tremaine and pull myself together. He needs me to be cheerful, upbeat. The doctors say he might be able to hear and understand what we say. So I square my shoulders, toss my hair and smile at the crazed clown. Just like that, Sennen's back. Back, and ready to fight.

I sit down on the chair next to Tremaine's bed and take his hand in mine. His big strong hand with the artist's fingers that deftly create such stunning seascapes. The same hands and fingers that hold me tight, caress my skin as if I am a canvas, setting my senses afire with a few delicate strokes. I feel my smile slipping, so pin it back in place and make sure it's there in my voice when I say, 'Good morning, my darling. How are you? Is today going to be the day when you give me that sign I've been waiting for? Come on, Tremaine. You've had plenty of time to rest now, you old lazybones.'

Tremaine says nothing. His chest rises and falls. Machines feed him oxygen and monitor his vital signs, his hand is warm in mine, but his soul? His soul is far away. I can sense it. He's probably surfing the Atlantic rollers or playing tag with an imaginary me on the forgotten beach. Perhaps he's painting or practising a few pots. Wherever he is, I hope he's carefree and not in pain. Leaning forward I kiss his cheek. I can't kiss his lips, as the oxygen mask prevents it. But at least I'm near him, beside him every step of the way.

'You will be well soon; I can feel it.' I tap the left side of his chest lightly. 'There's too much life in there waiting to be lived, and I'm gonna be walking alongside you. I'm not going anywhere fast, are you listening?' I move a strand of hair and place my lips gently on his forehead. A pang of sadness as sharp as any knife lodges in my throat. His familiar smell is gone. It's been gradually diluted by hospital soap, shaving foam and other toiletries unfamiliar to me since the first day he came in. Now there's nothing left of that distinct Tremaine smell. The orange and pear shampoo, the lemon and bergamot cologne, the fresh clean smell of his skin, sometimes infused with salt air. All gone.

Though I have tried to keep my emotions at bay, a tear escapes and falls on his face. Then another. I wipe them away with a finger and kiss his cheek again. As I move back, I see his brow furrow slightly. My heart skips and I hold my breath, stare at his forehead, will it to happen again. Nothing. 'Hey, are you waking up?' I say, and squeeze his hand. I nearly shoot through the ceiling when I feel a slight pressure in return. Oh my God. He's waking up. He's really waking up! Tremaine's eyelids flutter and a low moan escapes his mouth. Relief floods my system and hope lifts my heart. *Thank God. Thank God, it's happening!* But as I stand up to go and get a nurse, I realise something is wrong. Very wrong.

A twitch of the eyebrow spreads like wildfire to twitches all over his body. He's moaning, bucking, and his arms thrash themselves against the mattress. An alarm starts on one of the machines and after a second of fear-induced stupefying inactivity, I race from the room to find someone, but they're already running in. A doctor and three nurses block my view of Tremaine as they call out instructions and start to work on him. I scream as the enormity of the scene registers in my fear-numbed brain, and then I'm aware of a firm pair of hands on my shoulders as someone escorts me from the room.

A nurse with kind brown eyes sits me down, tells me to try not to worry and that they will do everything they can, but it's important that I must wait there. Then she hurries back into Tremaine's room. My whole body starts to tremble, so I wrap my arms around myself and stare at the white wall in front of me, read the same logo over and over on an NHS information poster – *One and All, We Care*. I look at the ceiling and make a plea to the heavens. 'Please let my Tremaine live. Please. If there's anyone listening. Please. I don't know what I will do without him.' Nobody answers. My brain goes into freefall.

Chapter Twenty-Seven

Six Months Later

The August sun winks off the rim of the parting glass as I hold it up to the blue heavens. I watch, fascinated as always, as the figures begin their endless dance when I twist the stem. How lucky am I to be sitting on a warm boulder on the forgotten beach in the height of summer? The rest of the Cornish coastline will be bursting at the seams with holidaymakers, but not here. On this beach it's deserted, pristine and quiet, apart from the ancient song of the ocean, and the occasional cry of a gull.

Last night, Gran came to me in a dream and told me it was time to put the glass back where I found it. Someone else in the future deserved to have the benefit of its powers, and to feel the thrill of past and present joining as one. I had been thinking it might be time to put it back where it belongs for a while, but Gran confirmed it. I've got a new metal box to keep it in. The old one was so rusted and damaged by time and salt air that it wasn't fit for purpose. But I will keep the old one safe and look at it from time to time.

I lower the glass and bring it close to my face so I can see the detail of the beautiful engraving. Now it comes to parting with the parting glass, I'm not sure I can. It brought me so much happiness, and I think back to that cold and starry night in December, only eight months ago, when I took a sip from it. And suddenly I'm back in the moment. I hear the church bells ringing in the New Year, feel again the fire through my whole body, every vein and sinew alive with an exhilarating energy, and in my heart, there's the unshakeable truth. My heart's desire is Tremaine. Tremaine, today, tomorrow and always. My beautiful Tremaine with the reflection of fireworks in his eyes and love in his heart. My man. The love of my life.

Out on the ocean in the distance, there's a little blue boat with white sails, gliding slowly past. I wonder if they can see me on the beach. I wave just in case. The boat looks so serene, sure of its destination. Like me, I realise. All of the uncertainty of the last few months, all the worry, anguish and heartbreak are over. At last, I know what lies ahead. I'm so grateful for all the love and support I've had over these past terrible months. Jasmine has been worth her weight in gold. Her crazy sense of humour and *joie de vivre* have lifted me out of many dark holes of despair and into the light of hope. Mum has been brilliant too. Her shoulder to cry on must be rusty by now with all the tears it's soaked up from me. I find myself smiling, and taking a deep breath of salt air I wrap the glass in a soft, thick cloth and place it in the new metal box. Then I fold the letter I've written for the next treasure seeker to find, and place it on top, with Gran's old one. I wish Tremaine was here on the beach with me. We could walk to the cave together, say goodbye to the parting glass together … but he isn't here. How could he be?

Before I close the lid of the box, I look up again and gaze out towards the hazy blue smudge of the horizon, welding sea to sky. I think of Victoria and Callum, Gran and Jory, me and Tremaine, and I tell the sky how grateful I am, and how lucky I am to have met Tremaine and fallen so hopelessly in love. But love is never hopeless, is it? Love and happiness are the greatest gifts of all. Victoria and Gran said so. I know now, more than ever, that Gran was right about ignoring her misgivings about her and Jory being too different, and going for her dream, despite happiness not lasting for ever.

The hours I sat by Tremaine's bedside were some of the most heartrending, and painful. I didn't know if our happiness would be short-lived, but I will never regret being there for him. Love gets you through, despite the heartache. I think about the time I'd held his hand and my tears fell on his cheek … and everything that came after. My heart squeezes and pushes a lump into my throat. Everything happens for a reason. Gran was fond of saying that too. Something tells me she and Victoria are waiting in the cave to help me say goodbye. Perhaps it's the glass on my knee conjuring their spirits again. Or maybe they will always live in my heart now. Perhaps they are a part of me. I hope so.

As I close the lid and get to my feet, I hear a shout from the top of the steps.

'Sennen! Wait, I'm coming with you!'

Turning and shielding my eyes from the sun, I see Tremaine holding onto the handrail with one hand and brandishing his metal crutch in the air with the other like a marauding pirate. 'Stay there! You can't manage the steps yet! You're supposed to be resting.' I run over to the steps and begin my ascent.

'I can!' He laughs. 'I'm perfectly fine if I hold onto the rail and use my crutch for balance. And I do nothing else but bloody rest. It's driving me crazy!'

Halfway up the steps I stop. There's no point in arguing. He's got that determined glint in his turquoise blues, and admittedly, these last few weeks since he came home from hospital he's been recovering at breathtaking speed. He was out of the wheelchair and on crutches much quicker than any of the medical professionals imagined, and he even had a go at painting yesterday with stunning results. 'Okay. But please be careful.' With my heart in my mouth, I watch his slow progress, a little at a time – a shuffle, a hop and a step, a shuffle, a hop and a step –until he's at the bottom and in my arms.

'Told you I could do it,' he says with a big sunny triumphant grin.

'Yes, you did. But let's sit on the boulders a while before we go to the cave, eh?'

'Anything you say, dear one.' I help him down and we sit and look at the waves, hand in hand. 'God, it's good to be on this beach again. There was a time when I thought I'd never walk again.'

I snort in derision. 'There was a time when I thought you'd never survive at all! Funnily enough I was just thinking about the day you woke up and went into seizure. It was one of the worst moments of my life, but then, thank God, you pulled through.'

He holds me close. 'I know. That must have been such a scary time for you. And I know you think it's mad, but I swear it was you who woke me, like a reversal of *Sleeping Beauty*. A magic kiss on my cheek and tears of love on my skin. You are my Princess Charming.'

I laugh. 'Yeah, it's mad, but I like it.'

'Yes. And you're amazed by the way I've quickly bounced back too.' He looks at me, pride in his eyes.

'Me and everyone else who loves you.'

He kisses the top of my head. 'Yeah. And I suppose on the positive side, Mother and Father have become much more like a proper mum and dad lately. Can't keep them away!' He laughs.

'Yes. I think it took nearly losing you to realise how much they loved you. Weirdos.' I laugh too. 'Actually, why don't you start calling them Mum and Dad? I'm sure they'd love it.'

Tremaine frowns and stares at the ocean thoughtfully. 'Hmm. Perhaps. It feels a bit odd though. Let's take it one step at a time.'

'Like you just did, coming down those?' I nod at the steps.

'Yeah. Exactly.'

'Bloody Olivia.'

'Yeah.'

'It doesn't seem fair that she got just twelve months' suspended sentence. All the heartache she caused.'

'I know. But then she would. She had one of the best lawyers.'

'And you didn't want to press charges.'

'No. It was an accident. Yes, I know she shouldn't have been here in the first place. But she was an addict. Olivia didn't know what she was doing most of the time. Now she's in rehab, she'll hopefully recover and never bother me again. She's lost her job, so it's not as if she's escaped punishment completely.'

A rumble of irritation at his – in my opinion – misplaced compassion passes through me, but I can't be bothered to argue about her. I say, 'If she does, she will have me to answer to. And you can be damned sure she won't come off best.'

'Ooh, I love you when you get feisty.'

I laugh. 'Do you love me when I'm not feisty?'

'I love you in all your moods, Mrs Nancarrow.'

I give him a gentle shove. 'I'm not Mrs Nancarrow yet, silly.'

'No. But you will be by the end of the summer.'

A shiver of excitement replaces the rumble of irritation. 'Do you think the beach is going to be big enough for all the guests?'

'Yeah. As I said last week, we can get married on the beach, and then people can wander round the gardens and in the house too. It will all be grand.' He kisses me. 'It just feels somehow fitting that we get married on the forgotten beach. This very spot brought you to me, after all.'

'It did. The beach and the parting glass, of course. Let's not forget that … or all those who've used it in the past,' I add, almost to myself. Because they did. I'm convinced their spirits drew me here, guided my hand.

'And now we've found each other, we can spend the rest of our lives loving each other and making a difference to the lives of lots of other people, with any luck.'

'Starting with the art classes in the October school holiday.'

'Can't wait.'

'You'll have to if you're not well enough.'

'Oh please. Look at me. Do I look well enough?' Tremaine wiggles his eyebrows at me and pulls a sexy pout.

'You look absolutely gorgeous as usual.' I chuckle, take his face in my two hands and place a kiss on his mouth. 'Wanna read the letter I've written?' I ask, nodding at the box.

'No. You read it to me.'

'I might cry.'

'Blub away. It's good for you,' he says, with a smile.

'Okay. I took the first and last lines from Gran's letter – it felt the right thing to do … as if I was continuing her story, you know?' Already I can feel a knot forming in my throat and hope it will untie itself so I can read it all. I look at Tremaine. 'Right. Here goes.' I take the letter out and clear my throat.

'To whom it may concern,

This glass gave me the truth I'd hidden from my heart. It gave me the courage to allow myself to love. To give myself totally, and utterly to the one I want to walk alongside for the rest of my life. Despite being from very different worlds, I knew deep within that our souls were one, forever united. Today, tomorrow and always. Brief or long lasting, love and happiness are the greatest gifts of all.

Sennen – granddaughter of Morwenna.'

Pleased that I managed it without crying, I look up to see silent tears trickling down Tremaine's cheeks. 'Looks like you're blubbing to me,' I say, in a wobbly voice. I sniff and dab at my eyes. 'Stop it. You're setting me off.'

'It's a beautiful letter, Sen. Just like you.' He lifts my chin and gives me a tender kiss. 'Are you putting your and Morwenna's letters together in the box?'

'Yes. I'm setting a new trend.' I laugh. 'Hopefully future generations will do the same.'

I fold the letter inside Gran's and put them both in the box and close the lid. This is it, then. Time to take the cup of kindness back to its home. I don't feel sad anymore that I'm parting with it. Not now Tremaine's here with me to say goodbye. I help him up and he puts one arm around my shoulder and the crutch under the other.

'Okay. I'm ready,' he says. And together we make our way towards the little cave on our forgotten beach. I smile. Except it's no longer forgotten. We'll make sure it's remembered, always.

Acknowledgments

Firstly huge thanks to my fantastic editor, Charlotte Ledger (Legend), who asked me to write a story with the title – *The Forgotten Beach*. On the one hand it was a little daunting, to be given only a title, but mainly it was a huge honour. She believed in my ability as a writer to take just a title and turn it into a novel! Thank you, Charlotte. Having you in my corner is half the battle.

A big thanks to my daughter Tanya and her partner Emma for helping me choose the Cornish names of the some of the characters. Emma is Cornish, so had lots of great advice.

To my fab writer friends who are always there to lend an ear or two, Mel Hudson, Linda Huber, Kelly Florentia, Celia Anderson and Lynda Stacey, to name but a few. And of course, thanks too to all my friends, lovely readers and bloggers who have given so much support to me and my writing over the years – you know who you are.

Last but not least, love and thanks to my husband Brian and wider family, I couldn't do this without you all.

Author's Note

The dedication is to Ronan who is now eleven. He was only ten last summer when we had fun sitting in a caravan, brainstorming ideas for this book. We were on a family holiday just down the coast from us near Hayle. Even though we were restricted in what we could do because of Covid, Brian, Tanya, Emma, Ronan and his younger sister Esmé helped made each day very special. Esmé is always up for an adventure and her boundless energy and laughter is infectious!

One morning, I got up early and sneaked out of the caravan before anyone was awake. There wasn't a soul on the beach and the sun was just rising over the Atlantic. Everything was calm and peaceful - the ocean shushed as it rolled into shore, and a few seagulls called to each other from the cliffs. Perfect. I could almost imagine I was on my own forgotten beach... and then the poem that opens this book just popped into my head! I videoed the scene with my phone and spoke the poem out loud so I would remember it later. A special moment which will always stay with me.

Thanks so much for reading *The Forgotten Beach*, and I hope you enjoyed it!

READ ON FOR AN EXTRACT FROM *A SECRET GIFT*...

Escape to Cornwall for another enchanting, heartwarming novel about friendship, hope and second chances...

'A charming and original concept'
Sunday Times bestseller Katie Fforde

'A highly original story with more than a hint of Cornish magic'
Celia Anderson, bestselling author of *59 Memory Lane*

A Secret Gift

CHAPTER ONE

The calendar on the kitchen wall tells me three things. It's February, it's Friday and you've been gone three years. The last one's a lie. Has to be. Because you're here with me always. In my heart, my thoughts, your essence alive in every room. Late at night, if I half close my eyes, I can see you sitting in your chair by the fire. I can hear your footfall on the stair, your laughter on the wind as I open the bedroom window. I stare at the scene on the calendar. There's a bent and battered tree on a hill by the ocean. Its stark branches are silhouetted against a winter sunset, fighting with the wind to remain anchored. The tree and I have a lot in common. Melancholy waits in my depths. It's seeking a chance to break free – swim to my surface, claim my day. I mustn't let it. I've a job to do.

St Margaret's Residential Home sits at the top of a rain-soaked Newquay hill. Its windows gaze out over the town to the far Atlantic horizon, which today is a charcoal line, joining together sky and water. I wonder how Hope Trebarwith is today as I hurry up the steps. The old lady hasn't been well at all over the past two weeks. I've grown so fond of her with her daft sense of humour and wise words. I hate to think of a time when she'll be no longer with us, but then losing lovely older people unfortunately goes with the job of being a carer.

I hang my dripping coat up and look at the roster. Hope's still with us, thankfully, but Doctor Kelly is popping in to see her later. I make a cup of tea and take it to her room, tap softly on the door.

'Come in … I'm awake.' Hope's tremulous voice is barely audible through the wood.

I step in and set the tea down on the nightstand, flick on the little lamp. Though today her room is as dark as the horizon, it's large, and has the benefit of a big bay window through which in summer, sunlight pours like molten gold. Hope's propped up in bed, her head's fallen forward as if her neck's too weak to support it. Too many pillows. 'Morning, Hope. You don't look too comfy there.'

'I'm not.' Hope's voice is muffled as her chin's on her chest. 'That young 'un got me washed. She's too quick. Comes in like a bloody whirlwind, shoves me up like this and buggers off. Can't wait to be elsewhere, I expect. Mind you, I don't blame her.'

A quick plump of the pillows – and removal of two – allows Hope to relax and make eye contact. For a woman of ninety-four she's still got remarkably animated eyes. The colour of moss in sunlit rock pools, and always ready to smile. 'That's better, Hope. Now, I've brought you a cuppa and a couple of biscuits.'

I sit by the bed and hand her the mug. 'Thanks, Tawny One.' I smile at her pet name for me. She says my hair's the colour and texture of a lion's mane. 'It seems ages since I saw you, Joy.' She takes a sip of tea, cocks her head bird-like, scrutinises my face as if trying to remember our last meeting. Her memory, like her health, is rapidly failing.

'It was my day off yesterday, but I saw you the day before.' The puzzle in her face makes my heart sad. She clearly can't remember that at all.

Hope takes a bite of her biscuit and points the rest at me. 'Your name doesn't suit you today. Joy isn't joyful. Why's that?'

I consider skirting round the truth, but what's the point? 'It's three years since Sean died today. Still can't believe it.'

Hope's bushy grey eyebrows furrow and she purses her lips. Then her eyes widen. 'I remember now! He was your husband – a fireman, died in a blaze.' She jabs the remainder of her biscuit at me in triumph. Then she lowers her hand, sighs. 'Sorry, Joy. Is there anything I can do?'

'Not really, Hope. But it's nice to chat to you. How are you feeling today?'

'Not so bad for an old 'un. My ticker keeps playing up – and I've got this cough at night. It won't be long for me now.' Hope's matter-of-fact tone makes me smile. She always tells it like it is.

'I think that's a way off yet. Doctor Kelly's coming to see you later and—'

'Smelly Kelly, I call him.' Hope's eyes crinkle and she gives a wheezy gasp that passes for laughter. 'He's got more of that perfume on him than a pox doctor's clerk. It's to cover up the stink of cigarettes. He's fooling no one.' She taps the side of her nose. 'Least of all me.'

I laugh and brush a few biscuit crumbs from the duvet into my hand, tip them in the waste-paper basket. 'Well, I'd better get on. I've got quite a few people to see this morning and—'

Hope grabs my hand. 'Come and see me tomorrow, Joy.' The strength of her grip and the urgency in her voice surprises me.

'Of course I will, don't worry.'

Hope's eyes hold mine with such intensity and she juts her chin out. 'I mean it, Tawny One. No matter how busy you are, I need to speak with you. It's important.'

I take one of her long bony hands, light as a bird's wing, caress the prominent blue veins under paper-thin skin with my thumb. 'I promise I will. And I'll look in again later before I go home.'

'No need for that. Just come tomorrow.'

As I'm about to leave, Hope starts to cough, and it's some time before she can get her breath. I give her water and tissues. Making sure she needs nothing else, I go about my business. But all the time I'm working, chatting to the other residents, completing my duties, I can't get Hope out of my mind. I wonder what she's so desperate to see me about tomorrow?

My shift over, I make my way down the long creaky corridor to Hope's room and meet Doctor Kelly coming the other way. He's a big round man in his forties with a moon face and a nervous smile. 'Hi, Doctor Kelly,' I say, standing to the side to let him pass and trying not to smile as a strong waft of aftershave follows me. *Smelly Kelly.* 'How's Mrs Trebarwith doing?'

His button-brown eyes look down at me. 'Not too good, I'm afraid. She's developed a chest infection, should really be in hospital, but she's not having any of it. Her daughter can't convince her either.'

'Oh dear. Is she on antibiotics?'

'Yes, three times a day. If there's no change she'll have to have them by IV.' Doctor Kelly's mouth twitches at the corners. 'Bye now.'

I tap lightly on Hope's door, but this time there's no answer. I push it open and pop my head round. Hope's propped up on more pillows than when I left her, but she's sleeping peacefully. I creep in and tuck her duvet carefully in around her feet; she hates it when they get cold in the night. I whisper, 'Night, my friend. See you tomorrow.'

She mumbles something that sounds like, 'Happiness is within your grasp.'

I draw the curtains against the darkening sky over the ocean and think about that. Maybe it is, it just doesn't feel like it today. But I promise myself that tomorrow will be different.

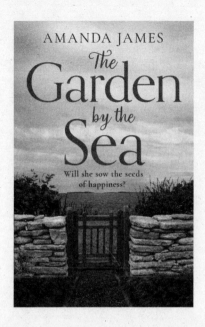

You will also love *The Garden by the Sea*...

Lowena Rowe's beloved mum always claimed her family seed box was special. Said to contain soil from Tintagel, the mysterious seat of the legendary King Arthur, whomever made a wish upon the box would have 'a beautiful garden, bountiful crops and love of their fellow man'.

Starting over in the Cornish village of St Merryn, Lowena can't help feeling lost and alone... but she isn't the only one. Now, as a community of misfits finds solace and friendship in the shade of her growing garden, she realises there might have been truth to the mythical box after all, and she may just be growing the life and love she's always wanted...

ONE MORE CHAPTER

One More Chapter is an
award-winning global
division of HarperCollins.

Sign up to our newsletter to get our
latest eBook deals and stay up to date
with our weekly Book Club!
<u>Subscribe here.</u>

Meet the team at
<u>www.onemorechapter.com</u>

Follow us!

 <u>@OneMoreChapter_</u>
 <u>@OneMoreChapter</u>
 <u>@onemorechapterhc</u>

Do you write unputdownable fiction?
We love to hear from new voices.
Find out how to submit your novel at
<u>www.onemorechapter.com/submissions</u>